WYOMING
SLAUGHTER

WYOMING SLAUGHTER

WILLIAM W. JOHNSTONE
with J. A. Johnstone

PINNACLE BOOKS
Kensington Publishing Corp.

www.kensingtonbooks.com

PINNACLE BOOKS are published by

Kensington Publishing Corp.
119 West 40th Street
New York, NY 10018

PUBLISHER'S NOTE
Following the death of William W. Johnstone, the Johnstone family is working with a carefully selected writer to organize and complete Mr. Johnstone's outlines and many unfinished manuscripts to create additional novels in all of his series like The Last Gunfighter, Mountain Man, and Eagles, among others. This novel was inspired by Mr. Johnstone's superb storytelling.

All Kensington titles, imprints, and distributed lines are available at special quantity discounts for bulk purchases for sales promotions, premiums, fund-raising, educational, or institutional use. Special book excerpts or customized printings can also be created to fit specific needs. For details, write or phone the office of the Kensington special sales manager: Kensington Publishing Corp., 119 West 40th Street, New York, NY 10018, attn: Special Sales Department; phone 1-800-221-2647.

ISBN-13: 978-0-7860-2805-4
ISBN-10: 0-7860-2805-X

First printing: October 2012

10 9 8 7 6 5 4 3 2 1

Printed in the United States of America

CHAPTER ONE

Oh, the coming new year harbored no joy in Doubtful, Wyoming. In fact, it evoked dyspepsia in more than half the businessmen in town and sickened the rest. A certain element was rejoicing as that fateful day approached, but the rest were plunged into a gloom so heavy it seemed to suffocate the whole town. There was anger, too. Talk of rebellion, talk of insurrection, talk of hanging a few earnest citizens, and most shocking of all, talk of lynching a dozen or more of the most respectable ladies in town, including a minister's wife and a midwife and the spouses of some of the most prominent businessmen in Puma County, Wyoming.

Still, the fateful hour of midnight, December 31, or rather 12:01, of the following year drew closer and closer, and with it, talk of revolution. A thundercloud hung over Puma County, threatening to turn into war, death, and mayhem. Ranchers were threatening to leave the county. Cowboys were threatening to quit and find work elsewhere. Certain businesses in town were threatening to shoot me, the sheriff, if I set foot on their property any time after one minute beyond midnight, January 1.

It was a mess, all right, and one that I hadn't the faintest notion how to solve. In fact I knew it couldn't be solved. The county was likely to engage in civil war and wouldn't stop the bloodletting until all sides were massacred. What's more, I had no help. Most of my own deputies had quit on this occasion. They said they'd sooner take a hike, or hand in their badge, than support me. So I would be entirely on my own, with no allies, and only one thing in my favor. I had sworn to uphold the law, and I'd do my blasted best to uphold it. I was sorry I'd croak so young, but that couldn't be helped. I was doomed, and they'd mutter a few words over me and plant me in the Doubtful Cemetery, where it was said the fate of those who rested there was plain doubtful, and Puma County would select another sheriff to be led to the slaughter.

But I'm stubborn, and that'll see a man through when nothing else works; so I did nothing. There was absolutely nothing I could do except sweat it out, as the clock ticked closer to the start of the new year. I didn't hunt up allies, or mark my enemies, or try to get the new law repealed. Nope, that wouldn't work this time. This problem was beyond the reach of law enforcement. It sort of hung there during the Christmas season, just dangled there making people irritable and pessimistic. Some store owners had giant sales, unloading everything they could push out the door before the start of the year. But other store owners thought things would be wonderful; they'd get much more trade in the new year than they had before.

One of the things everyone in town feared was a giant raid from the ranches, like it was the Rebs marching into Lawrence, Kansas, and killing most everyone in sight, as during the recent war. Most of the cowboys were Rebs anyway, and the idea of burning Doubtful to the ground and killing everyone in it was juicy, and good to think about during winter nights in their bunkhouses.

I hoped it wouldn't come to that. It would be me against lots of men from the surrounding ranches. I was willing to accept some tough odds, but that was too tough, even for the only sheriff the county had hired who had lasted more than a few months. But that probably wouldn't happen. I'd be shot in the back long before the invading army from the ranches rode in with nooses and revolvers. If I was alive that midnight, I'd stand my ground as best I could, and do what the law required me to do, which was to shut down every saloon in Doubtful, seventeen in all, right then and there, and forever.

One minute after midnight, the first of the year, Puma County would go dry. Dry!

It was awful to think about.

I didn't favor the law itself, but there it was, and my sworn duty was to enforce it.

Seventeen saloons would shut down. Six cathouses with bars in them would have to scale back. Six restaurants that served spiritous drinks would be in trouble. The Hotel Doubtful, home to whiskey drummers and barbed-wire salesmen, would fold. The ranch trade that Doubtful depended on would head for other county seats. This was serious stuff. They might as well just shut down Doubtful and let the dried leaves whirl through what was once a thriving little city.

It all began when Wyoming gave women the right to vote. That was the worst mistake Wyoming ever made, but few males understood all of it. Women had another trick or two in mind, which was Temperance, and drying out the wettest state in the nation. It was all so quiet that no red-blooded male knew a thing about it. First thing those ladies did was form themselves into the Women's Temperance Union. They were marching around with signs that said, "Lips that touch liquor will never touch mine." Given the way some of them looked, that was a pretty good proposition, but a man couldn't say that very loud.

Next anyone knew, the Temperance gals had set to work on their husbands and recruited them into the cause, on pain of marital troubles that no man wants to get into. So pretty quick there were all sorts of respectable businessmen who were being supported by the Women's Temperance Union, and running for any office that was open to them. And that's how three Puma County supervisors got themselves elected, and no one quite saw it coming. But there they were, put into office that November by their Temperance wives, and everything went downhill from there.

These new supervisors had hardly gotten themselves into office when they voted to go dry. That's how it would be. Beginning January 1, the sale or possession of spiritous drink, including wine, beer, and harder stuff, would be prohibited. And every place purveying illicit goods was to be shut down. And I, Sheriff Cotton Pickens, the law in Puma County, was to do the job.

It sure wasn't a job that I wanted. But that's what letting women vote had come to.

Puma County would be dry as the Sahara.

Of course all that stirred a lot of hot debate and hotter talk. Some businessmen approved. Every cent the cowboys didn't spend in saloons would be spent in their clothing stores or hardware stores or livery barns or restaurants or gunsmith shops. But a larger contingent of Doubtful businessmen figured that if the cowboys didn't show up with their pay at all, nothing would get sold. The cowboys would be spending their pocket change over in Medicine County or Sweetwater County, and Doubtful would turn to dust pretty quick. Nor was that the end of it. The saloon owners vowed to fight to the death. The ranchers vowed to overrun the town and install their own wet supervisors and string up the dry biddies. And the barbed-wire salesmen threatened just to skip Doubtful.

And that is how it all landed in my lap.

It hung over me like a guillotine blade. I thought about resigning, but decided I was too bullheaded to do that. So I made the rounds, trying to find some way out. The supervisor who had pushed hardest for prohibition, one Amos W. Grosbeak, offered no quarter.

"It's the law, boy. You're going to enforce it to the hilt, just as you're sworn to do. We're going dry. Not just dry, but parched. We're going to be Wyoming desert. That's the West for you. Someone wants to fuddle his head with spirits, let him go to wild Nebraska or someplace like that. It'll be a better world. No more drunken brawls in Doubtful. No more vice. Just peace and prosperity. Your jail will be empty. Once them nasty saloons are shuttered, you can sit back and play a harmonica and sing gospel songs and enjoy the fishing. You're going to do it. Shut seventeen saloons for starters, January one, and the rest of it, the bordellos and restaurants, the next day. The saloons must be padlocked. The bars in the other places locked. Or just close down the restaurants. No one should eat out anyway. We should all dine at our own tables in our own cottages."

Grosbeak was young and respectable, and clipped the abundant black hair in his nostrils, and waxed his mustache, and kept his fingernails clean. Doubtful had hardly known anyone with clean fingernails until Amos W. Grosbeak and his wife, Eve, showed up. She was the president of the Women's Temperance Union, and even her toenails were clean. At least most of Doubtful believed that was so. You just couldn't have a president of the WTU with dirty toenails.

"Well, sir, I don't have a kitchen table to eat at," I said.

"Well, you can remedy that by buying one," Grosbeak said. He owned the town's furniture store and was always alert to possibilities.

Having gotten my marching orders from the supervisors of Puma County, I passed them along to my last remaining deputy. "Rusty, you and me, we're going to shut down the saloons starting at midnight the first," I said.

"It ain't gonna be 'we,' Sheriff. It's gonna be you alone. I'm resigning at eleven fifty-nine the evening of December thirty-first, and that's not negotiable unless the dry law's repealed. I aim to live, and I'm just bullet fodder if I keep the badge."

That didn't bode well. The only good thing about it is that I wouldn't have to listen to Rusty practice bugle calls in the jail cell half the night. Bugling was his new hobby.

But if things were bad in the courthouse and the sheriff office, they were worse down on Saloon Row, where most of the thirst parlors catered to the ranching crowd.

I still patrolled there each evening, but the hostility was palpable. I usually stopped to say hello to my old friend, Sammy Upward, who owned the Last Chance Saloon. But now Upward was all frost.

"How's it going, Sammy?" I asked.

All I got back was a glower.

"Ain't so good, I suppose. You got plans after you close?"

Upward leaned forward. "Sheriff, why don't you just get out of here?"

"Seems to me a feller could set up shop across the county line, hire a few wagons to take the bar to a place where it's wet."

"Didn't I tell you to get out of here?"

"Well, my ma used to say a person shouldn't be asked more than once," I said.

I eyed the surly crowd, rank now with smoldering hatred for the man who would enforce the dry law in a few days.

Sammy softened a little. "Cotton, don't try to enforce that law. You could get hurt." The barkeep swabbed down his bar furiously.

"I know that. A feller's got no choice. I got a duty to do, and I won't cut and run."

"Just resign, Cotton. Just quit."

"You know something I don't?"

Upward stared a long while. "Yes," he said. "Just quit. That's all I'm going to tell you. If you don't, you'll wish you had. And I'll wish you had."

That was pretty plain.

"Something cooking for New Year's Eve, Sammy?"

The barkeep rubbed his hands on his grimy apron. The saloon had turned real quiet. There were a dozen cowboys from various ranches listening and waiting. It was like all the music stopped, but there wasn't any music.

Sammy leaned over the bar, wanting to say it real low so all those spectators wouldn't hear a word of it. "Cotton, this bar ain't closing. None of the other places are closing. None of the eateries is quitting. None of the ladies in the sporting houses is gonna quit pouring for their customers. That's the way it's going to be, law or no law, next year, the year after, ten years after that." He eyed me. "And not even the state militia will change a thing. You hear me?"

"No, Sammy, I kinda didn't hear it, and I didn't hear nothing coming out of your mouth."

The barkeep laughed suddenly. "Have one on the house, Cotton."

That was a safe bet. I didn't touch a drop on the job.

"Guess I'll be on my way, Sammy."

December was cold in Doubtful, and dark, too. The little county seat lay quietly, shivering in the relentless winds, a few lamps in windows supplying the only light. I thought a little bit about Christmas, but the holiday had been forgotten this time around. None of those fellers in that saloon were thinking about it, and not in any other saloon, either.

Up ahead, on Courthouse Square, was the courthouse, and on the square, the sheriff office. A lamp burned in that window. Rusty would be in there, at least for a few more days. It would be a temptation to hang up my hat and unpin the badge. That would be the safe way. And it'd leave Doubtful unprotected. Good people in their homes and shops needed someone to watch over them, and if I quit and played it safe, the whole town would be naked. There were some bad ones in those saloons, the sort who'd see all the troubles on New Year's Eve as a big chance to loot a store or rob a bank or steal anything they could.

"Ma, you always told me I was a little thick between the ears," I said to no one in particular. "I guess I'd better stick her out."

CHAPTER TWO

Well, it sure was a head-scratcher. All those buzzards in the saloons was simply gonna say no to going dry and defy anyone to do anything about it. I got through fifth-grade arithmetic, and knew that one sheriff going against thirty or forty angry men in every saloon wasn't very good odds. And I had seventeen saloons and a mess of other joints to deal with. It sure didn't look like it would be a happy New Year's Eve.

And I didn't have a notion of how to deal with it. I thought maybe I could ride out to the ranches and talk the foremen into keeping their men out of Doubtful that night. But to think it was to dismiss it. There wasn't a ranch owner or boss in Puma County that would do that, and there wasn't one in favor of going dry, either.

Maybe I could deal with it with a little sweetener. Those barkeeps that shut down proper as the new year rolled in, they could keep their spirits and wagon them off somewhere else the next day or two, but them that tried to stay open after the law shut them down at midnight, they'd have every bottle blowed away and every cask and barrel punctured and drained. Only trouble was, I didn't know how I'd break every bottle in Doubtful. Puma County was plain awesome when it came to drinking. It took half the distilleries in the country to keep Puma County properly lubricated and cheerful. It'd take more bullets than I had in my sheriff office to clean out all that booze. But maybe shotguns would do it. Even bird shot would wipe a swath through every backbar in town. A feller could dry up a saloon with a dozen shotgun blasts and a few six-gun shots into the kegs.

It sure was a mournful thought. But that seemed the best deal. Shotguns at the ready, a few solid citizens could dry up Doubtful real quick. But there'd be some men getting hurt, and I didn't much care for that, even if all them barflies deserved a little pain. A few loads of bird shot and Sammy Upward's Last Chance Saloon would be soaked in booze and its sawdust floors would be loaded with busted glass. It sure was a pity, all that waste. My ma used to tell me that booze wasn't for everyone, but just for those who didn't need it. That had me scratching my head a while, but I finally got the hang of it.

Twenty men with shotguns. That'd dry up Doubtful, Wyoming, faster than a trip to a fifty-cent cathouse. But before it was over, there'd be a few bodies, too, and that wasn't very enticing for a man sworn to keep the peace. It didn't matter who was at fault: saloon men vowing to defy the law, or the cabal of supervisors and their prissy wives who thought to force their notions on everyone else.

I scratched my head some more, but nothing else came to mind. I'd lived twenty-four years, but this was the first time I'd dealt with anything like this. There were scores of men in the saloons who were simply gonna say no to the law, and take the consequences. And when it was over, there'd sure be a mess of men who'd be mad at me, maybe fight-to-death mad, and that was something to consider, too. I'd sure like to live another twenty-four years, and then some.

Times sure were changing. The frontier was vanishing and settlers were settling.

I sure couldn't think of anything that might work. So the next step was to get myself a good posse. I thought I'd start with Supervisor Amos W. Grosbeak, get the names of them fellers who supported the Big Dry, as everyone was calling it, and line them up for the New Year's Eve fandango.

I trudged through a wintry afternoon, with the

air mean and northerly, and entered the court-house, which was almost as cold as outside. That's how justice was: cold and mean. A warm court-house would upset everyone's notion of how the world worked.

Sure enough, there was Grosbeak in his warren, plenty warm from a cast-iron coal stove.

"Yes? What do you want?" Grosbeak asked, plainly annoyed.

"Need to talk about going dry."

"Well be quick about it. I've got to hang this mistletoe." He eyed me. "Here I was, full of Christmas and you walked in. I guess I'll put up the mistletoe later."

"I ain't very kissable," I said.

That was the wrong thing to say. "You have ten seconds," Grosbeak said.

"I'm making a posse for New Year's Eve. That's the only way I'm gonna shut down the town and turn out the lights. My last deputy is quitting on me at midnight, and I can't do it alone."

"Posse? Why a posse?"

"Because no one's got any intention of shut-ting down, law or no law. They're gonna keep right on a-going, and they've told me if I mess with them, they'll bury me."

Amos W. Grosbeak frowned. "I really should hang the mistletoe," he said. "It's time to sing carols and crank up the holidays, and pour some wassail punch."

"What's that?"

"Why, ah, a little beverage flavored with spices, good health, and good cheer."

"Sounds like good booze to me," I said.

It was the wrong thing to say.

"Well, I expect you to do the job," the supervisor said.

"I need a posse. I need the names of all those fellers who feel real strong about us going dry around here. All them businessmen who wanted it. I'll deputize them for the posse. Thought I'd start with you. I found it in the books. I can make a posseman out of anyone I want, no matter whether they want it. Thought I'd swear you in."

"Me? I'm a public servant. I'm exempt from everything."

"You read me where you're exempt, all right?"

"Forget it, Sheriff. You can remove my name from your list. You can recruit plenty of men for the task, but I will be in my snug home, enjoying a quiet and prayerful welcoming of the new year."

"I'll need about twenty men with shotguns and a lot of bird shot," I said. "I'll give them barkeeps a little leeway and let them shut down for an hour into the new year. It don't make sense to shut down all them places on the stroke of midnight. Some of them barkeeps, they'll just lock up and start shipping their stock out of town the next day, but some'll want to defy the law and test me, and that's who I'm going after."

"You're not going to give any saloon any leeway, Sheriff. You're going to enforce the law to the hilt. At the stroke of midnight, Puma County will be freed from its prison of misery and crime."

Grosbeak was staring, a sprig of mistletoe in hand waiting to be attached to the kerosene lamp chandelier.

"Give me the names of ten good men I can deputize, men who believe the way you do, then. No, make it twenty able-bodied men."

"I'm not going to rat on anyone, Sheriff. I'm a public servant, and don't forget it."

This was going nowhere fast.

"All right, I'll just pick twenty of the town's top people and swear them in, and if they won't swear in, they'll get themselves a trip to my iron-barred parlor."

"Ah, Sheriff, those men won't be suited to the task. You want twenty good, law-abiding, God-fearing, prayerful cowboys for the task."

"That don't make a bit of sense. There ain't any, Mr. Grosbeak."

Grosbeak scratched his chin foliage a little and eyed the overcast skies, then examined the mistletoe hanging from his chandelier.

"You're a competent young man," he said, "and I have every confidence you'll enforce the law to a fare-thee-well."

"You got me there, sir. I never read nothing about a frothy well."

"Oh, forget it, Pickens."

"I keep trying to get myself educated, so I'd sure like to know about these frothy wells."

"A fare-thee-well is perfection. You are going to enforce county law perfectly."

"Learn something every day," I said.

There was no sense hanging around the court-house palavering with supervisors, so I headed across Courthouse Square to the chambers of Lawyer Stokes, the town's one and only attorney. No one ever called him by his full name, Timmaeus Pharoah Stokes, but just Lawyer Stokes. I had always sort of liked the feller and had wanted to call him Timmy, but my ma used to warn me about being overly familiar.

Lawyer Stokes had no receptionist and could usually be found reading law books or the King James Version, and that is how I discovered him. I removed my beaver Stetson and bowed and scraped a little.

"What is it, Pickens?"

"I got me the right to swear in a posse, if I want, and even if them folks don't want to be sworn, right?"

"Absolutely."

"Well, I'll be doing it then. I need me a posse New Year's Eve to shut down the saloons. There ain't one barkeep in town is gonna close up and toss the key away. They're telling me they ain't gonna obey the law and tough luck to anyone that tries to stop them."

"I see. Yes, that would keep the court dockets busy, I imagine. And since I'm the county attorney, I'd be pretty busy."

"Well, I'm sworn to uphold the law, and I'm gonna do her," I said. "I'm going to get me a posse, and it'll all be them fellers that pushed this law through, the dry law, so I'll swear them all in and we'll get her done. I guess I'll start with you, Lawyer Stokes. I'm hereby swearing you in and telling you to report at eleven, New Year's Eve, and bring your shotgun and plenty of bird shot that'll clean off backbars real fine."

Lawyer Stokes stared, aghast.

"I'm the county attorney, Sheriff. You can't swear me in. I'm immune."

"Show me where it says that; read me the chapter and verse, Lawyer Stokes."

"Why, there are abundant precedents, young man. There's no need. I'll tell you flatly I'm exempt, won't show up, and not even a court order will budge me."

"Lawyer Stokes, you lift your right hand and swear that you'll uphold the law and follow the directions of the head of the posse, namely me."

Stokes removed his spectacles, polished them, and restored them to their resting place just above the vast foliage of his beard. "You're a fine fellow, Sheriff, but a tad young and inexperienced. If you had a little more schooling, and a little more sophistication, you'd see that this is a bad idea. You are a peace officer. Your primary task is to keep the peace, prevent bloodshed, prevent violence."

"I thought it was to uphold the law without favor."

"That, too, young man, but the law has a little give in it, and you need to be judicious in the ways you apply it."

"Well, you're stuck. I'm swearing you into my posse, and you'll be there at my office ahead of midnight."

"Hell will freeze over first, Pickens."

That was pretty entertaining. I thought maybe I'd recruit the mayor of Doubtful, George Waller. He'd be a good man to have on the midnight posse. Waller ran a dry goods store and built caskets on the side, so I headed for the wood-working shop. Sure enough, there was the mayor, screwing brass hinges into the lid of a fancy rose-wood coffin.

"I don't know why you're here, Pickens, but you're up to no good and the answer is no."

"Merry Christmas, George," I replied. "You building that for somebody?"

"Let's hope it's not you," the mayor replied, screwing down the lid.

"I reckon I got me a mess New Year's Eve."

"Your mess, not my mess."

"You in favor of going dry in Puma County?"

"Don't pin me down, Sheriff. I refuse to be pinned down. There's virtues in it, and there's vices in it. The town might lose some business, but the town might gain some peace."

"That's all I need. I'm swearing you in for my posse. It'll take about twenty good men armed with shotguns and bird shot to close down all them thirst parlors. They're getting a little hot about it and saying they won't close, so we're just going to go ahead and enforce the new law. Now, George, lift that right paw and I'll swear you in, and then you show up armed at my office an hour before the new year starts."

"Jumping Jehoshaphat," Waller said. "Ain't you the card."

"Raise that paw, George. I got the right to put any man I want into a posse."

"I'm the mayor, and I'm proclaiming that Doubtful will stay wet until dawn, law or no law. That suit you?"

"Raise that paw and swear in, George."

"I'm not going to show up, so forget it."

"Guess my two cells are gonna get themselves to overflowing New Year's Eve."

Waller looked up from his coffin. "Over my dead body," he said.

CHAPTER THREE

It sure was annoying. All the gents who were making Puma County dry didn't want to help out when it came to enforcing the new law. I tried two or three more, like the banker Hubert Sanders, Doc Harrison, and George Maxwell, who ran the funeral parlor, and they just weaseled out.

"I'm not letting you off the hook," I said to Sanders. "I got the power to deputize you and put you in the posse, and I'm doing it. You show up at eleven, New Year's Eve."

"Tut tut, young fellow. I'm sure if you'd study on it, you'd find that your task is to keep the peace and that law enforcement requires a degree of moderation. If you cause trouble, there'll be widows made, and grief, and sorrow in Doubtful."

"I'm not the one causing trouble! Them saloon

men told me they won't obey the law, and they'll fight."

Sanders peered steadily through his wire-framed half-glasses. "Moderation, my boy. That's how to win the day. One little step at a time. You'll do fine if you just close one saloon at a time. Just put one out of business once in a while, and next you know, Puma County will be dry and clean and upright. So what if it takes a few months? Use a little patience, boy, and maybe shut down one a week, and everyone'll be happy."

"The ones I shut down won't."

"Well, they'll have time to move their bottles across the county line, if you let 'em alone a bit."

"They've had time to do that now, and I don't see any packing up and loading a wagon."

"Of course not. I have loans outstanding to several of the saloons. Mostly mortgages. We need to do all this moderately so these barkeeps have time to pay off their debts. I'd hate to foreclose on all those empty buildings."

I stared. "Guess I shoulda seen how it lies around here."

I didn't line up anyone for my midnight posse. And my threat to jail them if they failed to show up didn't faze them a bit. I was on my own.

I headed into the jailhouse with my temper up and saw my deputy, Rusty Irons, fixing to practice on his new bugle. He'd been learning Forward, Gallop, and Commence Firing.

"You're quitting me, too, you yellow-bellied punk. I should fire you now instead of letting you draw pay and then walk out the moment I need you."

"That's fine," said Rusty.

"What do you mean, fine?"

"I don't want to live in a dry county. I'm just staying on to do you a favor. I'm heading for Sweetwater on January one, and when I get there, first thing I'll do is have me a glass of redeye."

I didn't have much of an argument against that. Fact is, I thought maybe I'd quit Doubtful myself. Being a lawman in a dry county was about as interesting as watching an anthill. But I wasn't ready to forgive.

"You could stay long enough to help me shut down the saloons, but you weaseled out on me."

Rusty grinned. "Why get shot at for this? There's some laws that ain't worth spit."

"You swore an oath to uphold all the laws! So did I."

"That's why we're all quitting."

I couldn't stay mad at red-haired Rusty for long. The man had been a good deputy, brave and ready to pitch in whenever there was trouble. And now he was quitting, not because of cowardice, but because he didn't want to enforce a law that he opposed.

I didn't like the law, either. I thought it was full

of good intentions, but it would cause more harm than good. All them Temperance people, they wanted a peaceful town, quiet and sleepy and safe, and they wanted families kept secure, and people not to be impaired, and maybe the merchants wanted cowboys to spend their payroll in the stores and restaurants rather than in the saloons.

And there were all the churchy ones who thought Doubtful was the sinfullest place in the West, and they were determined to rid the community of everything that catered to appetites. There were some that couldn't stand it when someone else was having a good time, relaxing with friends. Prigs, that's what they were. Just couldn't stand the thought of anyone enjoying himself. I knew a few of those around town. But mostly, prohibition was based on good intentions, and a lot of folks supported it because they saw a better world if there were no spirits available. But that wasn't the way life worked, and most of them would be sorry some day, when Doubtful turned to dust and everyone moved away. Them Temperance folks, they just couldn't live in an imperfect world.

Well, it was coming to a head now. In a few days no one living in Puma County could sell or possess spiritous drinks, and there weren't no loopholes in that county ordinance, neither. And the fines were stiff, too. The county supervisors meant business, and if someone tried to get along just by paying a few little fines now and then, they were in for a surprise.

"Where do you reckon they'll all go?" Rusty asked. "Those cowboys get a big thirst, and they're sure going to take that thirst somewhere, and it ain't gonna be Doubtful, and they ain't gonna buy sarsaparilla at the ice cream parlor.

"There's no town anywhere within forty miles, but maybe one or another'll spring up on the county line. I've seen places like that. Bunch of shanties, green lumber, tarpaper shacks, doing business right on the county line."

"That and bootleggers," I said. "If I stick around here, I'll probably be chasing bootleggers halfway to Laramie and back."

"You could just wait and see," Rusty said. "Just leave the new law alone, and in a week or so the supervisors, they'll repeal it and Puma stays wet."

"Got to keep my oath of office."

Rusty sighed. "You're a hard man to work for."

I eyed the empty jail cells, studied the log, concluded it had been a quiet December afternoon and I wasn't needed there.

"I'm going to Saloon Row," I said.

"I'll send a coffin," Rusty said.

I bundled up. I could deal with winter cold, as long as the wind wasn't howling. When it blew, nothing I wore kept the cold at bay. It didn't matter what I bought; it was no good in arctic wind.

Saloon Row was clear over on the other side of town, and was the first thing that cowboys saw when they were riding in from all the ranches over there. It prospered, kept in business by a couple hundred cowboys, as well as Doubtful people. Some of the joints were rough, and some were pussycat quiet. Most of the joints were quiet most nights, unless some wild man got liquored up and started a brawl, and then I filled my jail-house.

I headed for the quietest, darkest, and most dangerous joint on the row, the Lizard Lounge. It was usually lit by a single kerosene lamp and was patronized by males who didn't like to talk. It was also patronized by people with no visible means of employment, mysterious males who drifted in and out of Doubtful, doing things beyond fathoming. It was owned by someone called George Roman, only in Doubtful he was called George the Roman, and was even more quiet than his saloon.

I went in. The door swung silently, admitting me to a scanty heat and thick gloom. Roman, sallow and bag-eyed, studied me.

"You closing up at midnight, New Year?"

"I don't announce my plans, Sheriff."

"Then you aren't. If you intended to shut down, you'd say so."

"You're very intelligent, aren't you, Sheriff?"

"My ma, she thought I was carrying a lot of wood in my head."

"You're a lot smarter than I am, Sheriff."

"I want to know what your plans are. I have two missions. One is to keep the peace. The other is to put the law into effect."

Roman smiled at last. "Contradictions," he said.

"You could stay open. Peddle other stuff."

"I've thought about it."

"The rest of the saloons, they're staying open after midnight?"

"How should I know?"

"I think you know."

"I hear you're recruiting a posse. All the bright lights. Empty out the churches and give them all a badge."

"Where'd you hear that?"

Roman sighed. "Sheriff, you could recruit the whole town. Every able-bodied man. Give them all shotguns. And you wouldn't be able to shut down the saloons. So forget it. Go to bed at midnight. You want a fight? You'll get a fight, a bad, drunken, whooping fight, with lots of lead flying."

That was the longest speech I had ever heard issuing from Roman.

"Thanks, Roman," I said.

"You have no smarts, Pickens; get some somewhere."

"That's what my ma always told me, but she always said I could make up for it by practicing the virtues."

Roman smiled. He was missing two lower incisors.

I let myself out. I blinked at the light. The Lizard was so dark that even an overcast December sky seemed blinding. I wondered what sort of men preferred to drink in the middle of a cave. Saloon Row wasn't at its peak yet, but it was always busy, twenty-four hours a day. I headed for McGivers Saloon, across the street, the only one owned by a woman. Maybe she'd close it down.

A gust of wind burrowed into my coat, hurrying me across frozen muck and dried dung in the road. McGivers was a bright place, but grossly overheated by a big coal stove. It would take little time before I had to undo my coat to keep from sweating in there. Sure enough, I walked into a blast of hot dry air with a little acrid coal smoke mixed in for atmosphere. Mrs. McGivers wasn't tending bar, but was sitting at a faro table at the rear, the chandelier spilling yellow lamplight over her bun of chestnut hair.

"I'm glad you came by, Sheriff. We're staying open."

"Against the law?"

"The law is an ass. Just stay out of here New Year's Eve. I can't guarantee that you'll feel comfortable in here if you wander in. And that goes double for the possemen."

"Word sure gets around."

"Don't try it. Don't come in. And if you do, wear armor."

"Does it matter to you that the ordinance was passed proper, and it's valid law?"

"Certainly it matters. It makes me want to hang the supervisors by their nuts, and gut their wives."

"You could pack up. Puma County isn't that big. Set up shop in Sweetwater."

"I like it here. I even like you." She eyed me, shuffled a deck without eyeing it, and smiled. "Like you a lot, Cotton. You just mind your manners. You're not going to take my livelihood from me. This is my living. I don't want to shoot your nuts off."

"There's some that say I don't have any."

She grinned. "Want me to find out?"

It sure was getting interesting. "Guess I'll have to shut you down. I'll start with you. One minute after midnight."

"Sure you will. You'll walk in here with twenty storekeepers and accountants, all of the scared shitless, and if I don't meekly nod my head and kiss your hand, they'll blow away my backbar with bird shot, and I'll be out a few clams." She laughed.

"Word does get around, ma'am."

"It sure does. New Year's Eve may just be the most fun we ever had in Doubtful, Puma County, Wyoming. I can hardly wait. Twenty merchants with wet pants, most of them half deaf from the shotgun blasts. I'm delighted I'll be first. We'll settle the whole issue right here. They'll all cut and run, and there'll only be you and me. I live upstairs. You come up and I'll show you my lithographs."

CHAPTER FOUR

I intended to hang some mistletoe from the top of the iron door leading to my two jail cells but thought better of it. I gave up on hanging it in the outhouse and also hanging it over my desk. But I did finally plant some at the top of the rack that held the shotguns and rifles. You never knew what might come in handy.

A little before Christmas I got a surprise visitor. Eve Grosbeak had never set foot in the place, and I hadn't ever expected her to. She belonged in a different world. She could sit in her comfortable north side home and run her Women's Temperance Union, and never know what life was really like along Saloon Row, or some of the alleys behind it.

But here she was, stamping fresh snow off her little boots and shaking snow off her bonnet and scarf. She eyed the room, the gloomy and smelly cells beyond that iron-barred door, and finally focused on me.

"Ma'am?" I said. I wasn't very good at polite, but I'd work at it some.

"Yes, this is about what I thought," she said. "We'll fill those cells New Year's Eve."

"Doesn't seem likely, ma'am."

"Don't ma'am me. It makes you sound servile. Call me Eve. It was just a happy coincidence that I was named Eve, and now I am Evening Grosbeak, just like the bird."

"You look like one, too, Eve. Nice big beak."

I had a feeling that I shouldn't have said that.

"Well, yes, young man, that's sweet of you. Now about prohibition . . ."

"It's a problem, ma'am."

"Aren't you going to invite me to sit down?"

"Wouldn't you prefer a tour of the jail? No one's in there sleeping with his pants off."

She stared and then nodded. I grabbed the big key ring and led her to the barred door, opened it, and invited her in.

"Two cells. Enough for Puma County, unless there's trouble."

"Don't you ever wash it down? The smell!"

"Well, it's a bad smell, all right, but it just makes 'em want to get out of here faster and makes 'em less willing to get stuck in here, so the smell's a good thing."

"But surely you attend to sanitation."

"Only when we're forced to, ma'am. The idea is to make a citizen's experience in here something he wishes to avoid the rest of his days. My ma, she used to say that a few days in the pokey cured my dad for good."

"I see."

"Not much to see. Just some iron bars, metal shelves to be uncomfortable on. Not so bad, though. I've slept here a few times in snowstorms. It won't match a hotel bed, though. Now, I could use some advice. I was thinking of hanging some mistletoe right there, over the outer door, but wasn't sure that was a good idea. What do you think?"

"Mistletoe? Door?"

"Right there."

"But who'd want to kiss anyone in here?"

"I see your point, ma'am."

I led her out, and she settled herself in the chair beside my desk.

"That's where your tax dollar goes, ma'am."

"Call me Eve, you young rascal. Oh, you're a card, all right. No wonder no laws are enforced in Puma County."

Oh, that stung. And from the supervisor's wife, too.

"Well, get on with it," I said, feeling testy.

"I've heard about your little posse. I've also heard that every respectable male in Doubtful is lily-livered. That means coward, doesn't it? I come from the East and I'm not sure about all these local terms. Lily-livered sounds good, though. Nothing but lily-livered males in Doubtful, including your remaining deputy, who is about to cut and run."

"I wouldn't say lily-livered is a very good way to describe him, ma'am."

"Call me Eve. I'll let you because you're a real man. You're not cutting and running. You're the only real man in town. You deserve to wear pants. You're the only man in town with the equipment."

"I do? I haven't ever given it a thought, ma'am."

"It's Eve, my boy. Now what are you planning for New Year's?"

"Right now, I'm treed, ma'am."

"I'll fix you up, boy."

"The best advice I've got is to deal with it gradual. Forget shutting down every saloon at midnight. Close them one at a time over the next days or weeks, and keep the peace."

"That's what cowards want to do. That's why you're the only real, true man in Doubtful. You're not going to do that. You're sworn to uphold the law, and you're going to do it."

"Ah . . ."

"We're going to turn Puma County into desert. We're going to abolish spirits of all sorts now and forever. We're going to spare little girls the shame of a drunkard father. We're going to rescue families from drunkard mothers. We're going to make everyone in Puma County a better citizen. We're going to close the jail because it won't be needed. Almost every despicable crime in the sorry catalog of human folly rises from spirits. It's the devil incarnate, young man. So no, we won't be moderate about driving the devil out of Puma County. If men won't do it, then women can. We're better suited anyway, being female. You can join us or not, but we're going to do it."

"Ah . . ."

"The ladies will proceed. That's all I'm going to tell you."

"I think you'd better tell me, ah, Eve."

"Now I'm Eve again, eh? All right. As long as I'm Eve to you, and you don't use that lickspittle ma'am word again, I'll tell you. Now you listen close, and get that jail ready, because the Women's Temperance Union is going to fill it to overflowing."

"Ah, I'm not quite catching on, Eve."

"Women are bulletproof."

"Ah, my ma used to tell me that women get notions."

"When we achieve full equality, we won't be bulletproof, you know. We will be like men, only smarter and better."

I sure didn't know what to make of all that, so I just sulked in my chair and waited, knowing it was going to be bad.

"If lily-livered men won't do it, women will. We're organized and ready. When midnight New Year's Eve rolls around, we'll attack."

"You can't do it with brooms, ma'am."

"There you go, saying ma'am. You need some manners."

She leaned over and touched my knee familiarly. As far as I could remember, no female had tapped my knee since I'd come into manhood. "Not even the most corrupt and craven and debased male in Doubtful will shoot women," she said.

"I wouldn't be too sure of it. My deputy, Rusty, he told me he'd as soon shoot a woman as a man."

"Well then, I admire Rusty. He sees us as equals. Now, the good souls in the Women's Temperance Union have divided into three-woman militias, three militiawomen for each saloon. Here's how it'll play out. At midnight, we'll enter, two of us with shotguns, one woman with a revolver to cover the rear and pick off snipers. We'll give the saloon man two or three minutes to shut down or not. If not . . . our bird shot'll clean out all the glass on the backbar, and not a soul will fight back. They're all as lily-livered as the town's businessmen."

"I'm not sure that's a bright idea, ma'am, I mean Eve."

"You're a slow learner."

"That's what my ma always said. But she said I make up for it. I'm quick in other ways."

"I bet you are," Eve said. "I can just see it in you."

"You'll get shot. You'll get sued."

"Oh, fiddle. Worrywart, that's you. Tergiverizing never won the day."

"Whatever that means," I said. "Look, ah, Mrs. Grosbeak, these ladies, they walk into the saloons toting the shotguns, and they're fixing to break a lot of glass, first thing you know some gent walks right up and takes their guns away, and that's that. And if they shoot in a crowded saloon, there'll be glass and bird shot and people are gonna get hurt, some real bad. If you gals show up outside some saloon armed like that, I'll just have to pinch—ah, hustle you off to one of them cells there."

She stared. "But you recruited men to do the same thing."

"No, ma'am. We'd move all them people outside, and then bust the glass afterward."

"You don't like women."

"Well, a good gelding's easier to ride."

She whickered.

"I'll get all them saloons shut down, one way or another. I don't like it. If you think life in Puma County will get better after all them bars are silent, you'd better think again. If you think that this law of yours is going to make a lot of families happier, guess again. There's some that shouldn't touch a drop, some that get mean or crazy, but keeping the bars shut won't help one bit. They'll get their whiskey one way or another. You shut down here, and there's going to be a lot of smuggling going on, and people will bring stuff in by the cartload. If I could talk you into it, I'd say repeal that new law before it gets started up."

"Typical male," she said.

"I got to deal with those saloons every day, and it's easier than trying to track down smugglers and little country cabins that get turned into a place to liquor up. That's more dangerous, and more trouble."

"I knew you'd find excuses," she said.

"If I had a good posse, I'd get her done fast. I don't. You'll have to be patient. Beginning at midnight, January one, I'll be the only man with a badge in the whole blamed county."

"You could deputize me," she said.

"That sure is an interesting idea."

She headed for the gun rack. "That's mistletoe up there, isn't it?"

"That's for anyone wants to kiss some guns," I said.

"You come give me a Christmas kiss."

"Ah, I don't think so, ma'am."

"You come here and give me a good smack on

the lips. You're the only man in the county who's not lily-livered, and you just barely make it."

I hesitated. She looked oddly delicious.

"Come on now. I'm not leaving here until I get a real Christmas greeting. If you want me to stand here until two in the morning, just ignore me."

I couldn't remember what my ma used to say about deals like this, but I figured the sooner I got it over with, the better. So I sort of sidled over to the gun rack. She was waiting there, and as soon as I got within shooting range, she grabbed me, delivered a big smoochy kiss on the lips, smiled, and let go.

"I like you," she breathed.

"I like you too, ma'am."

"We'll get along fine," she said. "You just need a real woman in your life."

I couldn't think of a response to that, but she just laughed, pulled her scarf tight, and headed into the winter outside.

That sure was something. I thought maybe I should deputize half a dozen women, and let them replace Rusty. Might be good for the county.

It was time to quit. I lowered the wicks until the lamps blued out and headed for Belle's Boardinghouse, where I had a front upstairs room with a good view of Wyoming Street. On a sheriff salary, it was all I could afford, but I didn't have anyone to look after anyway, so a room on the main street suited me well enough.

No sooner did I enter my boardinghouse than I knew I was in trouble. There was big old boisterous Belle in the parlor off the front door, and she'd gotten the two-burner lamp all fixed up with mistletoe.

"Come here, you big lunk," she said.

"I already got my Christmas kiss," I yelled.

"That mistletoe's not for you, it's for me. Gimme a big one, buster."

Belle was built along the lines of a bowling ball, and had a voice to match.

"I sure wish Christmas was over," I said.

"No you don't. New Year's Eve's going to be worse. Now, here's my motto: *'Lips that don't kiss mine can't live in Belle's Boardinghouse.'*"

She stood there, head cocked, her blond hair inches below the dangling mistletoe. I knew I couldn't get out of it. I would have to surrender. I would have to work up my courage and do her, and I'd have to do her proper.

"Maybe I need another landlady," I said.

She laughed, wrapped me in her commodious arms, and kissed me proper.

CHAPTER FIVE

I sure didn't know what to do. And that was getting downright embarrassing. I was supposed to be tough, commanding, and on top of things, but I was spending the season wondering how to resolve the mess. If I had my druthers, I'd see the new prohibition law repealed. If that couldn't happen, I'd like to bring on the dry times real gradual, one saloon at a time. And if that couldn't happen, I'd just like to get Critter out of the livery barn and ride into the sunset, and the hell with Puma County.

But I wouldn't do that. My ma, she always told me to stick things out, and not quit just when things got difficult. So come midnight, New Year's Eve, I'd still be sheriff, and still enforcing the law as best I could.

Which reminded me that it wasn't just the saloons on Saloon Row I needed to shut down. The cathouses all served hooch in friendly little side rooms and did a lot of business that way. Maybe I could get those shut down proper. The next day I bundled up against some real serious cold howling down from the north, pulled a woolen cap over my ragged hair, and plunged into the gale. It was blowing so hard that everything was swinging. Store signs rattled. Tumbleweeds rolled across Doubtful's streets and piled up against walls and fences. A man could hardly keep warm, even in a heated building. In my sheriff office, the jail was cold as a tomb, and anywhere more than ten feet from the coal stove was Siberia. Rusty was out patrolling somewhere; or maybe he was in bed with three quilts on top. Who could say? It wasn't going to be a big day for crime in Doubtful, Wyoming.

I let the wind blow me down Wyoming Street to Saloon Row and then cut south a block, past an alley, to another row of houses, their lamps and signs chattering in the gale. I thought I'd start with Denver Sally. She sort of reminded me of my ma, all cheerful and moralistic. I wasn't sure who'd be up in the middle of the morning; working girls usually slept all morning. But all houses were always open for business, so someone would be up.

I entered to the sound of a bell and found myself in a homey parlor with samplers on the walls and crocheted pillows everywhere. This was my favorite parlor because it reminded me of my ma's. There was a fine sampler, done in delicate needlework, with a red motto across the top: *"Better laid than never."*

Denver Sally's was famous for its plain girls. Any cowboy who wanted a plain girl, with an underslung chin or varicose veins or a pear-shaped figure, knew where to find one. But Sally's was also the home of the Argentine Bombshell. They did stuff differently down there in Argentina. I waited in the deep silence of the morning, in the half-light of December, and then indeed Denver herself appeared in a wrapper.

"Hi, there, Sheriff. Come for a bang?"

"Well, ah, you sure have nice ladies upstairs, Sally, but no, we've got to parley a little."

"Well, I should charge you for the time."

"This here is law business, not tomcat business. You know, Sally, I've got to shut down your bar room on January one."

"Crap," she said.

"Yeah, I know how you feel, but it's the law and I ain't got a choice."

She sighed, glared, and motioned me into the side room, which was fitted out as a small bar. "Look, it's only a few bottles, and it's on the house if the john gives us some business."

"You've read the law, Sally."

"I had it read to me."

"So I got to do it."

"It'll wreck my business. Pickens, you just leave us alone and we'll stay real quiet."

"It won't wreck your business, Sally."

"It will. There's a lot of men, you can't get them out of their pants until you pour a couple down their gullet. We've had some come in, look over the girls, and start out the door, and then we offer them a quick drink, and it's a mind-changer. A drink or two turns some knock-kneed Willy into a stud horse."

"And then you get some business."

"Business! Sometimes a couple of drinks will turn some timid little cowboy into the world's greatest loverboy, and then we collect for a week."

"Well, maybe you could make your ladies more enticing."

"What are you trying to do, insult us? Our merchandise is the best in Doubtful. I run them all through my personal coaching. I got classes I give to incoming ladies. Before they're graduated from the Denver Sally School of Amatory Arts, they're whizbangs."

I sighed. "I just hate to do it, Sally, but New Year's is it. If you have a quarrel, take it to the county supervisors. They're the ones passed the new law, not me. I just am stuck with making it happen, and that's going to mean pinching violators, and that means trials and fines and all the rest, which I don't like any but can't help."

Denver Sally was staring at me. "You're standing right under the mistletoe, Sheriff. Guess that means I gotta act."

"No, dammit, Sally, I'm just here for a palaver."

"Is that what you call it? Well, I'll give you a palaver you'll never forget."

She zeroed in on me, grabbed me in her commodious arms, and bussed me good and proper. I didn't mind that one bit, but it was the wrong kind of business. It took me a long time to extricate myself, and I thought I was being smothered until I came up for air, but eventually I got loose.

"See what you're missing, Sheriff?" she said, wiping my face with a handkerchief.

"You don't have to tell me about it, Denver. My ma, she always said—"

"You and your ma. Now you sit down in that horsehair couch and listen to me, and tuck your shirt back in."

I did as I was told. She settled across from me in the deep quiet.

"Me and the rest of the madams here, we've been talking about this, and we're not going to cave in. We're going to serve booze, law or no law. It's the only way to get some men out of their pants. So you'd just better get used to it.

"What's more, if the county tries to pressure us, we'll go on strike. Every cathouse in Doubtful will shut down until we can serve a picker-upper to them fellows that can't get it up and running."

"There's a lot of people on the north side of

town who'd say a strike is the best thing that could happen."

"That's what all those pious bastards want to think. But here's how it goes, Sheriff. If you shut down the saloons, and the parlors of paradise go on strike, you just ain't gonna have any business making a dime in Doubtful. There's maybe three hundred cowboys and ranchers out there, and they come into Doubtful to spend all their pay, and they just plain won't be coming here anymore. Sure, we get some of their pay, but so does every merchant in town."

"Strike?"

"Strike, idiot. We close our legs and tie 'em shut."

"But, Sally, that would be dumb."

"We'll pick up and go. No reason we stick here. It's not far to the next county. And we'll get twice the business."

"But you're licensed and taxed here."

"You're thick-headed, just like they say, Pickens. Now either drop your pants or head out the door."

It wasn't an easy decision, but I finally decided I'd head out the door, and maybe palaver with some more of them ladies. If it was true they was going on strike, I'd better tell the supervisors about it. Them women were the biggest source of tax revenue for Doubtful, and Puma County, and if they quit and moved, the whole blasted county would likely dry up and blow away.

It was one of the shortest days of the year. Even

midday, the shadows were long. On this overcast day, there was only twilight and wind. I let the wind push me toward Mrs. Goodrich's Gates of Heaven. It was the costliest joint in Doubtful, with nice, acrobatic ladies and a few who smelled sweet, too. Mrs. Goodrich required cleanliness, and the girls had to get into a hot tub once every two weeks.

She was sitting at a table in her bar, also located to one side of the parlor, knitting a purple scarf.

"I heard you were over here, dearie," she said.

"Word travels fast."

"Sheriff sets foot in the district, everyone knows it in two minutes."

"I'm letting all your nice gals know that you've got to shut down your bars on New Year's."

She smiled, her needles clacking, and said nothing.

"You going to comply all right."

She just smiled away.

"I'll be checking."

"You poor dear boy, why don't you just stop in. I'll give you a free token, and you can begin the new year with a whoop and a holler."

"That's real kind of you, ma'am, but I'll be on duty."

"So will we, my boy."

"I kinda have the feeling that it ain't gonna happen, ma'am, and if it don't, I may have to pinch you."

"That's the sweetest thing you've ever said, Sheriff."

This sure was getting nowhere fast. "I guess I'll have to bring in my posse, then," I said. "I was kinda hoping you'd cooperate."

"We're in the cooperation business, sweetheart."

"What about them other gals? Are they going to cooperate?"

"We all love to cooperate, dearie. Now, you move a little left, until you're under that chandelier, and I'll give you a sample."

I glanced upward, seeing a three-lamp fixture sporting some fresh mistletoe.

"Oh, no, I'll get outa here," I said.

But too late. She loomed next to me, cheer radiating from her mottled face, and clasped her long arms right around me and kissed me on both cheeks, the nose, the mouth, and was starting down my neck and chest when I wiggled free.

I collected my hat and backed away.

"You have a beautiful posse," she said. "You come riding in any time. I just love sheriff's posses."

I felt dumber than an ox, but there wasn't nothing I could do except retreat from there. I stepped into the mean December wind, decided I'd had enough bordello visits for a while, and headed for my sheriff office and the hot stove. I couldn't embrace the hot stove, but it would have to do, I thought.

"Where you been?" Rusty asked when I blew in.

"Talking to the sporting gals. They ain't helping me any."

"What do you expect? You're cutting into their business."

"The way they tell it, you can hardly get a man out of his pants until you've given him a drink or two. It sure makes them cowboys look like pansies. But that's what having a saddle pound on your parts all day does to you."

"That's why I'm not a cowboy," Rusty said.

"Rusty, I want you to go out and pull down every sprig of mistletoe in Doubtful. That includes every store, every saloon, every cathouse, every boardinghouse, and anywhere else it's hanging. I've declared war on mistletoe."

"War on mistletoe?"

"I been kissed more times today than in the last twenty years."

"And that's a problem?"

"It is when I'm on duty."

"I tell you what, Cotton. I'll go on a mistletoe patrol, but I'm going to buy some and hand it out to every blessed soul in Doubtful. If I get enough mistletoe strung up in Doubtful, no one'll notice it when we start shutting down the saloons."

"*We*, Rusty?"

"Yeah, dammit, I'll stick. We'll keep the lid on Doubtful."

"Don't you come near me with that mistletoe, Rusty, or I'll throw your ass into the cage."

But Rusty was just laughing away. "Say," he said, "Consuelo Bowler's in town and wants to see you. He's at the hotel and says he'll be there all day."

Bully Bowler, as he was called, was a big-time rancher south of Doubtful. "Did he say what he wanted?"

"Yeah, Cotton, he did. He doesn't like your plans for New Year's Eve."

"So what's he gonna do about them?"

"You better find out yourself, Cotton."

Rusty sure was acting nervous. "He was talking about hanging the county supervisors unless that dry law gets repealed real fast. And you know what, Cotton? He meant it."

CHAPTER SIX

Bully Bowler was actually the manager of an outlying ranch owned by Britons. His name was honestly earned. He was a massive man, fifty pounds heavier than me, and quick to make full use of his strength. He had massive fists, a thick neck, and a thicker skull. He ruled supreme out at his spread by simply pounding any cowboy who didn't toe the line.

Now he was in Doubtful, making noises I didn't want to hear. I donned my overcoat and hat, and plunged into the icy wind, headed for the Wyoming Hotel. Some said the hotel was the only good place between Laramie and Douglas, with two sheets on every bed and a tablecloth on every table. I wouldn't have known the difference, and didn't care. But I cared about Bully Bowler's threats, and that's what took me over there.

Bully never traveled alone, and I found him

with four of his skinny cowboys, sitting at a table in the dining room, smoking cigars.

"You were looking for me?"

Bully tapped some ashes over the remains of a pancake, smiled, and nodded. He said nothing, making me wait.

But I didn't press the man and stood quietly.

One of Bully's boys sipped coffee, looking a little smirky.

"Well, I guess I was mistaken," I said. "Someone told me you wanted to see me." I turned to leave.

"Pickens, stay put," Bully said, and still offered no explanation.

I yawned, waited a moment, and started to leave. The hell with it.

But a massive paw, lightning fast, caught my belt and yanked me back to the table.

"Now, Sheriff, you'll listen even if you're wetting your pants."

That's how it went with Bully Bowler. I had heard enough stories to fill a book or two, and none of them flattering.

Bowler let go of my belt just before I was about to do something about it.

"The boys are coming into town New Year's Eve. They're going to have a fine time. Every ranch hand in the area, three hundred, four hundred, in for a whoop-de-doo."

I nodded.

"You ain't gonna shut down the place."

"I'm glad you think so," I said.

"Because you won't want anything bad to happen to your supervisors."

I just kept quiet.

"Because that's what's gonna happen."

"Thanks for letting me know, Bowler."

"I ain't done with you yet, you little fart."

"I didn't think so," I said.

"That dry law, it's going to be repealed. And if it ain't, you ain't going to enforce it. That law's dead as poisoned wolf."

"You going to repeal it?"

"I already did."

"I haven't seen it published yet. Supervisors do it?"

"Pickens, I always heard you're thick between the ears."

"If it's not repealed, why do you say it is?"

"That law's gone away, sonny boy, gone. That's what I'm telling you. Now beat it."

"Just your say-so, is it, Bowler?"

"I'm tired of you."

"Guess I'd better protect you from them Temperance women. You better stop in at my jail and I'll lock you up safe and sound."

That started the crew laughing, but Bully Bowler stuffed out an arm and grabbed my shirt and yanked me forward. I hadn't seen it coming. Then the manager's iron arm shoved me backward, over the table, spilling coffee cups, plates, dead food, and silver. I landed on the far side, sprang up, and bulled into Bowler. I heard other patrons screaming. The floor was littered with food and tableware.

I hammered at the man. It was like hitting the door of a safe. Bully Bowler simply grinned, let me discover what I faced, and then lowered the boom. A few pops with those ham hands, a knee to the groin, a couple of elbows, and I was sprawled on the dining room carpet, discovering hurts I never knew I could enjoy and hearing the screech of waitresses and hotel guests. But Bully didn't quit. A few kicks with his boots caught my ribs. And that was the signal for his four henchmen to join the act. Every time I tried to get up, or fight, all five of them got in their licks. And I got the arithmetic lesson, and quit.

"Some sheriff you are, Pickens," Bully said, grinning.

I was more interested in all the ways I hurt than in my reputation.

"Gimme that rag," Bully said, and one of the henchmen handed him a tablecloth. Swiftly, Bully wrapped me in it and yanked another cloth from another table, and wrapped that around me until I was wrapped in a winding sheet that was tied tight with anything handy, including scarves and belts. I was as helpless in my cloth prison as if I'd been lowered into a grave. My arms were pinned so tight I couldn't get any purchase on anything, and my legs were wrapped to close that I couldn't even bend them.

"Let's show the town what kind of sheriff it's got," Bully said cheerfully.

One of the ranch hands pulled the pins out of a hinge and freed the wooden door into the kitchen. They loaded me on the door, and the pallbearers lifted the catafalque and marched into the bitter cold. One of those hands settled my hat on my chest as the cortege proceeded up Wyoming Street, through the heart of town, past the shops and eateries, straight up the one street where no one would miss the show, and toward the Courthouse Square, my sheriff office, and jail.

It might be December, but people flooded to windows and opened doors to view the horrible sight.

"Is he dead?" someone shouted.

"Might as well be," someone else said.

I eyed Mayor Waller and then spotted Turk, the livery owner, and watched Hubert Sanders watching the spectacle from his bank window. I saw Leonard Silver, owner of the Emporium, peer from his door and spotted Doc Harrison studying the parade from the Beanery, and there was nothing I could do. If they wanted a sheriff who strode through town with a six-gun at his hip, a sheriff whose frown stopped little boys from tossing firecrackers at dogs, whose squint deterred burglars, whose beckoning finger corralled drunks, whose bold gaze intimidated cowboys bent on shooting up the town for sport, they could only be dismayed. The young man they'd employed to keep the lid on Doubtful, and keep all the he-cats and she-dogs at bay, namely me, was being hauled through town like dead meat.

The message was clear. Doubtful was at the mercy of the ranchers and cowboys, and they intended to celebrate their New Year's Eve exactly as they always had, and if there was any trouble, they'd show the citizens of Doubtful just who owned Puma County.

Women emerged from doors, saw the awful spectacle, and herded their children inside. A carriage horse whinnied and reared, the spectacle too much for its equine temperament. Bully led the parade, smiling cheerfully but otherwise not acknowledging the crowds, while his four ranch hands carried the door, one at each corner.

"Whatcha doing in the winding sheet, Pickens?" asked Alphonse Smythe, the postmaster.

I could think of no answer, so I kept quiet. My ma used to say that there was no way out of a winding sheet. But maybe they'd let me go.

"Send me a postcard," Smythe said, enjoying himself.

I still hurt, and the cold was reaching me. I couldn't wiggle enough to keep warm.

And still Bully's parade marched onward,

turned, heading now toward Saloon Row, the very blocks where I, Sheriff Pickens, always walked tall and subdued rough men in a rough neighborhood. This was going to be the most painful of all. I'd kept order there mostly because troublemakers knew I'd whip them one way or another. But now every lowlife in Doubtful was going to see me wrapped tight in tablecloths.

The wind sure was getting to me. I rolled around on my wooden door, and the pallbearers were none too gentle about hauling me along, never looking to my comfort. Bully Bowler proceeded nonchalantly ahead, ignoring the cold but making sure the whole town of Doubtful knew the score: this sheriff is a joke. This sheriff couldn't enforce a law against stray dogs. Doubtful had no public safety. Those cowboys out on the ranches were going to do whatever they damned pleased on New Year's Eve or any other time.

My little funeral parade—that's how I saw it now—drew no followers. It was just Bully and his hands and me lying on the hotel door. But by the time we reached Saloon Row every barfly and tavern keeper was on hand. Somehow word had buzzed ahead, and the show had arrived. I saw Sammy Upward frowning and the whole McGivers Saloon crowd gaping at the spectacle. Some of them were looking pretty smirky. I spotted a few lowlifes I'd thrown into my iron cages a time or two, some for public intoxication, some for threatening with weapons, some for brawling. And now they were enjoying the sight of their nemesis bound helplessly on a door. What sort of message was all this? I resisted a sudden impulse to resign and load up Critter with all my worldly goods and head for Argentina or some place.

Bully Bowler steered his pallbearers toward Lovers' Lane, as some called it, and there the ladies flocked to the windows to watch. Some waved; some blew kisses. Most of them giggled, and a few flashed a little flesh. There was nothing like seducing a man tied up tighter than a hog going to market.

But eventually, the cortege slid past the bawdy-houses. Bully Bowler headed for the sheriff office, either tired of the sport or content that he had delivered an indelible message to the county supervisors. In any case, Bully and his boys entered the sheriff office, dumped me on the cold floor, stole one set of jail keys, and departed with the hotel door. Not a word was spoken. Not a warning, not a lecture, not a joke.

I lay on the cold floor, nearly helpless, but I soon found I could wiggle my fingers and arms. The long tour had loosened the bindings. It sure was cold in there, hardly warmer than outside because no one had built up the fire. I gradually freed my arms and hands, untied the rest, and stood, getting some blood circulating in my body at last.

I had complex feelings about the whole business. Bully and his four thugs had jumped me, deliberately planning the event. But that trip to town was what bothered me. I might as well turn in my badge. That was exactly the message that Bowler and his hooligans were sending to everyone in Doubtful.

I stretched, built up the fire with some kindling on hot ash, and pretty soon got a little warmth going. No one came in, and I was grateful for that. I wanted to think things over. I wanted to make some decisions. But I wasn't offered that chance. County Supervisor Amos Grosbeak stepped in, glaring at me like a thundercloud.

The supervisor examined the tangle of table-cloths and bindings, and squinted at me.

"Mr. Sheriff, I do believe an explanation is in order."

"Well, I pounded on myself until I was all beat up, and then tied myself tight in some table-cloths, and then hired some cowboys to haul me through town on a hotel door."

"Mr. Witherspoon at the hotel has already brought us a bill for seventeen dollars and sixty-eight cents, tablecloths, broken pottery. I told him I'd deduct it from your salary."

"That's mighty kind of you."

"What were you trying to do, Pickens?"

"Let the whole world know that I'm the friend of all cowboys and ranchers, Mr. Grosbeak."

"That's a poor way to do it. I imagine we'll be discussing this at the next meeting of the supervisors. What were you trying to prove?"

"That I'm the only sheriff in Wyoming that ever got a good ride on a hotel door."

"Pickens, you're acting very strange, I must say. We're relaxed in Puma County and think that cowboys will be cowboys, and boys will be boys, but we do expect our public servants to show some discretion, especially at Christmastime. Are you sure you wish to continue with us? We'll be discussing this, frankly, and it would help if you'd just tell me whether you feel you're up to the task. A sheriff needs strength and dignity, and that stunt certainly didn't inspire confidence in your abilities."

"Mr. Grosbeak, get the hell out of here."

"I'll put that on the agenda, too, sir. Do you think your deputy might be interested in stepping up?"

CHAPTER SEVEN

The next few days felt worse than a month of constipation. I hardly dared show my face on the streets. I was the same person as before, but now the perception of me had changed. Bully Bowler had robbed me of the thing most important in a peace officer—respect. That parade on a hotel door, wrapped in a winding sheet, had changed everything. Along Saloon Row, most of the people were smirky and insolent. Uptown, it was worse. People gave me long looks, looks that leaked dissatisfaction and worry.

It didn't matter that I was the same Cotton Pickens as always. What mattered was that the toughs in town were emboldened to test me, or ignore me, while the uptown people felt themselves naked and vulnerable. I sensed it. People who used to greet me cheerfully just sidled by. They were all waiting for the county supervisors to fire me, so there was no need to greet me cordially on the street. I was just another of the dozen or so peace officers Doubtful had hired and fired before I came along. And now I'd join the scrap heap.

Christmas was coming, but I didn't feel any cheer. In fact, I was lower than a snake's belly. All my friends had deserted me, too. The storekeepers who used to greet me now slid elsewhere. The clerks in the courthouse who used to share gossip with me were suddenly busy when I walked through. The ladies I tipped my hat to now replied with a frosty stare. Even my remaining deputy was giving me the fish eye now and then.

Well, the hell with it.

Christmas Eve arrived with no change. I told Rusty I'd take the shift; the deputy could have the evening off. And I'd probably pretty much shut the office Christmas Day. So I did the shift that eve, patrolled the town until the last caroler on the street vanished into the night, and then I shut down and locked up. People knew where to find me if they needed a lawman.

A good sleep at my digs in Belle's Boardinghouse looked good to me just then. Most of the lamps in town were turned off, and the whole town was dark and cold. I couldn't see Santa Claus anywhere, and would probably have to nip him for unlawful trespassing if I did, so I just hurried through the darkness, hearing the snow squeak beneath my boots and feeling arctic air frost my earlobes. There was a lamp burning in Belle's apartment on the first floor, but the rest of the place creaked in the winter cold. I scraped inside and was about to climb the noisy stairs to my room, when Belle opened her door and smiled. She was wearing a big red robe to cover her big pink person. The white of a flannel nightgown trailed below the robe.

"You come in here, Cotton. I've been waiting for you," she said.

"For a minute, Belle. I'm pretty tired."

"Of course you are. You're carrying more load on your back than anyone else in Doubtful."

I stepped into a totally female parlor. She had attacked every cushion with crocheting needles, and no stuffed chair was without lace doilies. But the coal stove glowed cheerfully, and the room seemed to cascade light and life over me.

"Time you had some Christmas," she said, maneuvering me gently until I stood under the chandelier. Too late I spotted the mistletoe and started to escape, but Belle was a lot of woman and surrounded me. She clasped me to her ample self, a self too large for me to encircle with my arms, and bussed me heartily. I quit resisting and enjoyed it. It was certainly a novelty. I could get my arms around every other woman I had embraced in my young life. But not Belle. She was in no hurry to quit, but then she sighed and let herself loose.

"There now. I've now turned a fantasy into reality," she said. "Sit down and have a Christmas cookie and a snifter of mulled rum."

She stuck a glass filled with something warm in my hand, and I sipped, finding the taste rather odd. I was game for anything, however, and besides, it was Christmas Eve and I owed my landlady rent, and she was good company.

"You want to stand under the mistletoe again?" she asked. "I get better and better at it as I go along."

"Let's wait a while," I said.

"Have a seat, and don't worry about being seen. I've pulled the drapes tight."

"I wasn't worried, not a bit," I said. "There ain't nothing worse can happen to me than already happened."

"Poor dear, hog-tied with a tablecloth on a door. If you'll stand under the mistletoe I have a cure for you."

"Let me see how this stuff goes down," I said, taking a fine gulp of hot rum.

"I just want you to know that I'm right there beside you, as long as you don't enforce the new law."

"I'm sworn to, Belle."

"Oh, fiddle. Just let the town be. If you drive cowboys away, I'll go broke. I can't run a boardinghouse in a ghost town."

"I was sort of hoping to do the job real gradual,

but half the town wants me to shut down the town one minute after midnight, and the other half wants me to forget I ever heard of the dry law."

"Between the devil and the deep blue sea," she said.

"I never heard that one before."

"I didn't learn it until about sixth grade," she said.

"That lets me out. But I got another. I'm between a rock and a hard place."

"Oh, that's about fourth grade," she said.

"It's about right, anyway. I don't know what I'm gonna do one week from now. I got saloonkeepers, I got Temperance ladies, I got a few hundred cowboys coming into town, I got half a dozen madams, I got county supervisors, I got hotel keepers and drummers, and they all got different notions about what I've got to do. And there's no escape."

"Then don't do anything, Cotton."

"Well, I might as well turn in my badge, then. What good is a sheriff that gets took around town on a hotel door?"

"That's sure eating you, isn't it, Cotton? You come here and get the mistletoe cure."

"I need to drown my sorrows first," I said.

I sipped more of that hot spiced rum. It sure was a novelty. I didn't even like warm beer before this, but this stuff wasn't too bad for a Christmas Eve. Some good cold redeye would be better, though, especially with ice hanging from every eave.

"If you enforce that law, I'm a cooked goose," she said.

"You don't look like a goose. More like a pig."

"Cotton, I swear, you need more schooling. I don't know how you got to be sheriff. But you've got to just ignore this here law and pretty quick it'll disappear. It'll be what they call a dead letter. A law on the books that no one pays any attention to."

"They carried me around, and I've got to get past that."

"What are you talking about?"

"They were funning me, and now I've got to get their respect. If I don't get their respect, I can't do my job around here."

"Cotton, what you need is another mistletoe session."

"I need respect. No one pays me any respect."

"That's what I'm saying. Come over to the mistletoe and I'll show you my respect."

"You have more respect than I want to see, Belle."

She tugged at me, and I reluctantly stood up and let myself be directed to the chandelier with its fateful green sprig. I thought that the hot booze did it. And I'd lost all respect. I didn't even respect myself. I was a failure. I didn't know one end of a horse from the other. I'd quit and saddle up Critter and ride to Nevada or some crazy place like that where I could start life over and hope no one asked any questions about my checkered past.

She maneuvered me until I was squarely under the kissing stuff, then undid her robe so it fell loose around her, and she was guarded only by a flimsy white Mother Hubbard that sort of bobbed and wobbled. Then she smiled, plucked my hot booze from my fevered hand, set it aside, and burrowed in.

There was too much Belle surrounding me. Her lips were finding mine, her arms were snaking around my back, but I couldn't embrace her because that was not possible. Pretty soon I was kissing away, and suffocating, and wanting more hot booze, but she kept right at it until I began sputtering and coming up for air.

"Okay, Belle, that's enough mistletoe stuff for now," I said, finding purchase on her shoulders and easing her away. She looked sort of pouty, but I didn't care. I could breathe. I wasn't smothered. And I could return to the task that had preoccupied me for three days, getting my respect back.

"Do you think I could do it?" I asked.

"Just give it a rip. I've got plenty of night-gowns," she said.

"No, I mean, how do I get to be sheriff again?"

"Let her rip, Cotton."

I sure was feeling bad. This eve hadn't gone in any direction at all, and the longer I hung around in Belle's parlor, the bleaker it got.

"Belle, you're just the sweetest old gal on the planet, but I gotta go to bed now."

She sighed. "You're leaving? I was hoping Santa Claus would come visit me."

"I guess I'd better git now."

I could never figure out women, and now I was baffled by the tears in her eyes. What was she doing that for?

She stood so desolately that I wondered if I might console her a little. "If that mistletoe's still up after New Year's, I'll come give her a try," I said.

"Goddammit, Cotton, get your skinny ass out of here," she snapped.

That sure puzzled me. One moment she was weepy, the next moment she was mad, and I still hadn't figured out how to get my respect back. "I'll bring you a bouquet tomorrow," I said.

She pushed me toward the door and into the icy hall, and the door closed hard behind me.

I started up the creaking stairs and then thought that I didn't really want to go to bed. I didn't know what I wanted. I turned around and slipped into the icy night, where the bitter air hit me like an avalanche. The clouds had cleared off, and the stars dotted the heavens like chips of ice. It was late, and Doubtful was mostly asleep, except maybe along Saloon Row, which never slept. Enough snow remained to coat the yards and walks with dim white. I didn't much feel like patrolling Saloon Row. Tonight Saloon Row could take care of itself.

The air cleared my head in a hurry, and I felt only a great quietness as I meandered through the silent town I had protected for two or three years. It came to me that it didn't really matter what the town thought of me. What mattered was what I thought of myself. What mattered was the sort of job I was doing. I had done a good job, at least until now when I was faced with an utterly impossible task. The prohibition law was tearing Doubtful to pieces, and hardly anyone agreed with anyone else, and hardly anyone was taking it peaceably. There was blood in the wind. And this trouble was ten times worse than anything I had ever dealt with. I hoped I was up to the task. If I did my best, that was all I could ask of myself, so I vowed to do just that.

I felt all right, then. That was a good enough Christmas gift. A man could like himself or not, and if he did, it was Christmas every day of the year.

CHAPTER EIGHT

The day after Christmas was sunny and warmer, but Doubtful seemed to slumber under a thundercloud. The new law was only days away, and the town was split down the middle by it. I had no business. There was no one in the jail cells. The town drunks were behaving. There hadn't been a fistfight for a week. No one reported any robbery. Some prankster reported a stolen kiss, but it wasn't prosecuted under a mistletoe amnesty. If it weren't for the law that loomed just down the road, one might have thought Doubtful was at peace.

I spent my hours keeping the fire built up and germinating an idea, which I finally tried out on Rusty, who was sleeping in the jail cells for lack of anything better to do.

"I think I know how to do her," I said.

"I hope you fail," Rusty said. "A dry Doubtful,

that's like moving back to Ohio. I come out here to get me some adventure."

"Well, it'll be the law," I said.

"Where have I heard that before?" Rusty asked.

"I think maybe timing is the way to do it. Not shut them down at the stroke of midnight. Let's let 'em rip until dawn. They'll be loaded and sleepy, and by dawn New Year's Day, they'll be pretty much snoring away and the saloons will be shut down."

"I see where you're aiming," Rusty said. "You're a rat. Striking when the whole town's hungover."

"I'll hardly need help," I said. "We'll just get us a good freight wagon, bust into them saloons, load up all the illegal booze, and haul it off. The town'll go dry when it's got hangovers and migraines galore, and then the job's done."

"They'll want their booze back."

"As of New Year's Day it's illegal booze, so they won't get it back, and if they try it'll make a good bonfire."

Rusty stared. "You're the meanest bastard ever held office in Doubtful. I don't know why I work for you."

"Neither do I," I said.

"You sure know how to stab a guy through the heart," Rusty said.

"Just you and me, starting about seven or eight in the morning, January one. We may have to bust into some places."

"You sure that's legal?"

"I can maybe get some search warrants. Illegal booze."

"What if one of them places has got drunken bodies lying on the pool table and everywheres?"

"They'll be too sore-brained to know what we're up to."

"That's a lot of booze. How are you going to carry it off?"

"All them Temperance ladies. They volunteered. I'll give them the word, and they can get that glass off the backbars and into a wagon before anyone sobers up."

"Somehow I think there's a hole or two in this plan, Cotton."

"Trust me."

"Trust you! I trusted you as far as fifth grade, and then you quit school."

That afternoon, when me and Rusty were catnapping in the empty cells, a visitor did arrive, and was about to depart when I emerged from the jail. I knew the man. It was Brigham Higgins, the manager of a big spread out at the far west end of Puma County. It was a big Mormon cattle operation, with thirty or forty hands.

The odd thing was that Higgins was dressed in a blue constable uniform, like it was from a ready-made clothing factory. I stared at him.

"You been made a cop?" I asked.

"No, but I'd like to have a little chat with you

about the prohibition law. We, of course, are for it. It would remove temptations from my Latter-Day Saints. We've managed to keep Utah mostly dry, to everyone's benefit, and now we see the chance to dry up Wyoming, starting with Puma County."

Rusty appeared, rubbed his eyes, and stared at the uniform.

"You going to be a policeman somewheres?" he asked.

"We thought we could help you enforce the new law," Higgins said. "I've a corps of thirty able men ready to serve as your deputies when the time comes. We've been drilling, and we can march as a company and load shotguns and fire them as a company. We're ready to help you rid Puma County of every last drop of spirits."

"And every last ounce of coffee and tea," Rusty growled.

"That, too," said Higgins

"Anything else you plan to get rid of?" I asked.

"We're at your service, Sheriff. At seven, New Year's morning, we'll march into Doubtful, thirty men on horse, all in blue, each with a shotgun in hand. It'll be the most impressive sight ever seen in Puma County. Call us the Mormon Battalion."

"If anyone's awake to see it," I said. "Tell you what. You leave your shotguns out on the ranch and come along with a few wagons, and you fellers can load up the bottles from each saloon and haul them out to the edge of town where we'll start a bonfire. I'm not gonna deputize you, so you won't be a posse, but you can help out all right."

"Under the circumstances, Sheriff, our men prefer to be armed."

"I'm not going to have a shotgun war around here, so just leave 'em home. But thanks for your help."

"And don't bust into the mercantile and grab the coffee beans," Rusty snarled.

"If coffee is legal in Doubtful, we'll leave it alone," said Higgins.

"I suppose you want pay for all this. I ain't got a spare nickel in the sheriff budget."

Higgins shook his head. "We don't want pay. We're glad to rid the county of vice. But if you want to do us a favor, in return, there's something you can do for us. After we clean out the booze, throw a ball. Have all the fine folks in Puma County bring their unattached daughters, and make sure all single women are invited. Two or three for each of us would be a start."

"I knew there'd be a hitch," Rusty said.

"I'm not much for dancing," I said.

"All the better," Higgins said. "You and your esteemed citizens can throw a fine party, maybe in one of those cleaned out saloons, with lots of sarsaparilla on hand."

"I'm not making any promises," I said.

Somehow I didn't like this deal, but it was the best thing I had going. And the whole heist would come while all the drunks were sleeping it off. By noon of New Year's Day, Doubtful would be cleaned out, the law would be in force, and it would all be done peaceably. All them cowboys would grumble and ride back to all the ranches that surrounded the town. Not a bad plan, I thought. It'd keep the peace in Puma County, at least until the other ranchers rode into the Mormons' ranch and hanged the whole lot and buried each one with a stake through the heart.

"I sure don't like waiting until the dawn," I said. "That dry law starts at midnight, and I'm sworn to uphold it."

"Cotton, you're an idiot," Rusty said.

"That's what my ma always told me."

I itched to escape Rusty, who was in a dour mood. So I clambered into my heavy coat, pulled a hat over my ears, and headed into the wintry town to do some patrolling. I'd freeze my butt, and frost my fingers, but Doubtful would get patrolled even on a peaceful winter's day.

There wasn't much happening. It was a time to huddle around the stoves, not a time to be galavanting. But when I got to Saloon Row, I found a freight wagon pulled by two frosted and ice-caked draft horses parked next to the Last Chance. I knew the wagon, all right. It belonged to Alphonso Flynn, who ran a big cow-calf operation east of town. Alphonso was a big, dark-haired bull-shaped man with pointy boots. Some whispered that he had Spanish blood mixed in with the Irish.

The wagon was being filled with cases of booze, twelve bottles to a carton, along with stout kegs, all of it being loaded from the Last Chance and the neighboring saloons.

"Whatcha up to, Alphonso?"

"I'm buying enough contraband to last until those pricks in the courthouse repeal the dry law."

"Ah, possession's gonna be illegal, Alphonso."

"Who says I'm gonna possess anything, eh?"

"Well, I might have to come looking."

"You set one foot on my outfit and you're likely to be mistaken for an elk, Pickens."

"I'm sworn to uphold the law, whether I like her or not."

Flynn paused. "Sure is a burden, ain't it?"

"I do what I have to do."

"Well, you come on out to the place and arrest me."

I watched weary saloon swampers drag crates of redeye and rotgut out of the old saloons and stack them in the wagon. In a few days, everything in that heavy wagon would be illegal. I thought it was strange, how the stuff sitting there was okay one day, outlawed the next.

Flynn loomed over me, menace exuding from him. "Look, Sheriff, I know you're just trying to do your duty, and I know you're not to blame. The supervisors made the law. But listen close now. That law's a dead letter. That law is dead on arrival. There's no way the people of Puma County, especially us out on the ranches, are gonna pay it any attention. This here law's generating hard feelings, Sheriff. Real hard feelings. This is not just fistfight trouble; it's worse. There'll be blood shed here unless you just back off. You want to keep the peace? You want to avoid blood? Then just step aside and let the law die. It'll die in its crib if the supervisors see that it can't be enforced. It's up to you, Cotton Pickens. You can have war, and blood, and deep trouble, or not. You can keep the peace or not. You start enforcing a bad law, and you'll have more trouble here than you've ever seen. You hear me?"

"I'm sworn, Flynn."

Alphonso Flynn sighed, shook his head, and turned away.

That was some speech. I felt halfway like that myself. I sure didn't want a blood-soaked whiskey war, and that was what I was getting. But I would either do what I had to do, according to my oath, or quit. I'd clear out the saloons on the first day of January, or turn in my badge.

I watched Flynn and two of his drovers climb up on the freight wagon and haw the draft horses. The big wagon lumbered through the rutted street slowly, spitting shards of snow off its big wheels, and turned east toward the Flynn place.

It wasn't going to end New Year's Day. Even if I got all the saloons in Doubtful shut down, there'd be new joints springing up all over the county, log cabin saloons in every rural gulch. I'd need more deputies to ride herd on all that.

I pushed into the headwind to get back to Courthouse Square and chose the courthouse itself to get out of the gale. I found Amos Grosbeak staring dourly at the drifts that were building up fast and threatening to shut down Doubtful.

"There isn't anything you can tell me," Grosbeak said. "I've heard every argument from you and all the rest. We're going ahead with the law, period."

"That's not what I'm here about."

Grosbeak peered upward, eyeing me over his wire-rimmed spectacles.

"I got to have me five or six more deputies."

"Are you daft, Pickens?"

"If you want the new dry law enforced, that's what I need."

"I'm sure you can do a fine job without all those subordinates, Pickens." He said it in a way that was loaded with doubt.

I recounted my encounter with Flynn and described the amount of booze that got loaded into a single freight wagon, and I didn't forget to tell Grosbeak what Flynn was saying.

"You want to turn this county dry? You want to shut down every log cabin saloon that's going to go into every gulch? You want to intercept nighttime shipments up from Laramie? You want to track down every beer party on every summer night in the county? You want to keep the booze out of a county the size of some eastern states, with just me and one deputy?"

Grosbeak eyed me levelly. "There's not a dime to be had. We just increased our administrative salaries, and there's nothing left over." He leaned forward. "We're putting our trust in you, Pickens. There's something you should learn to do, because you're not much good at it. You need to win the cooperation of the community. You need to organize watch and ward patrols, get informants, pay snitches. Get the women involved; get an earful of gossip and learn where the outlawed traffic is going, and then strike hard."

"All right, sir. I'll start with you. I want you and Mrs. Grosbeak to feed me anything you hear, every little rumor, and I'll track her down."

"We're too busy for that, Pickens. You get informants from people who have nothing better to do than spy on their neighbors."

"You going to give me a budget for that? For hiring snitches?"

"No, Pickens, you'll get help from all those people who are eager to do their civic duty. You'll get yourself in front of civic groups, like the chamber of commerce, and ask for their cooperation."

"This sure is entertaining," I said.

CHAPTER NINE

This sure was getting bigger by the hour. It was looking like war. At the stroke of midnight, New Year's Eve, the population of Doubtful would be reduced by about eighty percent, especially of women with shotguns waded into it. It was going to keep the grave diggers real busy. It was a good thing it was winter, because it would take a month to get all those bodies planted. They could be safely frozen in the meantime.

But that was speculation. I spent the next day shoveling out the sheriff office, which was inundated by a new storm that seemed to unload snow until the town slowed to a crawl. I hoped it would blizzard New Year's Eve and save the town from certain doom.

"You want to shovel for a while, Rusty?" I asked after putting in a good lick.

"I have a sore back, and the county's not paying me for that," Rusty said.

"We've got to keep the steps clear so we can get all the drunks into jail," I said. "We can't have them breaking their bones around here."

"They're going to be too loaded to know the difference. You could bring the whole lot in on toboggans," Rusty said.

I figured there'd be no one arriving in town that snowy day, but I was wrong. A company of men along with three or four big gold-gilded wagons came rolling in, snow-caked, cold, frost-bitten, and steaming the air.

I stepped outside, trying to fathom what that was all about. There were about twenty of the toughest hombres I'd ever seen, men with big walrus mustaches, bright red noses, long dark coats, square-toed boots, and a variety of caps that were mostly made of animal pelts. The horses looked worn; they had dragged those wagons through some tough drifts. A few men were carrying long guns, but whatever the rest were carrying was hidden under those big black coats.

The odd thing was the four wagons, which looked like they came from a circus. In fact, they were circus wagons, gilded and gaudy. One was a sleeper wagon, and three were rolling cages with iron bars. These were empty. The only time I had seen wagons like that, there were lions and tigers in them. It was so cold and blowing that not even the gaudy parade drew a crowd. Mostly people stayed inside, huddled around their stoves. But here was a company of men and wagons that defied explanation. They weren't doing anything illegal, and I figured I'd get the skinny of it pretty quick.

It didn't take long until the whole outfit was parked outside the sheriff office on Courthouse Square, and that's when one of the frostbit men finally detached himself, tipped a hat to me, and walked into the warm office.

"Goose Cannon here, out of Cheyenne," he said. "You the sheriff?"

"I am. Cotton Pickens."

"Good. We're here to help out. I didn't know if we'd make it in time, but we did. We got hired by the Women's Temperance Union to help you shut down all them saloons at one minute after midnight."

"Hired?"

"Yeah, they wired us for help. We're willing to work for anyone, long as we're well paid. We got us some of the best artillerists this side of Possum Creek. We butcher first and buy our hunting license later. The ladies said you'd deputize us, just to keep it all on the up and up. We'll just bust in, right after midnight, and shoot out the lights."

"Cannon, that's not what we've got cooking here, but thanks for the help."

"Don't thank me, thank the women. It don't matter whether you pin badges on us. At one minute after midnight, we're going to shut down Doubtful like it's never been shut down before."

"You're not going to do that, and you'll keep those guns off your persons. That's a city ordinance."

"Well, friend, your city ordinance is going to get itself ignored for a while," Cannon said. "See those circus wagons? We brought our own cozy little jails along. We heard you got just two dinky cells, which ain't enough to keep a few old souses safe, much less most of the rannigans off the ranches. So we brought our own, and we're going to fill 'em fast, and we'll let them freeze their asses in the cold until they repent, and then maybe we'll let them go."

"Sorry, Cannon, that's not how it's going to work, and if you pull some deal like that, you'll end up in those cages yourself."

"Them women, they knew you'd be on the wrong side, so they just said ignore Pickens; the head lady, she's married to the county supervisor, and that's all we need. You stay outa trouble, boy."

This sure was a pickle. I knew I wasn't going to get anywhere by arguing, not with twenty killers with more balls than a pawnshop, their hands not far from whatever lay on their waists under the buffalo coats and black slickers.

"Suit yourself. You can probably board those horses at Turk's Livery Barn, and maybe he'll let you sleep in the hayloft."

Cannon smiled. "I knew you'd be sensible." He turned to his bunch. "Follow the plan," he said.

"What plan?"

"Oh, relax, Sheriff. We got it all worked out. These wagons are going over to Saloon Row right now and are gonna be parked real conspicuous near all those houses of perdition. People are going to ask about them, and they're going to learn that the tiger and lion wagons are real good at caging drunks and rebels on New Year's Eve. That'll wet their britches for them. You're going to have the most peaceable New Year's Eve in the long, illustrious, shining history of Doubtful."

The company of toughs immediately started the frosted horses toward Saloon Row, black shadows in swirling snow.

"Who's got the key to them cages?" I asked.

"I do. I alone have the keys. I will play God on New Year's Eve, choosing who I send to hell. We're going to clean up this problem so fast it'll run like crap through a duck. Pickens, you got nothing to worry about. Them cowboys are no match for this outfit. A few minutes after midnight, the drunks will be caged, the booze in every bar poured out or shot out, the saloons locked tight, the new law enforced, and you can go to your little trundle bed and snore away the rest of the night." Cannon smiled. "Don't say we never did anything for you. We've solved every problem that's been eating out your gizzard."

"You heeled?"

"We're all heeled. You open our coats and you see a regular hardware store."

"I guess you better come with me, Cannon. We'll go over to my office."

"What for?"

I beckoned and Cannon followed, curious about what was up. The heat struck us as we entered, which was good. I liked that. I wanted heat. I took off my coat. Cannon stayed buttoned up.

"We'll pack them cells, boyo," Cannon said.

Cannon headed that way, through the jail door, and studied the cells. "They'll do," he said.

"We've got a law here. No guns inside of the town limits. You going to comply? You and your outfit?"

"That'd be like going naked in freezing weather, Pickens."

"There's pegs on the wall there. Good place for you and your outfit to hang up the guns. When you leave town, you can pick them up."

"Pickens, we come to help out. What's in your head except bone?"

"I got a law that needs some attention. Tell you

what, Cannon. You and me, we'll go out and tell those gents with you to bring in the hardware. That's what the rule is. It'll be safe here."

I picked up a scattergun I had lying behind my desk.

Cannon saw how it was. His greatcoat hung heavily over his own artillery. "I never forget," he said.

"Good. I guess you'll need to undo that coat one button at a time, while I stand behind you, and I guess you'll unbuckle your gun belt, and I guess you'll slowly let her drop, and turn around slowly with your hands high so I can see what else you've got. Then you'll head for one of them cells, you get your pick, and I'll write out a ticket, and maybe you can talk to Lawyer Stokes—he's the only one we got here—into defending you."

"You want to know what's gonna happen, Pickens? Those dudes out there, when they get wind of where I'm parked, they'll tear this jail-house to bits, and maybe you'll be lucky to get your ass into the woods before they do."

"Sounds like a threat to me, Cannon. My finger's itchy."

"Hell, Sheriff, my fists are itchier. Tell you what, Sheriff. If I give you my word that I'll bring the boys in, and we'll hang our hardware there until needed, would that do?"

"No. That 'until needed' part don't fly, Cannon.

Until you're fixing to leave town. Then you get it back."

"Fine way to treat friends, Pickens."

"You gonna give me your word? And you gonna keep your outfit legal?"

"Wait until them Temperance women hear about this! Pickens, there's no worse terror walking the earth than a Temperance woman. They scare the hell out of me, and they'll turn you into beeswax if they choose."

"You gonna give me your word?"

That room sure turned quiet. The bore of my pump shotgun never wavered.

"I can't speak for them others," Cannon said. "There's some that got born sucking on a gun barrel. There's some that consider their hardware their real, true private parts."

"You'll bring 'em in here and see to it that they hang their hardware on those pegs, and you see to it that they don't go out and buy more, and you see to it that you keep your word. If I need armed men on New Year's Eve, I'll decide. Maybe I'll ask you to arm. Maybe I'll even swear you as a posse. But that's my decision, not yours. If I let you walk out of here, do you agree to it?"

"You got me between a rock and a hard place, Pickens. Them women . . . they're expecting us to do our job. We don't get paid until we do it."

I shrugged. "Well, go pick yourself a cell, Cannon."

"I want to think about it."

"This is double-aught buckshot, Cannon. That greatcoat won't stop it."

Cannon sighed, stared, and finally whined a little. "I thought we'd be tight as ticks. We came to help out, and now this."

I waggled the shotgun.

"Oh, all right, dammit. I'll agree."

"You go write that down in the daybook. Put a date to it, December 29, and you agree to leave your arms here in the jailhouse and you're going to make all the rest of your outfit bring theirs in right now. And sign it."

Goose Cannon twitched and headed for the daybook, where there was a nib pen and ink bottle awaiting him. "You mind if I just put an X in there?" he asked.

"Why an X?"

"I can't think of all them letters and how to push them into a line."

"You're a man I understand," I said. "I got to shape them all up myself. But no, an X won't do. You'll write the thing down. Or we can wait until my deputy, Rusty, comes in, and he'll do it and witness your signature."

"Well, crappola," Cannon said. He dipped the

nib into the inkpot and began his task in block letters.

"How do you make a small A?" he asked.

"Just make it smaller than a tall A," I said. "Ain't any need for a college education here."

Cannon sweated and licked and blotted, and then shoved the log to me. It sure was a mess. But it did say, in crude print, that Cannon would leave his guns there and get the rest hung there real quick. He signed it with an X.

"That'll do, Cannon. This here's a quiet town, and you keep it that way."

Goose Cannon nodded, hung his matched revolvers on a peg, and fled. I thought the man was as slippery as a greased pig. Now I'd see if Cannon intended to keep the rest of his agreement and bring in the rest of those sidearms. It sure would be entertaining—if it happened.

CHAPTER TEN

Goose Cannon didn't return. He didn't bring his men in. No one showed up with a wheelbarrow full of gun belts and revolvers and rifles. I waited around, growing more and more morose. Rusty, damn him, was getting smirky over in his corner. The winter sun began to plummet, and still Cannon stayed away.

"You got took, Cotton."

"Looks like I did."

"You shoulda known better. Man like Cannon, you can't trust him as far as the outhouse."

"I did what I thought was best."

"Yeah, you trust people too much. You figure some skunk like that's really okay inside, and he'll not lie to you. Sometimes I wonder about you, Cotton."

"You picking on me?"

"Yep. You got hardwood between the ears sometimes."

"My ma used to say I made up for it."

"Well, you've got a gun ordinance and twenty armed men out there. And getting 'em in and their guns hung up, man, you've got a problem, Cotton. Too bad you didn't just lock the man up and hide the key."

"Yeah, too bad," I said. I wished Rusty would shut the hell up.

"We're peace officers," Rusty said, and that somehow tickled him, and he started wheezing his pleasure at the thought.

"If you don't like it, you go out and round up those dudes and bring them in—all twenty."

"You're the sheriff; me, I just mop out the jail. You're the one that's got the balls."

Rusty was enjoying himself.

It didn't seem so funny to me. "I'm supposed to be tougher and harder than the rest. I'm supposed to make those toughs think twice, or maybe shake in their boots. I don't know why I'm supposed to; people just think that way. But this isn't a dime novel. This is real life. I'm no different from anyone else, Rusty. I just try to work things out, keep the town peaceful, keep people from being shot. I don't know how to be twice as tough as anyone else around here. If that's what it takes, then I'll give the job to you."

"I don't want it."

"I trust a man to keep his word, and you tell me it was a mistake and I'm dumb."

Rusty turned silent.

"And if I threw Goose Cannon in the lockup, and his men started a war to get him out, you'd still be telling me I was dumb."

Rusty clamped his lips shut, like he had vowed to keep them sewn up tight.

"And if I lose a fight now and then, you'll tell me I'm not fit, and you'll get a new sheriff," I said.

Rusty industriously picked his nose.

I thought I'd go patrol. I would rather face the bitter weather than Rusty's cheery hostility. I wrapped a scarf around my neck, slid into a greatcoat, grabbed a sawed-off shotgun, and plunged into the cruel air. I headed into Wyoming Street, aware that the weather had chased sensible inside. If this evening was like any other this cold, I'd likely end up persuading the drunks to get out of the gutter before they froze to death. Drunks and cold weather seemed to go hand in hand. Usually, I corralled them all before their veins froze, but once I had failed to see a drunk lying in an alley. He didn't make it. He was so stiff the funeral parlor couldn't get him into a casket without a week of thawing. Maybe the cold weather was good. If it lasted through New Year's, there'd hardly be anyone braving it. Icy air would be more of a peacemaker than the Peacemaker holstered at my side.

There sure wasn't anyone wandering around. But then at Saloon Row I did see something a little odd. There was a pack train standing there. Five mules, all laden with stuff. Three of them carried wooden boxes, two to the mule, labeled DUPONT HERCULES. The other two mules carried other stuff, wrapped in canvas and tied down tight. I sure didn't know what was going on, but someone would. The mules were coated with a rime of frost and had icicles dangling from their muzzles. They were connected nose to tail by stiff lines. I dipped into the shelter of a recessed saloon door and waited, feeling my toes and ears getting frostbit.

The waiting paid off when two gents in buckskins showed up. Both had coon-tail hats and big cloth overcoats. They looked as frostbit as the mules, and they looked around, as if to see whether anyone was out in the twilight.

"You fellers need anything?" I asked.

They eyed me, eyed my sawed-off shotgun, and got the general idea I was a lawman even if the badge was buried somewhere under layers of wool.

"Nah, we're just casing them saloons."

"You mind telling me what's up?"

"You the sheriff?"

"Yes, Cotton Pickens."

"Well, that's fine. We're on our way to do a

little chore, and we stopped here to have a look at your town."

"What little chore?"

These fellers were so frosted up and hatted down I could hardly tell one from the other, but they sure interested me.

"Oh, just a little task is all. Nothing for you to worry about, Sheriff. We'll just leave town and keep on agoin'. Now me and my friend, we're drinking men, so we stopped for a snort. We're about ready to vamoose."

"You got names?"

"Oh, sure, I'm Ezra Panhandle, and this here's Scuffy Scruggs."

"And what do you do?"

"We're powdermen."

"What's that?"

"We work in the mines. We drill into the face, load a charge into each hole, usually a stick of DuPont with a cap, and run some Bickford fuse out of there. We get them all timed to go off at the same moment, and when it blows, the muckers have more ore to shovel."

"What are you doing in Doubtful?"

"Oh, just for a little while, Sheriff. We're here peaceable."

"Powdermen? That's what you've got on the mules?"

"Oh, we always carry. If we didn't carry, we'd feel as naked as a shootist without his gun."

"Could that stuff go off?"

"Sure could. If the stuff on them mules were to blow, there'd be no more Doubtful."

"And you carry it around town? You think maybe you'd better get out of here?"

"Aw, it's tough to set it off. It's not like nitro. This stuff is safe. Maybe a stray bullet might set it off, but nothing else, especially in this cold. It's so cold here that this stuff is half dead."

"A stray bullet. Along Saloon Row. Fellers, you bring that mule train over to Courthouse Square, and you and me are gonna have a little talk. You'd better tell me why you're here, who brought you here, and what you're planning to do."

"Naw, we're on our way," said Scruggs.

"I think you'd better walk in front of me and head for Courthouse Square. I think maybe we'll put all that explosive in a safe place."

"It's safe enough. And you don't have a powder magazine in Doubtful," Panhandle said.

"Tell you what. We'll get out of town right away. You can watch us go," Scruggs said.

"No, I think maybe we'll have a little fireside talk."

They shrugged, collected a lead line, and tugged the mules into the wind. The mules didn't like it, humped their backs, and made the DuPont cases dance on their backbones. But after a while, we all arrived at the square, and Scruggs tied up the mule outfit.

The powdermen headed inside, with me following, waving my sawed-off shotgun a little to hurry things along.

They stomped snow off and pulled hats from heads. It was the first real look that I got of the pair. Scruggs was short and thick; Panhandle skinny and bearded, with itchy fingers that kept flexing.

"Rusty, this here is Scuffy Scruggs and Ezra Panhandle. They're powdermen from the mines. They've got a mess of powder tied outside."

"What do you mean, powder?" Rusty asked.

"Six crates of DuPont Hercules dynamite, and all the fixings."

"Jaysas, I'm outa here."

"Couldn't be safer," Scruggs said. "It's just nitro and clay, formed into sticks. That's what dynamite is. You'd have trouble blowing up a house fly with it."

"They won't tell me why they're here," I said.

That stopped Rusty in his tracks. "They won't say?"

"Oh, it's not your business, long as we don't violate the law," Panhandle said.

"I think it's our business," I said. I waved them

toward some wooden chairs. "Why were you on Saloon Row with that stuff?"

"We're just a couple of wayfarers, lost in the cold," Panhandle said.

"You're a smartass. What were you there for?"

"To take a leak. There's an outhouse behind every saloon."

"Where were you headed? What's the powder for?"

"You sure are a nosy one, Sheriff."

That sort of fencing went on for several more minutes. It was plain that the powdermen weren't going to talk, and plain that I had no reason to hold them, and plain that they weren't going anywhere else. They'd come to Doubtful with the powder.

"All right, I'm escorting you out of town. We're going to move that powder far from here. Then you're free to return. Turk's Livery can care for the mules if you want."

"We ain't separating ourselves from our powder. What right have you?" Scruggs said.

"Public safety. That's right enough. You coming or do we do it ourselves?"

That galvanized them. In short order, they headed into the blowing cold, with me right at their side. They chose a creek bank out a way and unloaded the dynamite in an obscure area concealed by shrubbery.

"If this gets stole, I'm suing you," Scruggs said.

"That's better than blowing up Doubtful," I replied.

I steered them toward Turk's Livery Barn and let them go with a warning. "I don't want to see you around here tomorrow. Got that?"

"We're free men; we'll go where we want," Scruggs retorted.

I hastened back to the office, fearing that I'd frostbit my ears. The warmth was never so welcome. I hung up my greatcoat and warmed my hands in front of the cast-iron stove.

"What do you make of it?" I asked Rusty.

"If they were casing Saloon Row, maybe they were hired to blow up Saloon Row."

"They sort of showed up from behind the buildings when I was looking for them."

"Outhouses, like they say."

"Maybe. But if you was thinking of blowing up a building with that stuff, I guess you'd not want to do it on Wyoming Street, in front of everyone."

"Cotton, why is it that once in a while you make sense?"

"Rusty, my friend, your shift is about to get harder. We're going out."

"On a night like this?"

"Yep, colder than a frosted pump handle. You and me, we're heading for Saloon Row, and we're going to look for those powdermen and keep an eye on them. We're going to find them, and sort of ignore them, but keeping a sharp eye. I want to know why they're in town and what they're up to, and that means spoiling all the fun in a mess of saloons."

"There ain't a barkeep in Doubtful likes us hanging around his place," Rusty said.

"You take the north side and I'll take the south side."

"You mean I got to go out in this?"

"Yep."

"But I didn't put on my long johns."

"Now you're stuck."

"Are you going to carry?"

"No, but I'll keep my billy club under my coat."

"I'll freeze my toes," Rusty said.

"Serves you right."

With that, we bundled up and braved the merciless cold. I checked shop windows along the way, but Doubtful was hunkered down, waiting for spring, and so were the burglars, holdup men, purse snatchers, vagrants, and ladies of the night.

I had chosen the south side so I could visit with Sammy Upward in the Last Chance, one of the few saloon men who was semifriendly with me. And that's where I headed first. Sammy usually knew a few things.

The Last Chance was plenty warm and well populated with the usual ranch crowd. Sammy knew how to do business on a winter's night: generous shots and plenty of heat from the glowing stove.

I waited at the far end of the bar until Sammy slipped over to me.

"You know anything about two powdermen in town?"

"I heard about 'em. One's skinny, the other's short and thick?"

"Those are the two. They've got enough powder to level Doubtful."

"That's what I'm hearing. But the word is they're going to blow up Saloon Row at midnight, New Year's Eve."

"You know something, Sammy? I think you're right."

CHAPTER ELEVEN

That was all Sammy knew. If he knew any more, he'd tell me. He was the one man on Saloon Row who had some sense of keeping the place peaceful. No bar man can always choose his customers, but Sammy knew how to deal with most of them. He kept a few persuaders of his own behind the bar, ready to use. Mostly, the Last Chance was a peaceful place.

I had set myself a task, so I braved the subzero air and ventured down the street, entering each saloon for a look around. Those two powdermen would be easy to spot. There weren't many patrons in the saloons that evening. Most cowboys would rather nurse a big dry than nurse frost-nipped fingers and noses and ears riding into Doubtful. And most cowboys cared enough about their horses to keep from frosting their lungs by making them work on a night like this one. So the saloons were quiet, the bartenders yawning, the card sharps dozing at their poker tables, and the tinhorns staring into space beside their silent faro tables.

If there were powdermen around, they'd sure show up in a small crowd like this. I tried McGivers Saloon, where the barkeep, Buff Thorn, was no friend, but Buff just growled. There was only one man in there, a town drunk. I headed for Mrs. Gladstone's Sampling Room, one of the few saloons operated by a woman, but she had gone to bed and left the place in the hands of Rat Ryan, her swamper. Rat was a drunk who took his pay in booze, slept in the storeroom, and usually stank. But Rat was snoozing at the bar, a bottle in front of him, and two customers were huddled at the stove, worn out by talking when they had nothing to say, waiting out the cold until they could wash their winter long johns in the spring.

No powdermen there, either. The rest of the joints were the same.

I crossed the back alley and entered Sally's cathouse, but the girls were not in sight, except for a near-naked one behind the bar, shivering in the chill.

"You seen any strangers, tall and skinny, short and wide, come through?"

"All I look at is their pants," she said. "We haven't dished a screw all night. You want to try? A quickie, on the billiard table."

"I always want to try," I said, and backed out. "I'm a little slow, they say."

The other joints were the same. I doubted that the cathouses had done two dollars of trade that cold night. And no one had seen the powdermen.

I let the arctic air blow me back to the sheriff office and found that Rusty had beat me back.

"Nothing," Rusty said.

"Any rumors?"

"Yeah, them powdermen aren't friendly."

"Sammy says they're maybe gonna blow up Saloon Row."

"That's crazy."

"These are crazy times. I guess we got to follow the money. If someone's paying them for that, we ought to find out who."

"Seems to me we ought to be keeping it from happening," Rusty said dryly.

"Well, it's the same thing," I said, feeling a little sore.

"Powdermen don't show up by accident," Rusty said. "Someone got them here."

"Maybe they left town," I said. I was getting grouchier by the minute. "You go on over to Turk's and see if they're bedded down in the loft."

"Me? In weather like this?"

"You."

"But I'm still thawing out."

"You."

"I'll go if you go."

"Well, they're there. They wouldn't head out with them mules on a night like this."

"They haven't got their pay yet," Rusty said. "They've got to blow things up to get paid."

"Tomorrow, you go see if they're in Turk's hayloft."

"Tomorrow I'll pull the covers up and stay in bed."

Rusty was sure acting rebellious. I thought of firing him, then decided against it. "I'll fire you tomorrow, maybe," I said.

"That would be heaven," Rusty replied.

"Who do you think hired the powdermen?"

"The women."

"Like Mrs. Grosbeak?"

"She'd do anything to empty every bottle in town."

"They never should have let women vote in this state," I said. "It's ruined Wyoming."

"Too late now."

"My ma used to say that if women got the vote, she'd move to Texas. They'll never let women loose down there. Texas is not a good state for women and never will be."

I clambered back into my greatcoat, pulled a hat down, and headed out into the blistering cold. I had two powdermen loose in Doubtful, and I should never have let them go. If I found them, they'd answer some questions and probably enjoy my hospitality for the night. The more

I thought about the powdermen, the more it worried me. They could make the whole town disappear. I thought maybe I should go out to that cache of dynamite and try to blow it off. It'd sure light up the night.

Funny how this thing had gone from a prohibition law to a war. There sure were a mess of people who thought that going dry would cure just about everything that went wrong in the world. It was almost a religion to them: throw away the sauce and everyone, pretty near, would be happy and hardworking and responsible. And there were some steel-willed women in the town who believed it and were determined to make it happen.

I couldn't find any escape from that wind. It burrowed down my neck. It slid up my pants. It wormed its way into my waist. It nabbed my ears and nipped my nostrils and numbed my fingers. The only thing good about it is that it enforced the peace. I plunged into Turk's barn, which was almost as cold as outside. A lamp shown in the little cubicle that Turk called office and bunkhouse. The barn aisle was full of animals, welcomed into its shelter on this brutal night.

I rapped on Turk's door and heard cussing inside before the door opened a crack.

"I'm under six blankets and you come making trouble," Turk said.

"Yeah, it's a bad night. You got those powdermen up in your loft?"

"What men?"

"The ones put the mules in here."

"No, haven't seen them, Sheriff."

"Not in the loft?"

"Hell no. Not even a hay pile is enough on a night like this."

"Mind if I look?"

"Don't you be taking a lamp up there. Burn down the whole damned town. Yes, I mind. There's no one up there, and you ain't going to climb that ladder until there's light."

"They tell you where they'd be?"

"Closemouthed pair."

"If they come around, would you get me? I need to talk to them."

"On a night like this? Are you half crazy or all crazy?"

Turk jammed the door shut, cussing softly. You always knew where you stood with him.

It was black as spades in the barn.

"You up there, come on down," I yelled. "Sheriff speaking."

That met with silence. I stood there, full of a strange urgency I couldn't explain. I wanted those men, and wanted them before New Year's Eve, barely forty-eight hours away. I wanted to keep an eye on them night and day. My gut instinct was that the whole town, the whole county, lay in their hands. All they needed was a match.

I stood in that cold gloom, suddenly itchy and restless. I knew what I was going to do, and I hated it. But I had to do it. My instincts were howling. A white moon threw light into the barn, giving me what I needed. I worked through the restless animals sheltered there to Critter's stall and let myself in. Critter didn't like that and aimed a rear hoof in my direction. But I had anticipated that and dodged it. The hoof splintered wood.

"Cut it out," I said. "I'll turn you into dog food."

Critter leaned into me, pushing hard, driving me into the wall, squeezing air out of my lungs. I responded with a knee into Critter's belly. The horse whoofed and quit, and stood quietly for the moment.

"We're going out, whether you want to or not. So get used to it."

Critter bit me, then tried again, aiming at my kneecap.

"You've already told me that, but we're going. I'm going to stuff a cold bit in your mouth," I said.

I warmed the bit in my hand a moment and then tried to slide it in, but Critter was having no part of it. He bobbed his head and dodged the bit and farted.

"Cut it out! We're just going out for a few minutes."

Critter listened and quit fighting, and pretty quick I got the bridle on, and a saddle blanket, and then the saddle, which I cinched up tight, kneeing Critter to keep him from playing his usual games with the girth. Then I led Critter out of the stall, worked through the horseflesh sheltered in the barn, and stepped into a breathtaking, bitter white night.

Critter humped and shivered when I climbed on, but soon I was pointing my saddle horse toward the creek. There was something I had to find out, and fast, and that was whether the six cases of DuPont Hercules dynamite were where they had been unloaded at the creek bank under my watchful eye by the two powdermen.

The snow was so cold it squeaked under Critter's hoof, but at least the wind had slowed, and I thought I could make the whole trip without anything more than some frostbit earlobes and fingers. My ma would have scolded me for not bundling up.

There was nothing friendly in the moon that night. The white ground cover gave me plenty of light. Behind me, Doubtful hunkered darkly, asleep, barely a lamp lit. Smoke streamed from scores of stoves and bent to the wind. The night was as silent and secretive as any I had known in my life.

I saw no tracks. The wind whipped hoofprints away in moments. When I reached the creek and the brush along it, I hunted down the place where the powder had been cached and couldn't find it. I was sure I was at the right place. I had overseen the whole business earlier. But maybe the moonlight was tricking me. I rode up and down the bank, through brush, around naked cottonwoods, and found nothing. I stood at the very spot where the cases had been placed and saw not a thing. No imprint, no hoofprints. The dynamite was gone.

Just to be sure, I patrolled the riverbank in each direction but found nothing.

"All right, Critter," I said, and steered my horse back. Critter got the idea and settled into a sprightly jog, suddenly as barn sour as a horse could get.

This was probably bad news, unless the powdermen had simply left town. There would be an easy way to find out. The cold air harried me back, and I dismounted when I reached Turk's and let myself and the horse into the yard. I pulled open the barn door and led Critter to his stall, cleaned the tack off, and scratched Critter under the jaw. Critter bit me on the arm.

"Yowch!" I said, and got out just before a massive hoof crashed into the stall door.

"You're welcome," I added.

Turk allowed a bull's-eye lamp in the barn if it stayed on its wall hook, so I lit it, carefully extinguishing the lucifer. It cast a torpid light across the cavernous interior. There were maybe twenty animals there, their eyes on me, glowing like coals in the light. I was looking for the powdermen's mules, and I gradually picked them out.

They were good mules, well cared for, and I soon located all six. Some had saddle marks on the back, where the pack sawbucks had pressed into them.

So the powdermen were in town. And the dynamite was probably in town. Or at least it was no longer cached at the riverside, safely away from Doubtful. I wondered where it was and where the powdermen were. It was a puzzle.

I extinguished the bull's-eye lamp and waited for the wick to go black, and then slipped into the bitter night. Somewhere in this town were men with enough powder to turn Doubtful into history, and most of its people with it. I didn't know why they were here, what they planned, and who had brought them. I hadn't the faintest idea what the dynamite was for, but the best bet was blackmail: do what we say or we'll blow the place to smithereens.

CHAPTER TWELVE

It was colder than a pissant's mother-in-law the next morning, but I figured I'd better get busy. There were a mess of armed men in Doubtful, and two powdermen, and that made me a trifle unhappy. Wherever they were, they were all hiding, and that made me even more unhappy. Those three gilded wagons, parked near Saloon Row, sure reminded me that there might be a circus at midnight the next day. I bundled up and patrolled the town, but there wasn't a soul on the streets. It wasn't a day to be out.

The next best thing would be to have a little talk with them Temperance ladies. The armed men and the powdermen sure didn't get themselves hired to keep the saloons open. That meant a trip to the north side, to have a visit with Eve Grosbeak, wife of the Puma County supervisor and leader of the Temperance women. I sure didn't know what to say, but maybe I could rattle something out of her. I needed all the information I could get if I hoped to keep Doubtful from blowing itself to smithereens.

The Grosbeaks lived in a pleasant frame house with a white picket fence around it, and half a dozen peacocks. I had never been to a place with peacocks before and couldn't quite figure out the attraction. All they did was crap all over the yard and spread their feathers out. But that was the Grosbeaks for you. A pet often resembled its master. I got myself into my heavy coat, headed up there, and entered the yard, closing the gate behind me. The way to the house was barred by a big peacock, his tail spread out a yard or two, and he was making funny little waddles. Whenever I moved in one direction, the peacock dodged that way, tail spread. And no matter which way I moved, the big bird was quicker. I wished I'd brought a billy club so I could knock the bird senseless.

Then the bird leaped, landed square on my chest, and knocked me flat. Only then did I figure out what was what, and what the big bird was after. It sure was insulting.

"Get off me, you damned old stud," I yelled, but the peacock was doing strange things. I got to my feet, pushed the bird aside, and stomped toward the house. I saw a slightly parted curtain in a window fall into place and knew that some peacock-watchers were in there, recording the event for posterity.

I fantasized making the peacock species extinct and was giving it serious thought when the door opened, and there was Mrs. Grosbeak herself.

"Why, Sheriff, do come in. I just saw our rooster being friendly to you. That's how he is, you know. Friendly to everyone."

"Yeah, well, I'll shoot him if he gets any friendlier."

Eve Grosbeak's laugh was a tinkle.

She led me into a front parlor with flocked red wallpaper. A guest was there. I recognized her as Manilla Twining, the wife of Lester Twining, the chief cashier of the bank and one of the county supervisors. Manilla was famous for her campaign to bring suffrage to women in Wyoming, and also famous for having a whole platoon of gentleman friends.

"Why, Sheriff, you're just the man we want to see. Is everything going well?" asked Eve Grosbeak.

"Well, ma'am, no. There's a mess of armed men in town, and some powdermen, and three gold circus wagons. You want to tell me about all that?"

"Who, me?" said Eve.

"You, ma'am."

I turned to Manilla Twining. "I don't suppose you know anything about that."

"Young man, I deal with public policy, not circus wagons."

"What's public policy?"

"Oh, it's all over your head, Mr. Pickens."

"Well, I stand five feet ten, so not much over."

"Deduct a foot. Your head doesn't count," Manilla said. "But as long as you asked, I'll tell you. We're putting together an agenda for the Women's Temperance Union. Of course the first step was to obtain suffrage, and the second step is now about to occur, at least in Puma County. Prohibition. Absolute bone dry. Once we've achieved that and saved families from poverty and degradation, we will proceed to our next steps."

"I'm afraid to ask," I said.

"Oh, we'll tell you. But we must phrase it delicately in mixed company." Manilla and Mrs. Grosbeak eyed each other. "Why, we'll begin to remove anything that weakens family life, or causes gentlemen to stray from the bosom of wedlock."

"Ah, you'll have to make that a little plainer, ma'am."

"The places that have no name, my dear man. The places where no respectable woman would ever be seen."

"Oh, the fun parlors. They're all mighty fine, here, and I keep 'em well under wraps."

"They're a blot on our escutcheon, Mr. Pickens."

"Not on my escutcheon, they ain't."

"There's more, Sheriff. You may as well hear the whole agenda, because you'll soon be enforcing it. Next we're going to abolish smoking. Dreadful habit. Soon the lungs of wives and children will suffer less, and Puma County will be a better place."

"Yeah, and what else?"

"Why, gambling and horse racing, Mr. Pickens. Pernicious vices that sap the finances of families, create debt, and ruin children."

"That's it?"

"Oh, no, we have many more plans we're working out. "We're going to phase out restaurants. They are the vice of single men and weaken family life. Once we get them shut down, especially Barney's Beanery, we'll strengthen the bonds of wedlock in Puma County."

"What about me? I need a few restaurants."

"No you don't, boy. You need a woman in your life."

"I got too many of those already."

"Oh, aren't you the sly boy. Now, there's a few more things. We're going to eliminate coffee, tea, and card-playing from Puma County."

"Jaysas," I said. "What's a man to do?"

"Chop stove wood for his wife," said Manilla.

"I don't think I want to get married," I said. "I'd take the benefits, though."

"You poor dear, you only made it through fifth grade. Our agenda also includes putting all children through grade and high school so they can go out into the world better equipped to be mothers and fathers."

"You got any other plans?"

"Well, yes, but it's a bit radical. We firmly believe that men are the source of all difficulty, and that if men were disfranchised, and only women could vote, the world would be a peaceful, safe, and productive place."

"That makes sense. I always have to get someone to tell me what's on the ballot," I said.

"You're educable," Manilla said. "I'll say that for you. Now you come over to the settee here and sit between us, and we'll show you why you should become a family man, and why you should support everything we do."

"Sit between you on that red thing?"

They were both beaming at me. I sure didn't know where this was leading, but I edged down until I sat between them.

"We're going to show you how to kiss. So few men are any good at it," Manilla said. "This is just practice, of course. Consider it an important part of your education."

"That's fine with me," I said. "Only you got to take turns."

"We need to explain a few things first," Eve said. "We're hoping you'll be our ally. Our program requires friendly law enforcement. A peace officer against us could set us back a long way."

"Well, ma'am, I'm sure not for going dry."

"Well, dear boy, you would be if you were happily married. If you had a loving wife, and a little bundle coming along every little while, you'd see things our way. The trouble with single men is that they want all the wrong things. Saloons and other vices. Now, dear boy, Manilla and I have been talking about you for weeks, and we've come to some understanding. The thing that keeps you from wedded bliss is that you don't know a thing about women."

"That's what my ma always said."

"You got through fifth grade, but when it comes to women, you're still in first grade."

"You got some final exams or something?"

"No, child, but we are observing, and we've been watching you for months. You need some lessons, some samples of the joys that await you. And we're going to provide them—just little samples, of course, to start you in a new direction. If you take our lesson to heart, you'll be happily married in a week or two."

"I sure wouldn't want that, ma'am."

"That's why we're here. To show you a sample of what awaits you. Always with propriety and modesty, of course."

I discovered myself wedged between these ladies, who were gazing eagerly at me, and I decided it wasn't half bad after all. Nothing like a little lesson or two. They sure looked sweet, with loose lips and hungry eyes, and fluttery hands.

"Now, Sheriff, how long has it been since you washed your union suit?" asked Manilla.

"I put her on in the fall, and I'll take her off in the spring."

"That's what we thought. You are not fragrant. We'd suggest that you get another union suit and throw this away, and that you wash the new one once a week."

"On a sheriff salary?"

"You get a new one, and we'll arrange the rest. And while you're at it, Cotton, dear, you really should get a Saturday night bath at the Tonsorial Parlor. That would prepare you for all the good things to come, when you are courting and getting married."

"I'm not much for reform, Mrs. Twining."

"Call me Manilla, dear. Now, you could scrape your beard with a little more regularity, so that your cheeks are smooth to the touch."

She ran a hand over my cheeks. "Ouch! You really need to make your face more suitable for women," she said. "When we kiss you in a moment, we'll all suffer."

"You're going to kiss me?"

"We promised you a sample. Eve and I, we're dying to kiss you."

"Ah, I'm not sure about this. What if someone—walks in?"

"There won't be anyone walking in. Mr. Grosbeak is busy supervising Puma County. He's your employer, you know, and you'll do exactly as Eve and I require."

"Ah . . ."

"Be quiet, child. I'm going to kiss you, and Eve will give you pointers."

"But I might drown."

Too late. Manilla leaned into me, wrapped her arms around me, and began kissing me madly. I sort of enjoyed it, at least until she began probing with her tongue.

I busted loose. "What are you doing that for?"

"That's called French kissing, and it's sure to delight your future wife," Manilla said.

"I prefer the good old American type," I said. "I always knew foreigners do it different."

That didn't slow Manilla down. She went back to work, kissing away, and pretty soon she was breathing hard and carrying on, while Eve sat primly. I was getting so I liked the whole show and was ready for more lessons. But then Manilla suddenly pushed me away and sat there, breathing hard.

"That's your lesson, dear boy," she said.

She sure looked a bit wrought up.

"My turn," said Eve. "Are you ready for your lesson, boy?"

"I don't know, ma'am. I think I've had enough for one day."

"I'll show you a few things, boy."

She grabbed me and first kissed gently, eyes, nose, and lips, while she ran her arms up and down my back and snuggled in tight. She was real slow and steady, not all agitated the way Manilla was, and I figured that was just fine, so I kissed back, slow and steady, feeling warmer and warmer. It was sure strange, in the middle of winter, to feel so warm. Eve carried on that way for a while, her hands roaming far and wide, higher and lower, tugging at me, and I thought this was really good, and I was ready to get married after all.

But then, suddenly, Eve pushed us apart. She was sure acting like she'd run a race, panting away. She stood suddenly and bolted from the room.

"What'd she do that for?" I asked Manilla.

"Sheriff, you really are stuck in the first grade," Manilla said. "Now you just go find yourself a wife. I'm sure you'll make her very happy."

"I still don't know why she just bolted out of here. She want me to leave?"

"No, dear boy, quite the opposite."

"You want to try it again?" I asked.

For the longest while she stared, her gaze unable to meet mine.

"I think you've had enough lessons, Sheriff," she said, sounding like she didn't mean it one bit.

A little later, all bundled against the cold, I left the house, got past the peacocks, and went down the hill. I was feeling a little indignant. First grade, they said. First grade. They didn't know nothing.

CHAPTER THIRTEEN

The weather turned mild December 31, which annoyed me. I figured that bitter weather would make for a peaceable New Year's Eve and the start of the big dry in Puma County. If it was twenty below, law enforcement would be a lot simpler. But no, I was betrayed by a south wind, which raised the temperature into the forties.

I had a bum job that morning. The county supervisors had printed up a mess of flyers about the new law, and Amos Grosbeak had told me to post one on every road leading into Doubtful and then hand one out to each place in town that served booze. That was worse than going to the dentist.

I had been to the dentist once, and the dentist, Willis Hogbranch, had poked around and then told me my mouth was odd; I had no wisdom teeth. "That's what my ma always told me," I had replied. "But you can pull some others if you want. I got through fifth grade with them."

"If your wisdom teeth ever come in, you come see me," Hogbranch said. "I want to record it for posterity."

But I never got wisdom teeth, and now I had an armload of flyers to put up or hand out. I got a hammer and tacks, and put up a few on fence posts around the edges of Doubtful. I figured the first cowboy to ride in would rip down the sign. But if that's what the supervisors wanted, I'd do the job.

Next I headed for Saloon Row. It was still morning, and I wasn't sure how many flyers I could hand out when most of the places were locked up. But Sammy Upward was in the Last Chance, so I handed one to Sammy, who was re-stocking his bar.

Sammy spread it on the counter, read it, and then ripped it up. He didn't quit until he had ripped it into little pieces, and then he took the pieces, put them in an ashtray, and burned them.

"We've been friends, Cotton, but I'm warning you: don't come in here this evening, and don't shut me down. That law's going to be a dead letter real fast."

"I do what I got to do, Sammy."

Upward turned his back on me and continued unloading bottles.

It sure wasn't going to be easy, passing them

flyers out. And that was just for starters on this fateful day. I decided to cut through the alley to the bordellos. They were always open, and I could pass out the flyers over there. The bordellos sure looked quiet, with the sun warming their front porches, and all those busy gals snoring away after a hard night. It looked as peaceful as a Sunday school picnic there, but by afternoon things would be a lot different. Even on a cold day, there would be ladies sitting in the windows, smiling at fellers.

I thought maybe I would start with the smallest place first. That was Serena Sopworth's house down on the end of the line. It actually was a fine clapboard house, elegant by Puma County standards, with a big porch as well as four bedrooms, a parlor, a kitchen, and a well-stocked bar with a mahogany backbar. Serena was an Englishwoman from Manchester, and I liked the way she talked. She charged plenty, had pretty girls, and her clients were mostly Puma's businessmen. Cowboys couldn't afford Serena's wares, and she didn't really want cowboys in her comfortable place. There were even lace doilies on her armchairs.

Serena was the youngest of the madams on the line, and I figured she had yet to reach thirty. She wasn't exactly beautiful, but she had a slim, imperial body that plenty of men noticed.

I rapped a couple of times and a man in a black suit opened up for me.

"I need to talk to Serena," I said.

"Of course, Sheriff," the man said, waving me into the well-appointed parlor.

It took a few minutes, and when the lady appeared, she was wearing a gold robe, and her chestnut hair was tumbled about her neck. She sure looked just as pretty that way as she did all gussied up.

"I'm delivering these here flyers, Serena. They're written notice that you got to shut down the bar at midnight."

"Oh, let's see," she said. "Would you mind reading it to me? I don't have my spectacles."

"Ah, it just shuts down the bar is all."

"Well, you read it anyway."

"Ah, you can go ahead and read it when you get your specs."

"No, I'll have my man come in and read it."

The man in the suit materialized mysteriously, and Serena handed him the sheet.

"Notice. Be it enacted by the supervisors of Puma County that on the first day of January, 1883, it shall be illegal to possess, buy, sell, distribute, or manufacture spiritous liquors, wines, beer, or any other liquid or solid that contains grain alcohol.

"Be it further enacted, that all places of sale and distribution for such proscribed goods shall cease commerce, and as of January one, all licenses to engage in that commerce shall become invalid.

"Be it further enacted that the fine for any of the above infractions shall be up to five hundred dollars and three months in jail, and further offenses may be punished with fines up to one thousand dollars and a year in jail."

The man handed the sheet back to Serena and vanished into the rear of the place.

"There sure are a mess of fancy words in there," I said. "My tongue just don't wrap around some of them proper. Now you take that word *proscribed*. It's real hard to separate it from *prescribed*. And I don't get the difference between *infraction* and *infection*, but maybe you can help me get her squared away in my head."

"That's what I love about you, Cotton."

"Well, just because I get tongue-tied doesn't mean you got to love me, Serena."

"But I do, Cotton, even if you don't know the first thing about women."

"I keep hearing that. Mrs. Twining, she says I haven't got to first grade when it comes to women."

"Well, she's right, Cotton. You have a lot to learn. But that's what I love about you. You're such a fine, handsome man, so full of beans. If I can borrow a term from the Americans, you're a fine old fart."

"Oh, you can borrow it, all right, and I can cut loose any time if it needs proving."

"Really? You can do it at will?"

"Absolutely. I'll let one rip."

I cut loose with a long one that sounded like a railroad engine hissing steam.

"Oh, my, Sheriff," she said. 'I've never heard the like. You're a great improvement on British men."

"It's the only talent I've got," I said. "I can win any contest in any saloon in Doubtful. I did one for six seconds once. Word sure got around Doubtful. There's no one in town can match that. That was like rolling thunder. It made me famous. Well, I gotta go hand out flyers."

"Please don't go, Sheriff. I'd love to have you stay. If you've got a few minutes, you could make me very happy."

"With more toots?"

"I know the secret of life. A tooting man is good in the sack. It never fails. In my trade, you learn a few things."

"Serena, I don't know nothing about women."

"I'll teach you, sweetheart."

"Some other time, okay?"

She looked kind of pouty. "I don't know how you got into office, Cotton Pickens."

"Fast with a gun," I said.

"And slow with everything else," she replied.

I nodded and slid out just when she was about

to plant a wet kiss on my aching lips. But I escaped into the pleasant sunlight and headed toward the rest of the bordellos, where I had no trouble handing out the flyers. It was plain that the madams were going to comply with the new law. They said they'd shut down their bars and pack up the bottles at five minutes before midnight, then steer their customers upstairs. They didn't like shutting down, but that wasn't their main business, so they could live with it. But they sure were nervous about what those female voters would require next. The whole world was changing fast.

I thought of Serena Sopworth and wished I hadn't been so hasty. She was the only woman I'd met who didn't mind if I gassed the whole room. That was worth a lot. Maybe I should marry her. I'd greet her with a wall-banger every time.

The afternoon was bright, and I thought most of those saloons would be open and I could unload my flyers. I pretty well knew what would happen, but I had a job to do and I would do it. I tried Mrs. Gladstone's Sampling Room first, knowing they'd be civil before tearing up the flyer. I saw Cronk, the tinhorn, manning his green baize table at the rear and then found Mrs. Gladstone herself supervising the restocking of the bar.

"Howdy, ma'am. I've got a flyer for you. Supervisors want it passed around."

She eyed me. "I'm busy. Read it to me while I get these bottles up."

"It just says what's legal and what's not beginning at midnight, ma'am."

"And what's the fines?"

"Five hundred and three months first offense. A thousand and a year after that."

She pulled two more bottles out of a case and settled them on the backbar.

"I should go into the cathouse business," she said, and returned to work.

"I'll leave it right here, ma'am."

I put the flyer on the bar and walked out, knowing there were some in there who were watching my every step.

I headed for McGivers and found a new barkeep in there, a man I'd never seen in town. This one had jet hair combed straight back and had big hands on a skinny body. The bar was well stocked. The place had an overhead light well that threw sunlight into the room, which made it a lot more cheerful than most saloons. The man wiped his hands on a bright white apron and waited.

"I'm Pickens, sheriff here. You new?" I asked.

"I'm Addison McGivers, nephew of McGivers himself."

"Well, you won't be employed for long," I

said. "This here place has to shut its doors at midnight."

"Who says?"

"County supervisors passed a law. Here she be," I said, laying the flyer on the bar top.

"Read it to me, Pickens."

"Ah, you just get someone else to do that. I gotta make the rounds."

"What you're saying is, you can't."

"I can read her all right, except for a few words. But I ain't got time for messing around. This is the big night. I've got to get all my troops lined up."

Nephew McGivers smiled, wiped those knobby hands on his apron, and plucked up the flyer.

"Pretty stiff fines, Sheriff."

"That's what happens when women get the vote," I said.

"Amen to that. Now are you coming around at midnight? I need to know."

"I got to shut down Saloon Row when the new law starts up, Addison."

"Call me Mr. McGivers. I save my first name for friends."

"I'll call you Nephew. Yes, I'm coming, and I'm going to do what the law requires of me."

"You're likely to get hurt."

"I guess I knew that when I pinned on the badge."

McGivers smiled suddenly. "You go ahead and

do your job, Sheriff. I don't blame you. I blame the supervisors and their law. There's some around the row that blame you. They say you should just look some other direction, keep a blind eye on this place. What they're saying is, you should just be a toad and ignore your duty. I'm not one of them. You go ahead and do your duty, and we'll go ahead and try to throw that new law into the creek, drown it like a sack full of kittens."

"I'll be alone, except for my deputy. I haven't got any surprises for you. I haven't sworn a posse and don't plan on it. My first task is to keep the peace. Anyone breaks it, he'll get a trip to my jail."

McGivers smiled crookedly. "Good luck, Cotton Pickens."

"It won't be luck. It'll be people around here with common sense who won't let this thing blow up."

"Speaking of that, we hear there's some powder-men floating around."

"There are, and they've disappeared. They have six cases of DuPont hidden somewhere."

"Sounds like an exciting evening, Sheriff."

"I'da preferred a real cold spell, but it's not in the cards," I said.

"You mind telling what those circus wagons are for?"

"Some home-grown vigilantes brought them, and I've been looking for them."

"Little portable jails."

"It sure is getting interesting around here. You see an armed man anywhere, let me know, all right?"

"Maybe," said McGivers. "Maybe not."

CHAPTER FOURTEEN

Doubtful felt like a powder keg with a lit fuse. I prowled restlessly, looking for trouble, trying to find those two powdermen, hunting for the vigilantes I knew were filtering through town. But I saw no armed men on the streets. When the saloons opened, I plunged into each, looking for sidearms, but I simply saw nothing menacing. The cowboys from surrounding ranches were riding in, and the hitch rails were already full of broncs bearing several brands. The early-bird cowboys were already tossing down redeye and would probably be inert, sleeping it off in Turk's hayloft before midnight even rolled around.

But I was as itchy as chickenpox and didn't trust the peace for one instant. Finally I headed back to my office, wishing I had been able to thwart the trouble I knew was coming. But who was there to arrest? The ranch hands were settled back. The various outfits all had their favorite saloons, and that was good because it meant less brawling. But you never knew when some snockered cowboys might decide to visit the saloon next door to show that other outfit a thing or two.

"Any trouble?" Rusty asked.

"There ain't nothing but trouble out there."

"How many fistfights? How many murders?"

"Oh, go to hell, Rusty."

"I don't see you collaring anyone."

"It's only four in the afternoon. See if I'm collaring anyone around eleven."

"If they all ride in, we'll have about three hundred drunken cowboys on hand," Rusty said. "That should make the night entertaining."

"You'll stay here and handle the traffic, and I'll go out. I figure nothing much will happen until ten or eleven. And then, who knows?"

"You sure you don't want a posse?"

"No, they'd have guns, and I won't have it. No guns. This is a tinderbox. My business is keeping the peace. And that means keeping drunks from going for guns."

"You'll carry, though."

"No, Rusty, I'm going out with a badge and that's it. This ain't a night for guns."

"Seems a little crazy to me. You'll want all the powder you can get before the night's over. You can bet that every saddlebag on every horse has got some sort of gun in it."

"And that's where they'll stay if we use our heads."

"You should carry a scattergun, anyway."

"It'd just start wars, Rusty. No guns. And that includes me."

"How you gonna drag a drunk into those cells without one?"

"I'll manage."

Rusty sure looked worried. He was bursting with objections, but I just glared at him. I wasn't sure I was doing the right thing. A part of me wanted to carry a shotgun and a brace of revolvers. Another part of me said that there'd be some new graves out in the cemetery if I did that.

I headed back out on the streets late in the afternoon as the winter sun was sinking. It sure seemed quiet enough. The hard drinkers were already guzzling, but I saw no bunches of rowdies collecting in front of saloons looking for wild times. The mild air helped. It was above freezing, and everyone was happy. The horses were yawning, dozing at the rails, sometimes with a leg cocked.

Maybe, just maybe, the night would go peacefully. But I sure had an itch that was beyond scratching. I walked the alleys behind the saloons, watched boozy cowboys head for the stinking pisspots, eyed the cathouses slumbering in the winter's light, and finally watched the sun drop below the mountains and bathe the world in a final purple light.

So far, none of them vigilantes were floating around, which was good. It got dark fast, just a few days after the winter solstice, and by five it was full night. I prowled, ready to spring on trouble. But there was none.

I got to disbelieving my own senses. Three hundred drinking cowboys just didn't add up to no trouble. And they were still coming in. I watched big bunches of them ride up, hunt for hitch rail space, and sometimes make do with other arrangements. One outfit strung up a picket rope between two buildings and hooked their critters to it. It sure was getting crowded in Doubtful, but that was fine. The merchants would put some cash into their tills. And still there was no trouble at all. You'd think they were all serving sarsaparilla.

By eleven, the drunks were falling from the bar stools. Just about when I was ready to drag some of them to jail, their pals would escort the wobbly-legged ones to their ponies, hoist them up, settle them in the saddle, hand them the reins, and slap the horses. The barn-sour beasts would head home, with the loaded cowboy reeling like a dying top onboard but managing to hang on from sheer instinct.

"Guess that takes care of that," one of the ranch hands said, eyeing me. "Saves you a trip uptown."

"I guess it does," I said. "And there's no way that feller's gonna freeze up with that much booze in him."

Between eleven and midnight that was becoming routine. All I had to do was stand around while the cowboys loaded other limp cowboys onto their nags and sent them into the night.

But at eleven thirty there was a fistfight at McGivers; two real mean drunks were flailing each other while the crowd watched silently. Usually the crowd howled and encouraged, but this time no one was doing that. They were too intent on downing the last redeye they'd see for a long, long time.

I stepped in and separated the two. They were both too loaded to resist, though one bounced a fist off of my cheek, which bruised me some.

"Taking you in," I said. But neither of the pugilists rose, and it became plain that they couldn't rise and that walking uptown was not in the cards. And it wasn't worth it.

"Stretch 'em out on the planks and let 'em cool down," I said. "And when they cool down, put them on their nags. I want them outa here."

Some of the cowboys seemed happy to oblige. They hauled the carcasses outside, onto the plank sidewalks, and laid them down side by side. Both had bloody noses and one had a split lip, and the other was missing a piece of earlobe. Both had sore knuckles. They lay on their backs, staring up at the night sky, enjoying the ribald comments of the crowd.

Several cowboys from rival ranches hung around insulting the hapless warriors, which was fine. The bloodied men sprawled on the boards had earned it. Most everyone headed back inside for a final drink, and the barkeeps were pouring doubles even before being asked.

Time sure was running short. I peered around, hunting for trouble, hunting for those vigilantes, but I didn't see an armed man on Saloon Row. I wondered whether to get Rusty so the two of us could control the mob. But I decided against it. I wanted Rusty back at the jail. It got to be ten minutes to midnight, the brink of the new year, the beginning of prohibition in Puma County, and still nothing happened. I had it figured now. All them drinkers and saloonkeepers, they would do nothing at all. Let the good times roll.

But then about two minutes ahead of the hour, according to my pocket watch, a platoon of men, all in dark clothing, flowed like India ink into the district, each armed with a shotgun and revolver. Where the hell they came from I couldn't imagine. I headed toward the bunch, but even as I approached the platoon fell apart, two men posting themselves at each saloon, shotguns at the ready. It was an army maneuver, plotted out in advance. And suddenly there was a hell of a silence on the street and a dampening of sound in the bright-lit saloons.

I hastened to the ones nearest me.

"Come along now. There's a law against carrying arms in Doubtful," I said. "You head for the jailhouse. Either that or surrender those guns. Right now. On the ground."

They ignored me.

The others ignored me. I felt strong hands clasp me from behind.

"Don't resist, Sheriff. There's a ticket to hell waiting for you if you do."

It sure was getting quiet in all the saloons. A few men peered through the glass into the dark street.

"Is it midnight yet?" one of the dark-clad men asked.

Another, his face shadowed, pulled out the watch and tilted it toward the light spilling from the saloon. "Exactly," the man said. "Happy New Year."

"You're resisting arrest," I said, feeling like I was addressing a fence post.

"You stay out of it, and you might live," the

shadowed man said. "We're just helping you enforce the law, Sheriff. Call us a posse. Call us friends. Call us the strong arm of the law."

"I'll call you men in big trouble," I said.

Then another strange thing happened. Some guys with megaphones showed up. They opened each saloon door, lifted their megaphones, and addressed the revelers. But it was so quiet in the saloons that they didn't need megaphones at all.

"Head for the alley, watch the fireworks," the ones with the megaphones were yelling. "See the biggest show in town."

No one in the saloons moved. They stood at the bar, drinks in hand. They sat at the tables, drinks in front of them. The barkeeps stared, uncertain about it all.

"Watch the outhouse fly," yelled one with a megaphone. "And then watch the saloons fly."

That didn't make sense, but I couldn't do much about it, not with cold steel pressing in my back and two or three men pinning my arms. Finally, slowly, a few men headed for the rear alley, then more, and finally a hundred, from all the saloons lining the alley behind Wyoming Street. The men in black pushed me down a gap between saloons to let me see whatever was coming.

They sure were quiet. This was the quietest New Year's Eve ever seen in Doubtful.

"As the outhouse goes, so goes the saloons," said one guy with a megaphone.

A light flared near the biggest outhouse back there, a four-holer behind the Last Chance. Then a sizzle, sparks, a moving flame, eating its way through snow and muck, heading straight for the outhouse.

And then *kaboom.* A blinding flash, ear-splitting noise, white light, the outhouse rising into the night, falling into a thousand bits, stuff splattering everyone around. I got hit with some of that crap, and it didn't smell good. It dripped down my cheek and fell off my hands.

The shattered outhouse rose high and tumbled back to earth, even as the roar quieted down.

"Holy crap!" someone yelled.

The powdermen had been busy after all.

"Now, get out of the saloons. They're all ready to blow," yelled one guy with a megaphone.

"Jaysas," said a cowboy. He raced toward Wyoming Street to collect his ringy horse and get out. Then others were following. Soon it turned into a rout, those remaining in the saloons busting through the door to get out, running for their panicky horses, running as fast as their wobbly legs and booze-soaked lungs could take them. They climbed awkwardly into the stirrups and kicked their steeds away. The men in black didn't stop them; they waved the cowboys on until there were only the echoes of hoofbeats in the night.

That was the durndest thing. One minute three hundred cowboys were ringing in New

Year's Eve; a few minutes later the whole lot were collecting their horses and getting the hell out of Doubtful. It hardly took five minutes. Horses with riders on them vanished into the night.

"All right, you barkeeps, you get out, any still inside the saloons," the megaphone man yelled. "And don't try to be a hero. There's DuPont under every saloon, ready to blow."

One by one the reluctant barkeeps filed out of their saloons, some rubbing their hands on their bar aprons, most of them looking weary and defeated. The saloons looked forlorn, lamps guttering in the flow of cold air. Half-emptied glasses everywhere, a strange sadness issuing from them.

"Everyone out?"

"No, there's one in McGivers."

The shadowed men peered inside, and I did, too. Young Addison McGivers stood defiantly behind the bar, his arms folded, his white apron bright in the lamplight, unbudging.

"You, get out. The fuse gets lit at the count of three. One . . . two . . . three . . ."

A light flared around the back, on the alley. The fuse caught and hissed. McGivers saw the spitting sparks snake toward his uncle's saloon and bolted, making the street just as the saloon lifted bodily into the night sky and settled down in ruins. The explosion echoed through all of Doubtful, an odd, hollow thunder. The percussion slapped me hard. The tired old saloon settled back on its lot, a pile of rubble, dark in the night. McGivers stood in the street, tears in his eyes. It was over. Swiftly, the men in black pulled out hatchets and swept into each saloon, smashed bottles, crushed glass, chopped open casks and kegs, raided storerooms. In only a few minutes there was no spiritous drink left anywhere on Saloon Row. Prohibition had arrived right on schedule. The inkblot platoon slipped silently into the night, taking their wagons with them, and at the last they freed me.

"You see?" said one shadowed man. "We did it all for you. And not a life lost."

CHAPTER FIFTEEN

Well, Doubtful, Wyoming, wasn't the same anymore. And wouldn't be. The town woke up on New Year's Day a different place. There wasn't a saloon operating. There wasn't a lick of whiskey to be had, at least in a public place. It was so serene you'd hardly know anyone lived there. There wasn't any place for people to gather, so people pretty much stayed home. They could sit around the potbellied stoves in the stores and gab a little, but it wasn't like having a little redeye with your friends at the old clubhouse on Saloon Row.

Rumor had it that some of those madams who closed their bars a little before midnight had socked away some booze somewhere, but no one could prove it. As for the saloons, they sat forlorn, windows punched out, letting the snow and dust drift in and cover a sea of broken glass and busted kegs littering the floors. Some of the saloon men packed up and left Doubtful. One or two rummaged through the busted saloons, trying to salvage a thing or two, but they were mostly out of luck. It was like picking up after an earthquake.

It sure was quiet. The cowboys didn't come in much, or buy much, or hang around town much. That worried the merchants, and some of them were unhappy with the Women's Temperance Union, fearing they'd lost trade. But others argued that Doubtful was the only place for the ranching people to go. They were mostly five or seven or ten miles out, but if they went over to Sweetwater County, or some other county seat, they'd have to ride their nags a good fifty miles. So there was no need to worry. And besides, the cathouses were still in business, and that was enough to lure the drovers off the ranches.

But it was still a wait-and-see time. The merchants were eyeing their empty tills and getting irritable, and wondering whether Doubtful would survive. But of course it would. It was the county seat, with a courthouse and all. Why would it disappear?

Amos Grosbeak was happy as could be, mostly because Eve Grosbeak told him to be happy. He wandered into my office a day or two after it was all over and settled in the chair across from my desk.

"Well, son, you did it. You got us switched over to prohibition without any loss, except for

McGivers, and that wasn't any loss. No one got hurt. Every saloon in town shut down within minutes of midnight. The law slid into place real peaceable and quiet. You sure have my support for sheriff from now on."

"Well, it wasn't my doing, sir. My ma, she always said don't take credit when you don't earn it."

"Oh, pshaw, it was your doing. You didn't even have to put some drunk into these cells that night. The supervisors are going to meet soon, and I'll propose that you get a two-dollar-a-month raise, paid with our eternal gratitude."

"You should cut my salary because I got nothing to do," I said.

"Oh, you'll have some things to do. There'll be bootleg saloons springing up out in the hills, and you'll need to ride out there and shut them down. You can't expect a major change like prohibition without some effort to circumvent the law."

"Well, that'll be better than sitting here in a sleepy town playing checkers."

And playing checkers beside the office stove was about all I had to do as Doubtful slumbered through the winter. On my patrols, I made a point of hiking through Saloon Row, which stood quiet and forlorn now, the wind whistling through the sagging buildings. That outhouse blast and the one that leveled McGivers blew out the windows there, and now Saloon Row harbored nothing but rats and vagrants.

Mayor George Waller had a different viewpoint entirely. He complained that the city revenue of Doubtful had been cut in half. Saloon licenses paid for most of the town's budget; the only income remaining was the bordello licenses that the city collected every three months.

"I guess we'll have to begin with some property taxes now," he said here and there, which evoked horror. No one wanted that. Some businessmen proposed that the city invite another three or four madams to set up shop so the city would have more income. And others in town suggested that each girl should have to get a license, and at fifty dollars a quarter, that would make up for the lost saloon income. But other shrewd businessmen said that would only drive the girls away, and then where would Doubtful be?

It was a dilemma, all right. Some of the good folks rejoiced because Doubtful was dry as a desert, but there were others who sorrowed, who talked of furtive trips to Laramie to stock up on booze. It sure was a sorrow for some. And there was the town drunk to think about, too. His name was Rat Ryan, and I had let him sleep it off in a cell many times. But now Rat was sober, and shaking, and unhappy, and threatening to go somewhere else. He'd been a swamper in the saloons, cadging drinks, mopping the floors, sleeping on billiard tables. But now he was a trembling, tear-eyed old fool, wandering dazed through

Doubtful. I got to feeling so sorry for him I offered Ryan a stagecoach ticket to Laramie, but Rat just cried a little and wandered away.

The cowboys did return after a while, mostly to visit the girls, and it was rumored that the girls sometimes poured a shot for their most trusted customers. So that brought the ranch hands in, and they did spend a nickel or two in the stores, but it wasn't the same. They spent a lot more cash when Saloon Row was rolling.

One February day, I ran into Eve Grosbeak and Manilla Twining on Wyoming Street just as they were coming out of the Emporium carrying some gingham for dresses.

"Oh, Sheriff, this is so sublime!" said Eve. "Doubtful is peaceful and safe, and soon there'll be little children playing in vacant yards, and more Sunday school picnics, and nothing to worry about. I tell you what, Sheriff; the day will come when Doubtful won't even need a full-time lawman."

"Yeah, well, ma'am, that's fine for you, but not for me."

"Dear boy, we've been thinking about you," Manilla said. "Have you found a young lady to spark?"

"No, ma'am, Doubtful's short of young ladies. Least your kind of young lady."

"Well, we think you should get married. That's all you need. Once you're married, you won't be restless anymore. Have you tried to make yourself more presentable?"

"No, ma'am, I got the same old bad habits."

"That's what worries us, Mr. Pickens. You come over to Eve's this afternoon, and we'll work on that. We want you to be happy, and eligible. A young woman always knows when a young man is eligible."

"Well, I'll give her some thought," I said, and tipped my hat.

But when afternoon rolled around, I had a choice between playing checkers with myself or going over there to Eve Grosbeak's nice little place on the north side, and getting past the peacocks and getting a lesson again. That beat checkers.

I opened the picket fence and was attacked by the male peacocks, but a good kick or two sent them off. They considered me a rival, even though I wasn't inclined toward female peacocks. Eve Grosbeak let me in at once, and I followed her through the sunny, fragrant house to a sewing room off on one side, where she and Manilla were cutting their new blue gingham along the patterns that were pinned to the fabric. It sure was a female sort of room, white wicker, big windows, and sewing stuff all over. I had never been in a room like that before and hardly knew what to make of it. But females had to do something in life, and maybe this was what they did. The room sort of solved a mystery about them.

They eyed me appreciatively. "Would you like some Earl Grey, Sheriff?" Eve asked.

"Is that some scotch?"

They laughed. "No, dear, it's tea, and much better for you."

"There's nothing better for me right now than some redeye, or the like," I said, meaning every syllable.

"Poor dear. You live with low expectations. We want you to learn what's available to you, so you live with high expectations. Spirits won't do you any good. A wife would. You need to take a wife, Sheriff."

"Well, it's crossed my mind, but I can't afford just me on a sheriff salary, much less me and a woman."

"You'll find that wives save you money. Think what you'll save not having to spend a nickel on spirits. Or not having to spend two dollars whenever you walk into, ah, one of those places."

"You can have a five-dollar pleasure for free if you're married," Manilla said.

"Or a ten-dollar one," Eve added. "Of course, it's up to you to find the right woman."

"My ma always said I was no good with money."

They walked around me as if I were a dummy in a store window, studying and nodding, and pointing. It sure made me curious.

"How long has it been, Cotton?"

"That's kind of personal, ma'am."

"I mean, how long since you washed your long johns?"

"Since Thanksgiving, ma'am. Got the pair at the Emporium."

"We think you need to wash them. You can't go sparking in dirty long johns."

"Oh, they're good to spring, ma'am."

"No, Cotton. I can see grime peeking through. You can't go sparking a girl until you dress for it."

"I didn't know you had to be dressed to spark," I said.

Manilla laughed like a tinkling bell.

"You step behind that screen there and hand us your long johns, and we'll wash them," Eve said.

"I couldn't do that. Not in front of women. And it'd take a long time to dry. I'd be stuck here for two days, bare-assed."

"No, no, no. Mr. Grosbeak has several old pairs, and I'll give you one, and we'll wash yours and return it to you in a few days."

"Well, ma'am, the Chinaman on Utah Street does a fine job, and I'll get these to him in the spring."

"Get behind that screen, young man. I'm going to bring you a spare pair. They'll fit just fine."

Eve vanished and I slid behind the screen, while Manilla pretended not to look. Truth to tell, I couldn't even manage one button, much less everything I wore.

"I'll come help you if you want, Cotton," she said.

"I'll need to do it in the water closet," I said.

"You just don't know anything about women," she said.

"Well, thank heaven for that," I said.

But I did manage at last, and peeled out of my boots and smelly stockings and shirt and pants. Then I got up my courage and pulled off the union suit. It sure was sort of clammy, now that I thought about it. I pitched it over the screen just when Eve showed up with a spare of Amos's. She set it atop the screen, and I snatched it and plundered my way into it, and pretty quick got myself back together. That new union suit felt soft and warm, and I had to admit I liked that. Eve took the old union suit away, holding it with two fingers, and I wondered if I'd ever see it again.

"There now," said Manilla. "You're on the road to sparking."

"You certainly are more fragrant," she said. "I'm going to put a little witch hazel on you, just to improve the flavor."

She had a bottle of that stuff, and pretty soon she was dabbing me here and there, behind the ears, on the neck, and on my wrists. Not bad. No worse than what I got in the tonsorial parlor over on Colorado Street.

"Now, Cotton, you'll need to buy some nicer clothing. We'll have Leonard Silver fix you up. We need to get you out of those, ah, slightly soiled trousers, and that, ah, ancient hat, and that, ah, frayed shirt, and those, ah, too comfortable boots."

"What for, Mrs. Twining?"

"So that you can find a sweetheart and be properly married and settle down in a lovely little cottage with rambling roses and a picket fence and lots of cheerful little children."

"Ah . . . but I only got through fifth grade."

"This is America, Cotton. Everything is possible. Only believe."

"Ah, but that's too many diapers, Mrs. Twining."

"Well, you'll need to progress. You can evolve, you know. You can continue your education. There are mail-order institutes that will send you materials. When you are suitable, you'll be filled with wedded bliss."

"Ah, madam, it's time for me to vamoose. I've got a hot game of checkers going."

Eve Grosbeak stayed me. "No, Mr. Pickens. We want you properly prepared for our next stage. Puma County is still in dire need of reform."

"It's already parched, ma'am. I don't know how it can get dryer."

"Dear child, this is just the first stage. When we are done, Puma County will be a land of milk and honey, with no crime, joyous families, lots of churches, children going for Sunday strolls, mothers pushing perambulators on paved streets, big shade trees plantcd along all our boulevards, and happy schools, filled with beautiful teachers and joyous students. Civilization will come to Puma County. The barbarous frontier will soon slip away forever. And you will be a part of the great step upward."

"I think I could get as far as eighth grade," I said. "I'd have to really give it a shot."

"We're trying our best to prepare you for what's next in the county. The Elysian fields of happiness."

"Well, ma'am, I'll give her a try."

"Good! At the next meeting of county supervisors, our dear husbands, the supervisors, are going to ban houses of ill repute in Puma County, and make it an offense to sell, buy, solicit, or engage in, ah, relations outside of the marriage contract. We'll want you to enforce the new law rigorously."

"Holy cats," I bawled.

Chapter Sixteen

The county supervisor Amos Grosbeak himself showed up in the sheriff's office one afternoon, interrupting my game of checkers with Rusty.

"Ah, it's perfect," said Grosbeak. "Playing checkers."

"What's perfect?" I asked.

"There's no crime. Nothing for you to do. Puma County is as peaceful as a graveyard. Playing checkers all day is the very signature of our success."

"It's a bore," said Rusty, jumping my piece and taking the game.

"It's heaven. We're succeeding in creating a piece of paradise here," Grosbeak said. "And now we're ready for the next step. At the February meeting, the supervisors will enact another ordinance, this one prohibiting all carnal relations in the county, apart from holy matrimony, of course. We will make it illicit to buy, sell, procure, or give away any fleshly vice. It will be illegal to operate, own, or rent a house of ill repute—or opium den. We don't have any, but we plan to prevent it anyway. This will be effective March one, and after that, violators will be heavily fined and jailed. Up to a year in jail ought to persuade the sisterhood to go elsewhere, as fast as their dainty feet will carry them."

"What for?" asked Rusty.

"So that we may advance matrimony, and keep predators and assorted vices and criminals out of Puma County. We shall have a serene county, filled with yeomen and their beloved wives, and the riffraff can all go elsewhere."

"And what will single men do?" I asked.

"Plant vegetable gardens. A little hoeing, a little weeding, a little stoop labor, a little collecting of cabbages and digging up potatoes, and plucking peas, sir. Put a cowboy to work in a garden, and you've got a good citizen in the making."

"Have you talked to the cowboys about this?"

"We don't need to. It is the most advanced thinking to be found, issuing from universities. A lot of scholarship has gone into it."

"So I'm supposed to shut down the parlor houses?"

"It'll be easy, Pickens. You did a masterful job with the saloons. See how peaceful we are now, with no trouble at all. You can get started by visiting those, ah, ladies and telling them what is in fate for them beginning the first day of March."

"So you want me to take the bad news to the madams?"

"Who else, Sheriff? You're the man of the hour, the hero of New Year's Eve. So we'll leave it up to you to inform them, and with any luck they'll all be shut down and the ladies will have caught the stage for Laramie even before March one arrives."

"You gonna tell me what the fines are if they resist?"

"Multiple fines, Pickens. For operating a house of ill repute, a hundred dollars for each offense. For soliciting, twenty-five. For, ah, servicing, fifty. Each offense, of course. Beginning with second offenses, jail time stretching into many months. We'll post it all after we've passed the law."

"You got all the supervisors with you?"

"Myself, and Twining. Reggie Thimble wavers a little, but he'll come around—or face the wrath of the Temperance women."

"So the gals got three weeks to sell their buildings and move out?"

"That's more time than they deserve, Sheriff. They've bilked innocent males out of a fortune. We're cleaning up Puma County."

"Seems that way." I turned to Rusty. "Set up another game."

"No, Sheriff, you'll be doing a lot of groundwork," said Grosbeak. "Beginning immediately, you'll visit all the operators of those houses and inform them what is coming. Don't delay. The sooner you tell them, the easier the transition. We'll put the frontier behind us and make Puma County the proud, serene, agricultural capital of Wyoming." He gazed placidly into my eyes. "Someday, the frontier and all its vices will be forgotten, and the past buried, and all the world will ever know of Doubtful is that it is the farmer's home, the supplier of all the neighboring wheat and livestock enterprises, filled with whitewashed churches, the paragon of everything mankind has dreamed of from the beginning of time." He studied me a moment. "Here, in this very place, those jail cells will go unused. Your days will be filled with checkers and chess and pleasant strolls through town."

"You know, you ought to give them ninety days. They've got property to sell."

Grosbeak smiled. "The wages of sin, my boy. If they have to sell at a low price, don't you suppose they earned it?"

"Who's gonna buy?"

"That's valuable land, and those are solid structures. I know of half a dozen of Doubtful's upright men eager to bid."

"For half price, I'd guess," Rusty said.

"Ten percent," Grosbeak said. "It'll benefit the town."

"Guess a mess of them gals will be getting married fast," I said.

Grosbeak frowned. "We won't encourage it. Puma County's going to be the most reputable place in the entire West, a model of virtue. No, we'd encourage all such women to depart swiftly."

"Okay, what's gonna finance the city?" Rusty asked.

Grosbeak glared at him. It was a delicate and cantankerous subject. "Mayor Waller will have to propose other means," he said. "If you are a stalwart at your job, Sheriff, you'll improve the city coffers."

Doubtful's entire municipal budget derived from quarterly saloon licenses, bordello licenses, bordello inmate licenses, and fines levied in municipal court.

"I'm not going to pinch anyone doesn't deserve to be pinched," I said.

"Well, I'm sure Mayor Waller will give you some new opportunities," Grosbeak said. "He's resourceful. We've had some chats and have some dandy ideas. We'll soon have a clean municipal budget, and here's how it'll happen. The mayor and the city council are about to enact an anti-spitting ordinance. Spit anywhere in public, and you'll get fined five dollars. Now there's a sensible law. Keep Doubtful de-spitted, and keep the coffers full. You'll be able to nab most any cowboy riding into town on that one. They all spit like rabid dogs."

"Me? You want me to arrest them?"

"Who else, Pickens? You're the finest lawman in Wyoming, the hero of New Year's Eve, the man with the shiniest badge in the West. Of course you will. We're going to give you a spitting quota. You'll arrest ten spitters a day, fifty dollars a day for the till, and that'll pay for most of the town budget."

"Not me. I ain't gonna haul a man into court just for laying a gob on some grass."

"You're sworn in as a peace officer, Pickens, and you'll enforce the law to the last jot and tittle."

"I'm not sure I want the sheriff office to be the source of the whole city budget," I said. "That ain't quite right."

"Sheriff, you're such a ninny at times. There's money to be made. Waller's going to propose a restaurant licensing tax. Fifty a quarter to operate a restaurant."

"Why? What have you got against restaurants?"

"They're public nuisances. They attract drummers and whiskey salesmen. People should eat at home, with their wives at the stove."

"What about the poor devil who's not got a wife?"

"Like yourself? Get married, Pickens. That's

going to solve all bachelor difficulties at once. Food, intimacy, baths, you name it."

"Well, I just don't figure out how wrong makes right. How pinching some innocent feller to raise money for the city does anyone any good."

"You'll understand better as time goes by, Pickens. You're still in your twenties and wet behind the ears." He eyed Rusty and me. "Now I have another matter to discuss, strictly confidential. And you'll both be involved in this. There's a new bootleg saloon opened up on the county line, at the place where the Cheyenne Road crosses the North Platte. The ferry house. It's on Puma County land, so it affects us. And you're going to ride over there and put a stop to it before it gets going. I hear they're set up to move the whole saloon across the river whenever trouble arrives. If they see you coming, that entire booze parlor will be ferried over to Medicine Bow, safe and sound. You can imagine what that means. You've got to pounce. You've got to get in there and bust it up and haul the guilty back here for trial."

"I can do that. But you tell Waller to go hire a town constable to enforce his spitting law."

"No, I won't tell him. Mayor Waller's a progressive man who sees a need and fills it. He's considering another option, a smelly outhouse fine. Any property owner who fails to lime his privy and creates a public nuisance, stinking up Doubtful, that's worth seven dollars in municipal court for each offense."

"I can sure go along with that," Rusty said. "The jailhouse outhouse, you'd get a fortune out of Cotton here. He heads in there and stinks up Courthouse Square."

"I don't have a budget for lime, Mr. Grosbeak."

"Well, I guess the town's gonna fine you."

"Or you. It's your outhouse, not mine."

"Oh, tut. The main thing is, there's lots of ways to raise revenue for Puma County and the city of Doubtful, and that'll keep you plenty busy."

"That's what I'm feared of."

"That's all, gents. Cotton, my boy, you go spread the word among those fine ladies, and urge them to vamoose fast, and tomorrow, you boys ride out to the crossing of the Platte, and see if you can nip that devil's work in the bud."

Grosbeak smiled broadly, clapped his derby on his well-clipped locks, and departed into a mild afternoon.

Rusty and me, we stared at each other, the checkerboard forgotten.

"I'm not sure I like this here job in a dead town. I'm a peace officer, not a cemetery officer," I said.

"What are you gonna say to the madams?"

"You go say it, Rusty. I'm heading for Barney's Beanery."

"No, it's your job, and he asked you. I ain't

going. You're going. Those ladies are my friends. They get about ninety percent of my pay. I ain't going over there like some hangman with a noose in my hand."

I was stuck. Rusty wasn't budging.

"Oh, all right. I can maybe do it before business hours."

"It's always business hours over there, Cotton."

"Maybe I'll just quit. It ain't any fun wearing this badge anymore. Maybe you and me, we could go over there together. You do the talking and I'll do the smiling."

"Not me. You want a deputy? You're about to lose one."

This was getting serious.

"Rusty, go get some beans at the beanery before they shut it down."

I wandered over to the bordello district, wondering which of the houses to visit first. I finally chose Mrs. Goodrich's Gates of Heaven, mostly because she wasn't likely to skin me alive when I opened my mouth. The place slumbered quietly in the February light and looked oddly forlorn, not at all like the gates of heaven.

I walked in, setting off jangles, and Mrs. Goodrich appeared at once. "Oh, it's you, dearie. The girls aren't up yet, but I'm ready, any time, any place. You want to try it on the front porch?"

It wasn't a bad idea, but my ma always told me

to take propositions under advisement, so I told her I'd consider the matter.

"Mrs. Goodrich, I, ah, got real bad news."

"You got the clap?"

"No, nothing like that. I got sent here by the county supervisors, in fact the chairman, Amos Grosbeak."

"They're gonna shut us down."

"Well, yeah, but they'll give you a little time."

"March one."

"Well, yeah, three weeks."

She began laughing, but it turned into a snarl. "Sweetheart, I've been there. Almost every town I've worked. Sooner or later this rolls through the door."

"I guess the saloons showed what was coming."

"The bitches of the north side. They got the vote and used it."

I nodded.

"I'm tired of running. I'm gonna make it as hard for you as I can, Cotton Pickens. Go ahead, kick me out."

"Well, I was thinking of making it as hard for you as I can, Mrs. Goodrich."

She laughed, the gravel grinding in her throat. "We're a pair," she said. "You could always come work for me."

"I guess I'd better go tell the rest."

"Don't bother. They knew this was coming. After Saloon Row, what else could it be?"

"I still think I'd better spread the word."

"If you want anything else spread around here, just speak up, sweetheart. It's on the house."

I nodded, retreated, and heard the door jangle behind me. Oddly, it was easier than I had supposed. The whole row was waiting for this. But I headed for Denver Sally's place just to make it official.

"Sally," I said when she let me in, "we got to talk."

"I already know," she said.

"How could you know?"

"Lester Twining blabbed it out yesterday. He said the supervisors were making big plans, that it would affect the Row. Lester's not one to keep a secret. Stick around, Cotton; how about the Argentine Bombshell? On the house?"

"Aw, Sally, I got work to do," I said, feeling blue.

Chapter Seventeen

The weather was agreeable the next morning, so I headed for Turk's Livery Barn. It would be good to escape dolorous Doubtful. Critter was in an ornery mood, having been stuck in jail for much too long.

"You want to go for a long walk?" I asked.

Critter kicked the stall wall and then the stall gate for good measure.

"If you don't let me in, we're not going anywhere."

Critter sawed his head up and down and clacked his teeth.

"I'm coming in. If you kick me, you're dog food."

I opened the stall door cautiously. A hoof hit it so hard the shoe left an imprint.

"Things are about normal," I said, sliding along the horse with a bridle in hand. "Now hold still."

Critter leaned into me, jamming me against the stall wall, crushing the air out of me.

"Stop it," I said, and kneed Critter in the belly. The horse went *whoof* and settled down. I slid the bridle in and looped it over Critter's ears. That pleased Critter, and he dropped some apples. After a bit I eased the horse out, brushed his back, loaded on a blanket and saddle, kneed the air out of the horse and tightened the girth, and then added a travel kit behind the cantle. Some bad-weather gear, a shelter half, a hatchet, and a few fire-starting items.

"You gonna be gone long?" Turk asked.

"Back late tonight or early tomorrow. Going to the Crossing."

"That's the new county seat," Turk said. "That's what I hear."

I boarded and let Critter hump and thump a while. Actually, Critter enjoyed the show and waited eagerly for it with every trip. I yawned. Then I steered Critter smartly away, and soon I was headed for the Crossing, some thirty miles distant. It would be a fine trip if the weather didn't turn.

There was enough frost in the trail to keep it hard, so Critter was having a fine old time of it, lurching along like he wasn't barn sour. But I knew better. Inside that cunning equine brain was a ferment of plotting, and with the slightest care-lessness, I would find myself out in the middle of nowhere, on foot, while Critter waltzed back to Turk's, laughing all the way. So I kept a tight rein and was extra careful when he stopped to wet some sagebrush along the way.

It sure was a dandy day to ride, and the frost hard trail made it easy. Around noon I spotted a group of riders angling in from the Admiral Ranch, so I pulled up and waited. Sure enough, there were six cowboys rippling with good cheer.

"Howdy, fellers, going my way?"

"Howdy, Sheriff. We're off to the Crossing for a little sizzle." That was Spitting Sam talking.

"What's at the Crossing?"

"Why, bottled goods, Sheriff. Lots of bottled goods."

"Well, that's where I'm heading, too. Mind if I join you?"

"Come right along," said Sam. "Join the party."

"How long's the Crossing been serving?"

"Ever since they shut down Doubtful," Sam said. "They got the Crossing up and running in a week or so, and had it all worked out. It sure is just fine."

It amazed me that the bunch should be so open about it. Booze, after all, was outlawed from one border of Puma County to all the other borders. But that didn't bother this crowd. Some had even donned a new bandana, just to get all gussied up for a little saucing.

"Is Yumping Yimminy still running the place?"

"Him and Jimminy Yimminy."

"That's his wife?"

"Well, I wouldn't go that far. But she's keeping us happy."

"What kind of place they got?"

"Same as ever, Sheriff, but more of it."

"What do they charge to take a wagon across?"

"Fifty cents, last I knew."

"On the flatboat?"

"Yep, but they got a bigger flatboat for the saloon."

"What do they charge for drinks?"

"Well, that's a sore point. They want two bits. Now, in Doubtful, it was a dime or one bit. But I guess they got transport problems out there. So we just pay up."

"Lots of ranch hands go out there?"

"More and more, Sheriff. But it's pretty far from them as ranch on the other side of Doubtful. For us, it's about the same, Doubtful or the Crossing, dozen or fifteen miles."

"Your bosses, they still buy supplies in Doubtful?"

"Some, yes, but Jimminy, she's loading in a lot of stuff and hardly can keep it on a shelf. It sure beats going to Doubtful. Pretty soon now, she'll have a whole mercantile going, and then no one'll go to Doubtful except to get married, which means no one from any ranch."

"Aw, you can still have a fine time in Doubtful, Sam. There's the ice cream parlor and the horse-shoe tournament."

Spitting Sam cackled. "Sheriff, they always said you was a little thick betwixt the ears."

"Well, cowboys ain't interested in women, Sam."

"Sometimes they are."

"No, if they wanted women, they'd not live in bunkhouses on ranches. Truth is, there's hardly a cowboy in Wyoming that cares a thimble about women. And don't tell me otherwise."

"Then what about Doubtful's sporting district?"

"That's for temporaries, not real wifey women. Your Admiral Ranch bunch, they go to the sporting houses much?"

"They got more important things to do in Doubtful," Sam said.

They were traveling in a jog, a gait that covered ground but didn't tire the horses. The trail led through long foothills, around the lip of gulches, into cottonwood parks, and up rocky grades, while off on the horizon loomed the Medicine Bow Mountains, chocked with snow, bold against a glowing blue heaven. Wyoming was a pretty good place, even Puma County, and I always got recharged when I got out into the country.

But it sure was a barren land. From some

perspectives, one could gaze in any direction and not see a tree. And not see much sagebrush, either. We ate up the miles through the day, and when the winter sun began to sink, we spotted the Crossing down a long grade leading into the Platte Valley, and the ranch hands turned real smiley.

By then, I was wondering about something. Why was Spitting Sam and that crowd so open about this bootleg saloon operating in dry Puma County? Why did they talk freely to the sheriff? Why weren't they tight-lipped, and trying to divert the sheriff? So now that the place was in sight, a mile away, I asked Sam.

"You sure have been gabby about an illegal saloon, Sam. You fixing to tie me up and toss me into the river?"

Sam, he just laughed. "See for yourself, Sheriff."

So we kept heading down that grade, out of the plains, with the big, wide river sparkling in the sun. One could see where the road on the other side snaked southward, but it would take a ferry ride to get a man and horse or wagon over to that trail. It sure was a distant corner of Puma County, and as far from the law as anyone could get. So I was wary. There might be big trouble boiling up fast, and I had to be ready.

But no one was paying any attention to that. The Admiral cowboys, they put spur to flank and broke their ponies into a trot, and then a lope, with a few wild yells to celebrate their arrival on the banks of the North Platte.

I took my time, even if Critter wanted to join the fun and go walloping in like all the other nags he'd befriended that long trip. But I thought that a little close observation might be the best thing, so I just jogged along, falling a half mile back as the rest whooped their way in.

Some of the place was as I remembered it. The big house, built of twisty cottonwood logs, was the same. That's where the ferry-keeper Yumping Yimminy and his wife lived. There were a couple of cabins for travelers that wanted shelter, and these were unchanged. There was a corral and a haystack and an open-sided shelter mostly used by the once-a-week stage line from Laramie. But there was now a long log structure with smoke issuing from a chimney, and it reminded me of the bunkhouses I'd seen on a dozen ranches. I saw no sign of a saloon anywhere, at least not in the old log house or the outbuildings. But the ferry was sure different. It was twice as big as the old one, a flatboat that had a regular cabin on top, tethered to the bank. This new ferry was a busy place, with smoke issuing from a stovepipe in the cabin and cow hands coming and going, up a gangplank from the riverbank to the cabin.

There was a hitch rail along there, and the

Admiral horses were tied to it, some of them steaming from the run down the long grade. I tied Critter well apart, knowing that my nag would bite pieces of flesh out of any other nag he could get his teeth into. Critter was my burden, my cross to bear, but I bore it manfully. I didn't want any other nag.

I dismounted and was immediately greeted by Yumping Yimminy. "Hey, yah, it's de sheriff! Welcome to de Crossing, Pickens. Come on in and wet your whistle."

So that was it. This was a floating saloon, at the edge of the county, if the county's boundary stopped at the edge and not the middle of the river. I didn't know for sure, so I wasn't going to be hauling the owners back to Doubtful any time soon. I'd ask Lawyer Stokes about it before I did anything rash.

Then I figured out the rest. This floating saloon was simply a river barge tethered to the shore. It wasn't used to ferry wagons or stock or men; the old ferry did that. This was a thirst parlor on a scow. It had been thrown together of raw planking, a hasty, crude saloon cut from green lumber, as raw as the redeye it served.

I found a compact tavern inside, with a rough plank bar, some tables, and a barkeep pouring drinks. Stumps served as seats. A black sheet-iron stove warmed the place and threatened to burn it down. The place was well patronized, with maybe twenty ranch hands swilling hooch, playing poker, or just rocking along with the river flowing under their feet. A man could drink and then retire to the cottonwood bunkhouse. All in all, a fine resort for the surrounding ranches on both sides of the county line. And making money, too.

I checked faces against my memory of Wanted posters and then decided that most of those pres-ent were not running from the law. Only one or two wore sidearms.

"Sheriff?" said the barkeep, a man who had worked at the Lizard Lounge in Doubtful only a few weeks earlier.

"A sarsaparilla," I said.

The keep slowly shook his head. "We don't have one. We don't plan on getting none. It's not ever going to happen here. This is the Crossing. Drink or go home."

"That's a pretty good motto: *Drink or go home.* You could frame it and put it behind the bar."

"Comic, are you?" The barkeep poured some-thing amber from a bottle and set it before me. "Two bits," the man said.

I sipped a little, letting the fiery stuff clean out my throat. But I was mostly interested in who was there, who wasn't, and what the place felt like. The truth of it was that the Crossing was thirty miles from any law. Even farther if one looked for law in the adjoining counties. It was a hangout for whoever wanted to steer wide of authorities. I didn't like the place. There was something sinister about it, something I couldn't dismiss. I sipped the redeye a little more, set the half-emptied glass on the planks, and slid out into late afternoon light. I wanted some daylight to look the place over. I didn't know what I was looking for, only that I wanted to case the place, stroll the grounds, poke into the cottonwood-laced river bottoms there, see what there was to see. So I wandered up and down the riverbank, watching snowmelt tumble down the North Platte on its way to the Missouri River. I studied the old ferry, tethered and ready to pole across the river. I wandered into the new bunkhouse and saw the crudest sort of shelter, a sod-roofed structure with raised plank bunks. A cowboy was on his own for comfort. A tin stove offered all the heat that place would get. I looked into the two older cabins, a little more civilized, with corn shuck mattresses and homemade chairs. An ancient outhouse served the buildings. The saloon on the scow didn't need one. I retreated into the deepening twilight, wandered the grounds, looking for whatever there was to see, trying to explain my itch to shut the place down. All I needed was a burial ground. A few graves would do the trick, all right.

Then I made a decision and walked over to Critter.

"You ready to go?" I asked. "It's a long way back to Doubtful, and you'll get tired of hauling me."

Critter aimed a hoof at me, missed, and let me mount. I rode out, without saying good-bye.

CHAPTER EIGHTEEN

I sure didn't want to go to that monthly Puma County supervisors meeting, but I had no choice. The head man, Amos Grosbeak, told me to come. The supervisors would hold the final hearing on the new ordinance and then vote.

So that February afternoon I made my reluctant way toward the courtroom in the Puma County courthouse, where the awful deed would take place. It was cold out, and the windows would be shut tight, and that would only make it worse.

The bill was entitled An Abatement of Public Nuisances. I could hardly figure it out, and Rusty wasn't much better, but the county attorney, Lawyer Stokes, would read and discuss the bill, and I hoped to garner some idea of how it worked. I knew it prohibited "immoral commerce" and closed down all them nice old parlor houses along Sporting Row, back when the saloons still existed. Saloon Row was now a forlorn stretch of abandoned and ruined buildings waiting to burn down. Vandals had swiftly removed anything of value from them, and the weather had done the rest.

But the parlor houses had soldiered on, their welcoming lamps swinging in the winter winds, at least until now. Somehow, Doubtful wasn't the same, and now it would seem even more strange, if this thing was enacted. I knew it would be. Each of those supervisors had him a dragon for a wife, and they all belonged to the Women's Temperance Union. Those gents were greatly put upon and also scared to be voted out of office, now that women had the vote, at least for all Wyoming state offices. Things sure were changing fast.

I ascended the creaking courthouse stairs, and at the top I hit a wall of perfume. The air was thick with it. There were enough lilacs and roses and marigolds and jasmine, and all that to floor a man. I had no choice but to breathe it for a while, so I made my way into the courtroom. And wasn't surprised to see the spectator benches all filled up, row upon row, of Women's Temperance Union members. They were all gussied up, too, most of them in subdued suits buttoned right up to the neck, or brown suits, or tan suits. A few had blouses and jabots. I didn't know the name of them at first; there was a mess of fabric collected at the throat, like some giant cravat, as if women were envious of neckties and had to have one ten times larger. The perfume emanating from that quarter was beyond description and made my poor throat raw. I yearned for fresh winter air, pine forests, lakeside panoramas. But there would be none of those, and not even an open window. The potbellied stove was burning away, turning all that perfume into darts that laced my nostrils. It sure was something. And every one of those gals wore a hat, too. They looked like a flower garden. Not a one of them wore a bonnet, in the old way.

There was one other gal standing there, and she was austerely dressed in funereal black, with tiny satin buttons running clear up to her neck. She wore no necklace, no ring, and no hat, unlike all the rest of that bunch. And there was no seat for her among the spectators, so she stood patiently. She was Mrs. Goodrich of the Gates of Heaven Parlor House, and I was secretly glad to see her.

Pretty soon the three supervisors, Grosbeak and Twining and Thimble, emerged from the chambers and settled themselves along the dais. Lawyer Stokes also emerged from the chambers, carrying some documents. The officials arrayed themselves like hangmen, and then Grosbeak rapped his gavel and the game got under way.

Soon enough, Grosbeak announced that this would be the final reading of the proposed ordinance of abatement; there would be a time for comment, followed by a vote. Old lawyer Stokes, his voice as raspy as a hand lathe, took to reading the ordinance, which sure seemed a few thousand words longer than necessary. The ladies fanned themselves, some with their hats, and blotted up all this stuff. It was too full of big words for me to get the measure of it, but the first section described a wide variety of felonies and misdemeanors, buying and selling this or that, running a disorderly house and stuff, while the second section described all the penalties, fines and jail terms and confiscations of property, for offenders. I thought that the county was going to get rich, even if the city of Doubtful went broke because it would lose all its license fees, which had been the larger part of city income.

The ladies fanned away, eyed me, while I smiled and suffered, and thought that I would prefer a room full of farts. When the county attorney wound up, Grosbeak invited comment. At first no one spoke up. The Temperance Women sat smugly. It would have been unladylike for them to comment about things beyond mention, so they just smiled and waved their makeshift fans.

Mrs. Goodrich firmly raised a hand, and Amos Grosbeak affected not to see it. So Mrs. Goodrich took to waving her arm, while the three supervisors studied the window and the ceiling chandelier and the American flag.

But Mrs. Goodrich was not to be denied, and

after Lawyer Stokes whispered a thing or two, Grosbeak discovered her presence.

"Madam, you wish to speak?"

"I do."

"Will it offend public sensibility?"

"It might."

"Well, I will gavel you to a stop if you do. Seat yourself there in the witness chair, if you wish, and be on with it."

"I am Elaine Goodrich, also known as Mexican Marie, the owner and proprietor of the Gates of Heaven Resort on Sporting Row, also known as a whorehouse."

That brought a rap of the gavel and a twitter of delight among the Women's Temperance Union ladies.

"I wish to make several points. The first is that if men don't get regularly laid, they tend to go bad. It's like a steam boiler without a pressure valve on it, and eventually deprived males simply blow up."

"Madam, your language is out of bounds. This is a proper public place."

She nodded. "I'll watch my tongue for these broads. Now, then, it is unfortunate but true that most men can find little pleasure in wedded life and soon need to stray. That old boiler is building up a head of steam. I am present to accommodate them, and the results are immediately visible. Family life becomes serene. Children are better treated. Wives are respected and honored. There is less likely to be a harsh hand lifted against a man's own flesh and blood. In short, a parlor house acts to produce tranquility and good order."

"Ah, are you quite finished?"

"Nope, I'm just starting to rip."

"Well, we'll take your views under advisement. Is there any other comment?"

"I'm not half done yet. You going to let me speak my piece?"

"Well . . . be brief."

"Over half the income available to the unincorporated city of Doubtful is derived from licensing fees for the houses and for each lady within each house, and these are renewed quarterly. Close us down and the City of Doubtful will need to levy property or other taxes upon all of you. The city has already lost its saloon licensing income, which totaled four thousand seven hundred dollars before the recent calamity. It lost another five hundred from licensing gambling tables.

"Now, there's more. Close the parlor houses and the last attraction for the ranch trade will vanish, especially because rival towns and county seats are already gearing up to welcome drovers and cattlemen and whiskey drummers and all of that. What will bring the ranch trade to Doubtful? Not a thing except proximity. You think you have an advantage because the ranches are mostly within a few miles, but you will be surprised. I already know of peddlers who will visit ranches with vital supplies, from horseshoes to flour, in their wagons. And Doubtful will lose that trade."

I spotted Mayor Waller standing against a wall, nodding his approval.

The Temperance Women stared at Mrs. Goodrich, fascinated by her and her trade.

"Are you quite done?" Grosbeak asked.

"Not at all. I'm just getting cranked up. Now consider that ladies in my profession are really educators, teachers, mentors, who improve a man and give him practice in all the happy arts. We help poor wretches become manly men, enable them to bring delight sublime to their wives. That's why my resort is called the Gates of Heaven. Take it from me: many a grateful man has returned to my house with happy stories about the improvement of his domestic life, and the smile on his wife's face, and the love blossoming in her gentle eyes."

There was a considerable stir among the ladies. Some looked stricken. A few smiled. Some fanned themselves furiously.

"Modesty prevents me from naming the names of these satisfied customers, but I see some here and know that there are many more who are hoping that Sporting Row may continue to benefit the entire community of Doubtful."

"Are you done, madam?"

"I'm getting there. This ordinance is much too hasty, and therefore unjust. It requires us to dispose of real property in two or three weeks, if enacted, or see it confiscated. Like all of you, we have engaged in hard and perilous work, and have invested our proceeds in property, but now we are threatened with grave loss. If you enact this ill-advised ordinance as it stands, you will profiteer at our expense. It is akin to theft. If you must enact this law, at the very least provide us with six months to divest our real property and any other goods."

"We've heard enough! This is becoming redundant."

"Well, thank you. I am, of course, opposed, and hope you will vote that way. Shall I leave my list of customers for you?"

"What list?"

"Why, my patrons. I copied them off. You'll see that I have widespread support in Doubtful, and even wider in Puma County."

She waved a few papers before the crowd. The women of the Temperance Union stared, fascinated. For once, no one was fanning.

"I think we're done here. Sheriff, would you escort the lady to the door?"

"Who, me?"

"Do we need a new sheriff here?"

I got up, began toward the door, but Mrs. Goodrich had already exited, her jet dress rustling softly.

She had left a heavy shawl in the anteroom, and wrapped herself in it.

"You suppose it made a difference?" she asked.

"Yes, ma'am. Some of those wives, they got educated. But I don't know it'll affect the vote any."

"Well, we're packed and ready to leave. We should be off tomorrow, if the law goes through."

"Where you headed?"

She smiled. "I don't think it is prudent to tell you."

"I'll sure miss you, ma'am."

"You're about the only man in Doubtful we never took to bed. You're an enigma, Cotton Pickens."

"Whatever that is," I said as she slipped down the stairwell. The stairs didn't even creak.

I returned to the courtroom just as Grosbeak was calling for a vote.

"Aye," said Twining.

"Aye," said Thimble.

"And aye," said Grosbeak. "The ordinance is enacted. Sheriff, see to it. On the first day of March, you will close any remaining violators. Distribute notices as soon as we get them printed up."

The perfumed women all stood at once, stirring the air in that overheated room, and I watched them drift out, most of them pensive. They weren't quite as frisky about all this as I might have thought, and I knew Mrs. Goodrich's little argument had not gone unheeded.

"Well, Pickens, you ready to shut 'em down?" asked George Waller.

"I do what the law requires," I said. "I've heard that the ladies are going to outlaw tobacco next. Next thing I know, I'll be nabbing people who chew."

"Well, that's going too far. A man can do without spirits. He can do without women. But no man in his right mind, of normal body, can do without a smoke or a chew. If that's the plan, I'll fight it. Doubtful needs tobacco. Doubtful needs Bull Durham. Doubtful needs real men, who chew and spit and smoke up a storm."

"You aren't going to tax it?"

"No, it won't work. Pickens, you'll see most everyone in sight move out. There won't be a Doubtful anymore. I've got another revenue source in mind that'll work better. I'm going to have the city council outlaw public spitting. It's a disgusting habit, spitting. We'll put a five-dollar fine on it and start you to enforcing it. If you ticket ten spitters a day, that's fifty dollars in the coffers each and every day. We're going to depend on you, Cotton. You'll slow down a filthy habit and keep Doubtful in buffalo chips."

Chapter Nineteen

I sure didn't want to take the word to the madams. They probably knew they were doomed in Doubtful, Wyoming, but it was my official duty to give them all notices. They had to shut down before March 1 or face the music. And that went for the gals in their houses, too.

They knew, of course. Mrs. Goodrich had told them, even though she wasn't present during the vote. But still, I had to make it official, and now that the notices had been printed up by the *Doubtful Advertiser* I had to stuff them into the hands of the owners, and maybe leave a few around for the girls to pick up and study, always assuming they could read. Reading wasn't easy, especially public notices that used big words and were just as pompous as any lawyer could dream up.

So one February afternoon I loaded a sheaf of them in my arm and headed for the sporting district. It wasn't doing so well since the saloons had

been shut down, but it was lively enough, getting
trade off the ranches. I thought I'd start with
Denver Sally. She had the biggest house, two
stories, with a dozen rooms upstairs and a parlor,
kitchen, and closed-down saloon, along with her
private suite, downstairs. It was right nice in
there, with an upright piano and red damask
drapes with heavy tassels, and doilies on the
horsehair furniture. It was a real nice place for a
feller to select a girl. They drifted in, wearing
gauzy stuff, and a feller could sit in a horsehair
sofa, just like he was at home, and study the
shadowy figures of the girls under that gauze
and point to one or another, and pretty quick
Sally would have two dollars and that cowboy
and his temporary bride would be climbing the
creaking stairs. Old-timers could tell if she was
busy just by listening to the stair creak or feeling the whole place vibrate. There were cowboys
who could make the whole place thunder for a
moment or two. It sure was a nice, homey, cheerful place that reminded most of the cowboys of
their family parlors.

But since the saloons got shut down, Sally's
trade had diminished a little, and she had let two
of her dozen girls go. She'd paid them off, given
them a mud-wagon ticket to Cheyenne, where
they could reach the railroad, and the gals just
sort of vanished from town. That was pretty
normal; there were all sorts of ladies coming

and going from the district, but this time a few cowboys had broken hearts. Sally encouraged cowboys to fall for any gal, real hard, except that she sometimes had to ban some feller or other when he got jealous and didn't want a girl to work her trade. That's when Sally got stern. She had a small list of gents who were not welcome, and she had a burly hooligan who enforced her will with a knout and brass knuckles and a black-jack and boot knife. But only rarely did a cowboy ever get cut up, and he usually deserved it.

I walked in there just after noon, when the place would be real quiet and the girls were either sleeping or painting their toenails, and sure enough, the jangle of cowbells on the door drew Sally out of her suite. She was dressed just as gauzy as her girls, and that made life interesting for me because Sally was a real pretty forty or so, not much older than all the gals she imported, mostly from Denver.

"Well, if it ain't the sheriff. How's your pecker, Cotton? Need a little exercise, does it?"

"Well, ma'am, I come to give notice."

"That's not how most people do it. Tell you what, Cotton, you come on in here and try a free one with me."

"Ah, ma'am, I just stopped by to tell you."

"Oh, I've known about it for days. Come on back where the merchandise is ready. Sheriffs get it for nothing. It's a perk of high office."

"Denver, you've got to shut down at the end of the month. This here notice says so."

"Read it to me. I'm better horizontal than upright."

"Okay, I memorized it anyway. It says you got to quit, and that you can get fined real heavy and thrown in the slammer if you don't."

She steered me into the parlor and sat me down in one of those horsehair chairs, and then she tucked her robe tight, hiding all the joyous views.

"They did it deliberate. Do you think I could sell this parlor house in two or three weeks? Hell no, unless I give it away. I got a lot invested in this. So what do I do? Walk away? There's plenty of gents who'd like that. They'd get themselves a nice building in good shape for a song. It'd take no time to condemn it for taxes or something and arrange a quick little sale, even if I still got the deed. It was deliberate, you know. That's the fate of working women. We get screwed."

"It's not very pretty, Sally."

"Not pretty! Once you climb into my world, Cotton, you find out you ain't got any of the rights guaranteed by the Constitution. You think I don't know about that? I know plenty. You get pushed into a half-world, like slaves. Slaves were three-fifths of a human in the Constitution, but we aren't any fraction at all. We get to walk away and leave our property behind. There's a few ways out. You want to marry me? You marry me, and they wouldn't take my stuff. I'd be Mrs. Cotton Pickens, and you'd own me and the parlor house, sort of anyway. You want to get married? Hell, we can walk over to the judge and tie it in five minutes, and you've got me and a twelve-room cathouse, and a free lay the rest of your life."

"I just stopped in to give you the word, Sally. It's not my idea of what's right, but I got no say in it."

She laughed. "No one's got a say in it. We live in high-minded times. When the whole world is high-minded, there's a lot of places like mine. When the times are low-minded, and females are available, there ain't hardly any parlor houses. Who needs 'em? All I need is a change of view-point. All those ladies on the north side, they're against us here. They want to make the world a perfect place, only life isn't like that. Hell, Cotton, half of them secretly are glad we're here. They don't like marriage, not this part of it. High-minded women, they'd just as soon get babies via the stork and never get touched by a male. But they can't ever say that. They can't say to their husbands, go over to the district for your animal needs, and leave me to my lofty ideals. Nah. But they're over there."

She eyed me. "I like my business. Always have. I like men. I like bedding them. I like the money, and I like being my own boss—at least if they let me. But hell, Cotton, those girls upstairs, most of them are there because they got no choice, because they're desperate. There's girls upstairs got abused by their old man. Girls driven off of farms. Girls who got pregnant from a boyfriend and got kicked out of their homes. Girls fleeing from killers and white slavers. Girls who are a little crazy or slow. Girls, hell, Cotton, they're just all the hard-luck women in the world, no less or more moral than the respectable ones, but much more desperate. And now Doubtful, Wyoming, is going to get rid of them, and they'll flee from here and end up in some worse place, or maybe just go off and die of some disease somewhere, and get buried in an unmarked grave in some potter's field. So Doubtful will boot them out and feel superior, and think that it's a better town, and now everyone will be virtuous and it's going to be like paradise in Puma County. And you know what, Cotton? It'll be darker and meaner than before."

"Well, Sally, I got no choice."

"I do. I'm staying."

"But Sally—you can't."

"On the last day of February I'm going into a different business. This here parlor becomes a rooming house. I'm going into the boarding business. I'll fire all the girls. I'm going to run an ordinary house, and my first tenant's gonna be you. I'll make you a better room and board deal than your pal Belle, and you'll get some nice quarters. And if you want me, you've got me just for fun."

"You're going to fire all them gals?"

"Tough, ain't it? I just got through telling you how they got beaten down, and now I'm gonna beat 'em down some more."

"What if they want to stick, and rent a room, and find work as a chambermaid or something?"

"They're welcome. My price is ten a month for a room with breakfast and supper. But Grosbeak and all them, they'll just drive the girls away and bring up charges against them. That's how it goes. They'll say I'm still in business and the girl's in business and the rooming house, it's just a false front, and it's really just a cathouse. You ready for that?"

"Now I am. If they put any heat on me to charge you, I'll just tell them to prove it. You gotta have some evidence."

She eyed me for a while. "You sure you don't want to get married, Cotton?"

"No, I'm not sure of anything."

"You want a sample?"

She laughed, knowing I did and that I was a little slow about everything.

"I got to deliver these notices to the rest of the houses," I said.

"Stop by after, and tell me what they say."

"They'll all try to get my pants off."

"I knew I liked you, Sheriff."

I headed into the sunlight. It sure was quiet. The ruins of the saloons stretched along the alley, visited by reform. And now the reformers were striking again. And the funny thing was, Doubtful seemed to be croaking along with the reforms.

Next door was Mrs. Goodrich's Gates of Heaven. And even though she'd been at the supervisors' meeting, I had to give her official notice anyway. So I drifted that way, enjoying the pale sunlight. It sure seemed eerie, this part of Doubtful without a horse tied to a hitch rail, and without a sound issuing from the saloons.

Mrs. Goodrich, perpetually in black, greeted me coolly.

"You've come to serve notice," she said. I handed one of the sheets to her. "You want to read this to me, or should I read it to you?"

"I guess you can figure it out," I said. "I got to fifth grade and know a few words beyond, but not many."

"I've debated it for three days, and am not sure what to do. This building, it's worth four thousand and a half. Or was. It's worth about ten cents now. One of your town fathers will end up with it. Maybe Mr. Twining, since he stopped here all the time to untwine himself." She smiled. "That's how it is in my profession. Make a friend and he has you for dessert."

"It's not any law I want on the books, ma'am. I'd just as soon let you all bang away, night and day."

She brightened briefly. "But you have to enforce the laws, and you're not going to play favorites, and you're going to do your best, and you'll be fair and square. That's what I like about you, Sheriff. Well, I tell you what. Come March one, this place will be inhabited by rats and garter snakes. I'll take my girls with me, every one. I won't abandon them. They're some of the best girls I've ever had, and they've been good to me. We're going to get a couple of freight wagons and take our beds and bedding with us, and we'll set up shop somewhere . . ." Her voice trailed away.

"Where's somewhere, Mrs. Goodrich?"

"I wish I knew," she said. "Somewhere. Maybe a mining town."

I felt sorry for her. She hadn't asked for this turn of fate, and now she was being hounded out of Doubtful by some triumphant reformers who never paused to wonder how many people they were ruining along the way to their paradise on earth.

"Don't worry about us," she said. "But maybe blow the girls a kiss when we leave. There are a lot of cowboys who are sweet on some of my gals, and some of my gals are sweet on them. There'll be a few tears, Sheriff."

CHAPTER TWENTY

Well, the madams didn't put up much of a fight. Maybe that's because they were used to it. Most madams had gotten kicked out of five or ten towns, and Doubtful would be no different. Their trade was barely tolerated, and often isolated or confined to special districts, where it would be mostly invisible to the rest of the burg.

About half of them houses were already gone before the March 1 deadline rolled around. Lillian Labrue, who ran Lucky Lil's, a cowboy favorite because she charged a dollar, with regular fifty-cent specials, was one of the first to pack up.

"It's not been the same, not since they shut down the saloons," she told me. "Cowboys used to roll in here, drink a few and come for a visit, and times were good. But now the whole place is dead, and my trade's down to ten percent of what it was. Not that it was ever tops. Doubtful is not a real good place for a parlor house. Too many cowboys, not enough other sorts around here. You spend your life on a horse, and your equipment knows it. There's not one cowboy in ten that's up to snuff. My poor girls would try real hard, but most of the time it was just wishful thinking for the cowboys that would come in." She eyed me. "I hope you don't ride that horse of yours too much. You can be salvaged. I could work with you. But you turn yourself into a cowboy, riding broncs all day, and you're not gonna get yourself a wife or family. Look at the ranches. Hardly a woman or a child on them. There's a reason for it."

She had hired a good coach and a freight wagon, and her six girls waited patiently in the coach while Lil stopped to tell me she was pulling out. She was abandoning her place.

"Let the vultures take it. They'd find a way anyway, sooner or later. No one made an offer, and no one even asked my price. That's how it goes, Cotton. In my trade, you make your bundle in two or three years, get it away from town, and then call it quits. I stayed in it too long. But I'm not broke. These girls there, they're young, and they'll do all right. I let the ranchers know they could be married, if any cowboy wanted one. Hell, I'd get married myself if any man wanted me. You want me, Cotton? You can have me for a two-dollar silver band."

The coach and freight wagon were attracting a crowd on Courthouse Square. There were plenty of women in town who'd never set eyes on a bawd, and now they were openly examining the poor frails sitting quietly in the coach, frails banished from righteous Doubtful. I watched the Temperance Union gals study the frails furtively, sniff and glare, and then walk away. A proper lady could not be overly curious about things she artfully knew nothing about, at least in public.

"Well, Lil, you have yourself a good trip. I sort of envy you. You'll go somewhere and start over just fine."

"Any mining town will do," she said. "Miners, they don't lose it the way cowboys lose it. I can get back on my feet in two or three months in a place like Butte, Montana. And miners pay more. I can charge two-fifty or three bucks and get it. Cowboys, they hate like hell to spend a dollar fifty for a girl, not if there's any sheep around. You know what, Cotton? This is the last cow town I'll ever come to."

"Well, you have yourself a fine old time, Lil."

"Better than you will," she said.

I lifted my battered hat and settled it, while she clambered into the maroon-lacquered coach, and her little caravan started off. A little punk spat at the coach and then leered. I corralled the kid by the scruff of the neck.

"I don't allow spitting, kid."

"Whores," the kid said. "I shoulda fired a bigger gob."

"What's a whore, kid?"

The kid looked stricken. "I don't think I'll tell you," he said.

"Then don't spit at them."

"My ma says you're dumb."

"That's what my ma said, too. And that's what you'll be if I start to shake you until you rattle."

I let go of the kid, who fled.

The coach rolled out of town, on the road north. Probably heading for Montana. I thought about Lil for a moment. Tough gal, but no trouble. She dealt with drunks and rough men without help. She never called the sheriff. Lil was the toughest of the madams, and now she was gone. It sure was quiet. The town women nervously scattered, their day's excitement over. I wondered what they were feeling. They could hardly miss the fear in the drawn and pale faces inside that coach. Those girls wore their profession like sackcloth and ashes, most of them, and the happy woman was a rarity among them.

"What was that?" asked Amos Grosbeak.

"Lucky Lil pulling out."

"What about Denver Sally?"

"She's turning her place into a boardinghouse on February twenty-eighth."

"No she's not, Sheriff, she's just playing a game with us."

"She's letting her girls go."

"Baloney, Sheriff. How can you be so dense? She's just going to stay on and sell flesh the way she always has."

"You know that for a fact?"

"I don't need facts. It's plain as the wart on my nose. Here's what you're going to do. Come March one, you're going to serve papers on her telling her to abate her illicit business, and haul her into your jail."

"She says she's going to run a boardinghouse, and I have no reason to doubt her. She says she has too much invested in that building. That's a big place, two stories, well built, and she can't find a buyer."

"Of course she can't. Who'd buy it?"

"She offered it for a low price, she told me, and didn't get an offer. So she's staying."

"You get her out of there."

"That's not my job. My job's to enforce the law and keep the peace."

"You nail her on March one, Sheriff, or there'll be hell to pay."

"If I'm made aware of a violation, I'll do it. But I'm not going to invent reasons to pinch her."

"Sheriff, get this straight. Even if she goes straight, runs a real boardinghouse, we don't want her type in Doubtful. She may be an ex-madam, but she's carrying all that baggage and hasn't changed an iota. She'd be bad for the town. Bad for everyone. The reputation of that place would taint anyone who wanted to stay there. Memories don't simply disappear, Sheriff. Some innocent might move in there and the whole town would draw conclusions. But that's obviously not the way it'll be. She's just playing you for a damned fool, and she's going to go right on selling flesh, and you'll turn a blind eye to it."

"Well, make her a decent offer for her building, and she'll sell. She's not fond of Doubtful."

"Why make an offer? It'll be an abandoned building shortly, and the city can seize it."

"And then what happens?"

"It'll be sold at auction. Maybe someone can turn it into a good hotel."

"Like who?"

"I could list twenty of our outstanding businessmen who'd be glad to pick up the building at a price that would make a venture out of it."

"I thought so," I said. "I just thought that's the way it's going to shake out."

"You will act. You will remove that disreputable woman immediately. You will do so or face disciplining by the supervisors."

"She keeps to the law, she stays," I said. "She violates your law, she gets to go to court and pay up if she's found guilty. She violates the law lots of times, maybe the judge will move in on her.

She runs an orderly rooming house, she pays her taxes, she keeps to the ordinances, I'll leave her alone. Maybe I'll even move in myself."

Grosbeak glared. "This isn't over," he said. "In fact, it's barely started. Consider yourself warned."

I watched the county supervisor plunge into the courthouse. They didn't care if Sally had gone legal; they just wanted the building and they intended to euchre her out of it, even if there wasn't an iota of justice in it. Some bunch of reformers they were. Doubtful wasn't being reformed; it was being pillaged. Some respectable people were using the law as an excuse to enrich themselves. Already, all the lots the saloons stood on had been sold, in some sort of furtive maneuver that I didn't understand. I'd only heard a few whispers. Most of those structures could be fixed up, turned into stores. And they'd been bought for nothing much. What saloon owner had gotten a nickel out of them?

I sure didn't know what to do. I watched the maroon coach climb the hill out of town and vanish, another one driven out. Lil was predatory, and tough, and maybe she cheated when she could, so I didn't plan to shed any tears, but now her building was up for grabs, and some one of those upright, virtuous, moral, ethical, sterling businessmen in Doubtful would have himself a nice building and lot for just a few pennies on the dollar. It sure set a man to thinking about reforms. Who benefits? That was a good question to ask about any reform. Who stands to gain from it? I'd never been in a place full of reformers before, and it all was an eye-opener to me. I thought maybe these reformers simply had a vision of a good world, and were pursuing it, but now I knew there was more to it. Reform hurt people. Reform transferred a lot of wealth from one hand to another. Reform turned some people into social outcasts. It had never occurred to me before, but there it was.

I found Rusty in the sheriff office.

"You may be sheriff pretty quick," I said.

"I'd quit. No one's gonna pin your badge on me."

"Pretty quick, all the businessmen in town are going to own Sporting Row."

"How can they do that? It's private property."

"Watch and see," I said. "They've already got ahold of the saloons."

"They're gonna open the saloons?"

"No, turn them into stores and stuff. There's one or two with rooms above, maybe rent rooms."

"Who's got them?"

"I don't know. They'll show up on the county records pretty soon, but maybe not until things settle down a bit."

"You look blue, Cotton."

"Oh, I just don't like the way things are going around here. You want a job? You can have it."

Rusty stood suddenly. "Cotton, don't you go quitting on us. You're the only one strong enough to keep Doubtful fair, and that means plenty to me. I'm talking out of my hat, I guess, but just don't quit. Don't do it."

"I may get fired."

"Then we'll both of us make sure the whole town knows why."

"And then?"

"And then if anyone cares, you've got hope. And if no one cares, it's time for both of us to bail out of Doubtful, Wyoming, and go where the air is clean and the privies don't stink."

That evening a mess of cowboys rode into town, from all the ranches, including the Admiral and the T-Bar. I hadn't seen so many cowboys since the saloons got shut down, but there they were. I knew plenty of them. Spitting Sam and Big Nose George. Alvin Ream. Foxy Jonas and his brother Weasel. Wiley Wool, Rudy Beaver, Zelda Zanada. And that was just for starters. I sure didn't know what was happening. They didn't stop at Sporting Row, but rode straight toward Courthouse Square, where they seemed to collect as if they were expecting something. There sure were a mess of drovers, and some were armed. They'd have to hang up those sidearms if they were going to enter any merchant place, including the sporting houses.

But more and more kept coming, more cowboys than had been in town since the saloons were running wide open.

Then one of them, Smiley Thistlethwaite, a tough customer if ever there was one, along with Big Nose and Foxy Jonas, all pierced into my bailiwick.

"Gents?" I asked.

"We got news for you, and news for the supervisors," Big Nose said. "Here's for you. You're going to leave them women alone. You're going to steer clear and let them run their places, just like before. And if you don't, if you send them out on March one, we're going to tear Doubtful to pieces. We'll tear every store to bits, we'll pull this here jail of yours into scrap iron, and we'll maybe hang a supervisor or two. Got that? Now we're gonna go to the courthouse and we're gonna give the same message to Grosbeak, Twining, and Thimble."

"You got to check your guns in town," I said. "You can hang them up right here, on them pegs and pick 'em up when you leave."

"Pickens, you're nuts," Big Nose said.

"Probably so," I said. "Since I'm going in there with you."

CHAPTER TWENTY-ONE

Well, it sure was plain that this wild bunch wasn't going to be hanging its artillery on pegs while they were in town. With the saloons all shut down, there was hardly a peg to hang a gun belt on anyway. All of those drovers were standing there, itching to do something if I started the ball rolling.

Instead, I palavered. "Now if this was one of them dime novels," I said, "I'd be some sort of lantern-jawed man with two revolvers, and I'd whip them out fast as lightning, and I'd have you all buffaloed real quick, and you'd back off and quit with your tail between and betwixt your skinny legs."

That sure got their attention.

"Only this ain't a dime novel. This here's a real place, Doubtful, Wyoming, and this isn't a story. You want to take your message to the supervisors, right? Okay, I'll help you do it. You choose two fellers to do the talking, and we'll go talk to the supervisors. You pick two, and those two leave their gun belts with you, and the three of us, we'll parley with whoever you want. I know Grosbeak's in there, and maybe the others are, too."

Pretty quick they agreed to it, and Big Nose and Smiley Thistlethwaite got themselves elected to give the word to the supervisors. Sure enough, the pair of them unbuckled their artillery, and it was real good steel they were leaving behind. Big Nose had a Colt Peacemaker with a filed-down trigger, and Smiley had a sawed-off twelve-gauge pump-action scattergun that he handed to one of those fellows.

"All right then, we'll just walk on over," I said, and soon the whole mob of tough cowboys was cornering the square. The mess of them settled in on the courthouse steps, while me, Smiley, and Big Nose went in, our steps echoing in that place with high ceilings and a lot of varnish around. Up on the second floor, I led them into a rather grand office, and sure enough, there was Amos Grosbeak, scowling up at us from behind a mess of papers.

"Make it quick," Grosbeak said, rattling a sheet. The supervisor eyed me, and then eyed the two cowboys, without acknowledging that he knew who they were, although he did.

It was odd how tamed those cowboys were. With their gun belts off, the bluster went out of them.

"Well?" asked Grosbeak.

"It's about pushing them nice gals out," Smiley began. "Every drover in the county's agin' it. You should just take back that new law and let them live in peace. They ain't harming a thing there, and they're friends of ours, and this here law is real hard. I mean, it don't seem to be the way we feel."

Grosbeak was smiling.

"I mean, you repeal that law and we'll do business here in town. At least what's left of it. Ain't much to buy anymore. There's no call to treat them poor ladies like this."

"And what else?" asked the supervisor.

"Well, if you don't pull that law off the books, it'd be real unfriendly around here," Big Nose said. "There'd be fellers like the ones out there, they'd maybe not be very happy to come to Doubtful, and maybe they'd not want to spend a nickel here anymore, and maybe they'd ride over to the other towns, even if it means traveling a piece, where a man can have a drink and a screw."

"Ah, now we're getting somewhere," Grosbeak said. "If we don't repeal the ordinance, you'll take your business elsewhere."

"That's the gist of it," Smiley said.

"And all those gents standing outside, fully armed, would not threaten to tear the whole town apart," Grosbeak said.

"We'll, they've been talking it up a little."

"And none of them really wants to tear Doubtful apart, hang the supervisors, shoot the sheriff, and stomp away, with nothing but women and children left in the ruins of the county seat."

"Where'd you hear that?" Big Nose said.

"It's been rumored for days. There are big ears listening, my friends. Big ears connected to big lips that spill secrets in my ear. There's not a thing I don't know about your talk, your dreaming, your plans."

"Well then, you can take heed," Big Nose said. "You've been warned. You let them women alone, and we'll all be happy. You don't, and there'll be trouble in the streets."

Grosbeak yawned, deliberately, and smiled. "Get your skinny butts out of here and don't come back. Don't threaten elected officials. Don't threaten the sheriff. Don't try to defy the law. Don't expect it to be repealed. Don't think that a mob will change anything at all. If you don't like it in Puma County, we'd be pleased to see you depart. Good afternoon, gentlemen."

Those two drovers, they just stood stock still, like they'd been poleaxed and didn't know when to die.

Grosbeak nodded to me, so I gestured the drovers toward the door, and sure enough, the cowboys exited, me behind them and Grosbeak smiling blandly. It sure had been something to see.

We exited the courthouse in the bright sun and saw the mob of cowboys waiting at the foot of the steps. "Well," said Big Nose, "what we learned was we'd better ride on over to Sporting Row and spend every last dime while the spending's good."

"They gonna repeal?" asked one.

"Nope. They're gonna clean up Doubtful and invite us to take our trade elsewhere. If we don't like Doubtful, we're free to leave. That's what old Grosbeak said. Go on, git, find some other outfit to work for."

"Well, ain't that something," said another.

"We oughta maybe tear it up right now," said one.

"We could, but chances are, no one would get two minutes with one of the girls."

"Is that all the time you take?" one asked. "I'm good for five, and repeats."

"Naw, you're done in thirty seconds," another claimed.

"Let's go on over and find out," said Big Nose.

That sure did it. The mess of them shifted their weapons around and started down Wyoming Street. Those ladies would do some box office business that afternoon.

I watched them head for their horses. Pretty quick the cowboys were out of sight, and Doubtful settled into its usual gloom that peaceful February afternoon. People appeared on the streets. Store owners in aprons studied the retreating cowboys. One-Eyed Harry, over at his beanery, stood in the road looking disappointed. Usually, when cowboys were in town, he did a good trade. They all liked his beans. He claimed his beans and side pork produced more satisfying music than any other food on the planet, and there were plenty of cowboys who liked to prove it.

Women reemerged, some of them with wicker baskets. It was an ancient habit in Doubtful that when cowboys were on the loose in town, its womenfolk quietly made themselves invisible. I watched ordinary life reassert itself. A farmer loaded up bags of Golden Harvest flour on his spring wagon and covered them with a tarpaulin. I decided things didn't need looking after. Those cowboys down at the sporting edge of town would stay there and not raise any more hell. In a way, I could understand why the ordinary folk of Doubtful wanted to shut down the sporting district entirely. They wanted a peaceful life to commence, even at the cost of some business in the county seat.

I was just about to return to my bailiwick when Eve Grosbeak and Manilla Twining caught up with me.

"Oh, Sheriff, that was grand," Manilla said.

"What's what?"

"We saw it all from my husband's window in the courthouse. There you were, down below, facing an armed mob, fifty cowboys, and you just standing there courageously, like some hero of a dime novel, standing there without a gun in your hands, unafraid of them."

"Well, ma'am, I was actually a slight bit nervous."

"And there you were, talking with the ringleaders and next thing we knew, they were unbuckling their gun belts and handing them to the other ruffians, and you were leading them into the courthouse for a peaceful consultation. We understand you took them to visit with Eve's husband, and he made peace with them, and sent them on their way. You're a hero, Cotton Pickens. You're our dream of a fine sheriff and a fine man."

"Well, ma'am, all I done was try to keep from getting myself shot."

"We saw it all. We saw them turn and leave, and now they're on their way home."

"Well, I guess you could call it home if you want, ma'am."

"They're not going away?"

"I don't keep track, ma'am. They're coming and going all the time."

"Pretty soon they won't come at all, and Doubtful will be all the better for it. I can hardly wait for the first day of March, when the last of the sinners depart and we will be a fine place for families."

Eve Grosbeak looked me over. "Have you made any progress, Cotton?"

"I'm always making progress, when I'm not going backwards, ma'am."

"Finding a wife? Finding a suitable young lady and starting a family?"

"No, ma'am, I've had a few offers, though."

"Well, perhaps that's because you need a little more refining. You come with us and we'll get you washed up and mend your clothing. You can't expect to find a proper woman unless you smell just right."

"Well, I really should get back to the office and relieve my deputy, ma'am."

"You come with us, Cotton Pickens. You need another lesson in domesticity."

"What's that?"

"It's what all fine men possess, and make their ladies happy. Domesticity means that you'll sit at the hearth and read the paper and take tea with your wife, and discuss how the children are doing."

"I sure don't know if that's what ought to be on my platter, ma'am."

For an answer, Eve Grosbeak tugged at my coat and led me toward the north side, with Manilla tugging on the other lapel. I thought it was better than if they each had ahold of my earlobes and were dragging me over there.

We walked through the gate and were instantly surrounded by peacocks, but Eve had her way with them, and they let Eve and Manilla and me pass by without pecking and fanning their tails. Pretty quick they had me in the sun parlor again.

"All right, dear boy, you just slip behind that screen and hand us your duds, and we'll start heating up some water for your bath."

"Ma'am, the Hero of Courthouse Square doesn't need a bath. He's only three weeks from his last one."

"You just obey us, and be quick about it. Manilla, you bring hot water from the stove reservoir, and Mr. Pickens, you just hand us your duds and step into that little tin tub there, and we'll come and get you all scrubbed up, and fragrant for any proper girl you chance to meet."

"I don't know about this, ma'am. I've got to relieve Rusty."

"Don't be shy, Sheriff. It's something you'll get used to as soon as you're married. Men were made to live with women."

"I never did hear that before. My ma, she used to say the opposite."

"That women were made to live with men?"

"Naw, that men can't stand to live with women most of the time."

"Well, there's some truth in it, dear child. It takes an artful woman to keep a man happy," Manilla said.

She vanished into the kitchen and returned

with a pail of steaming water, which she dumped into the tin tub, and then went for another.

"While we're waiting I could teach you how to kiss," Eve said. "You definitely need more lessons, because you sort of, well, failed last time."

"Well, ma'am, I've kissed Belle under mistletoe, but that's over until next year, and I don't think I should be kissing anyone until Christmas rolls around."

Eve sighed. "You're a very difficult student, Sheriff."

"I got to go relieve Rusty, ma'am. He's all alone in the jail, and there's no one except me to cut him loose to go eat dinner."

Manilla returned with more hot water, poured it into the tin tub, and tested it with her hand. "It's a little hot still," she said. "But maybe you like it that way. Are you ready? You just slide behind that screen and get yourself ready, and we'll close our eyes when you step into the tub, and then we'll get you all soaped up."

"Ah, ma'am, I got to go keep Doubtful safe. Like you say, I'm the Hero of Courthouse Square."

I jammed my hat on and fled, managing to evade the peacocks by running to the gate.

But I wished I could have just stayed on there and let them scrub me up real pink. They sure were nice ladies.

CHAPTER TWENTY-TWO

One by one, those madams pulled out, wagons of stuff and a few girls in hired coaches with the shades drawn, so no one in Doubtful got a peek. Whoever was inside those coaches sure didn't want to be seen in bright sunlight. They usually pulled out at dawn, before the town was awake, and next anyone knew, another parlor house was shut down tight.

By March one, the day the new ordinance took place in Puma County, they were all gone. Word was that some had gone to Cheyenne, but most of the gals headed for Montana, especially Butte, where there were lots of miners and plenty of business.

Doubtful sure was peaceful, or so it seemed. The county had some way of condemning all those buildings and putting them up for auction, so the gals who owned them didn't see any return on them. I wasn't sure how that was done and meant to ask Lawyer Stokes about it, because he did it, and the auctions all took place about two or three days after the madams and the ladies left town.

But there was the new boardinghouse owned by the madam who called herself Denver Sally before, and now called herself Sally Sweet. It was mostly empty. She'd rented to a few vagrants for two bits a night, but she wasn't getting much trade. The gals had gone, and she was alone in her suite on the first floor. But she wasn't budging, and she owned the building, and she was legal, and she wasn't violating any law that I could think of. It sure wasn't illegal to run a boarding-house and rent out rooms and serve up break-fasts and suppers, which is what Sally did.

I didn't have any notion that there was trouble afoot until Amos Grosbeak called me in one day, maybe two weeks after all the ladies of the night had fled Doubtful and were gone forever.

"What are you doing about the boarding-house?" Grosbeak asked.

"Not a thing. Sally's as legal as anyone can get."

"I think you should put a little heat on her. We don't really want her kind in Puma County."

"What's she doing wrong?"

"Just being here, with her reputation, gives the town and the county a bad name, Cotton. We don't want that sort of female anywhere around. We've got a real nice little paradise going here, and she sort of sits there like a reminder of the past. Get rid of her."

"You tell me what law she's violating, and I might have something to pin on her."

"Find a way, Sheriff."

"Not if she's legal."

"I said, find a way."

"And I said, she's legal."

I was getting a little huffy about it. If anything graveled me, it was abusing justice. Maybe I wasn't the brightest light in Puma County, but I knew an injustice when I saw one, and I wasn't going to permit it if I could help it.

Oddly, Grosbeak didn't press it. Instead he settled back in his quilted leather chair and gazed out the window. The snow was melting, and the promise of spring lay upon Doubtful.

"It's a sweet little burg, isn't it, Sheriff? Here we are, deep in the West, building a small paradise where people can live in peace and beauty. We have our wives to thank for that. They saw the need and organized their Women's Temperance Union, and set out to weed the town of vices that disturbed our fair city, that filled citizens with fear, and which led our children astray. Now we're almost done. The county supervisors will enact Sunday Closing Laws at the next meeting. Our wives inspired us once again. No matter what your belief, we should all have a day of rest, when no business remains open and people can contemplate all the good things that have been placed before us. Yes, it will be a day to halt all commerce."

"What commerce?"

"Stores and restaurants will be closed. Public transportation will cease. No stagecoaches on Sundays, Cotton. No employed person shall work on Sundays. No boardinghouse can serve meals."

"A feller's got to eat, Mr. Grosbeak. If I don't get fed by Belle, I take my meals at Barney's Beanery."

"Well, fasting will be good for you. We all need moments of sacrifice."

"I guess that means me and Rusty don't work Sundays."

"That's right. There will be no crime on Sundays. We've driven out the criminal element."

"Well, there's always mean schoolboys roaming around, looking for trouble."

"They will be kept at home by their loving parents on Sunday. There's going to be nothing for you to do."

"That's getting enacted real quick?"

"March meeting. And we'll enact the anti-tobacco law, too. That was inspired by Manilla Twining, who came to us with the idea. Tobacco means a lot of foul smoke and spitting, and it's hard on people. It's a costly vice. And we're against vice. So we'll outlaw it. Truth to tell, some of our friends and allies smoke, and they're a bit testy about it, but they'll get used to it, and once freed from the demon, they will rejoice and thank us. They can spend the money they save to buy beautiful bonnets for their wives."

"Well, I hope it's not up to me to arrest some feller for smoking a cigar."

"Oh, it will be. The fines will help pay the county budget, and George Waller says that when the city enacts the spitting ordinance, the fines will pretty much pay all municipal costs."

"Maybe I won't nip some feller for spitting."

"Of course you will. The law's the law, and you'll enforce it."

I wasn't so sure I would, but I kept quiet about that. This was getting serious. I was going to have to stash food to eat on Sundays and pinch people with a wad of chew in their cheeks. I knew who the victims would be. Traveling salesmen dropping into town. They'd get themselves fined, and the fines would pay the city and county expenses.

"Now, what arc you going to do if a mess of them cowboys off the ranches ride in on a Sunday and want to tree the town if they can't get themselves a meal or a haircut?" I asked.

"Arrest them. The Sunday Law's going to have a quiet clause, a provision against unseemly, boisterous, unruly, or unregulated conduct."

Amos Grosbeak was smiling, and looking so dreamy that I thought he was voicing the very thoughts Eve Grosbeak had whispered to him from her pillow beside him. That Eve, she sure was changing the whole world.

Doubtful had changed, no doubt about it. When I wandered out onto Courthouse Square, the place seemed almost dreamy. I wandered up Wyoming Street and saw ranch wagons parked in front of the mercantile, and ranch hands loading in flour and sugar and oatmeal and molasses. At the Emporium, Leonard Silver was helping the Admiral Ranch load up.

"You're still in business, Leonard," I said.

"I thought we'd get hurt, but it's not happening. Ranches still need supplies, and still send their crews in to buy them. It's just the saloons and tonsorial parlors got hurt."

"You approve of the change?"

"Didn't at first; now I do. Town's better than ever."

"They're going to enact some Sunday laws, I hear."

"Don't bother me none."

That's how it went. Doubtful was happy. The wildest town in Wyoming had settled into the most pacific one. It sure was strange, I thought. I didn't even need a billy club, much less a sidearm. There was so much civilization around that I was pretty near choking on it.

Still, I had a whole county to patrol, and maybe I'd better start taking little tours around the area. There sure would be a temptation to open up little grog shops in hidden valleys, where the bozos could get a drink or two. I thought I wouldn't mind getting one or two myself, and I knew Rusty positively pined for a snort.

The only cloud on the horizon was Sally Sweet and her new boardinghouse, but I was pretty sure that if I ignored Amos Grosbeak's threats, that would go away. Who cared what sort of past Sally had? There were plenty of wives of respectable businessmen in Doubtful who had a past as colorful as Sally's past, or even more so, but that didn't faze the county supervisors.

I headed south, thinking to check up on Sally. Maybe I could learn a little about what sort of heat the supervisors were putting on her and do something about it. It sure was a benign March day, with the snow vanishing, a few birds celebrating the warmth, and a few rowdy crows protesting my every step.

The whole sporting district looked sort of forlorn, but Sally's boardinghouse flew the Wyoming flag from a staff, and the steps were swept.

I entered to the jangle of cowbells.

"You gonna arrest me for something, Cotton?" she asked.

"Nope, but you can pour me some coffee and tell me how business is."

"Business is so thin I'm losing weight," she said, bustling about. She had a speckled blue pot on her wood-fired range and poured some into a mug. It tasted like varnish.

"You hanging on, Sally?"

"They sure are hungry, ain't they, Cotton?"

"Who's they?"

"Stokes. County Attorney, but also a lobo wolf if you ask me. He wants this building so bad it's like a permanent hard-on in his mind."

"This place? Why?"

"Cotton, this here's the finest building in Doubtful. I built it that way. It's a natural for a hotel. Twelve rooms, suite, parlor, dining, kitchen, indoor plumbing, water closet at the end of the hall, copper roof. You know what I spent? Five grand and change. You know what Stokes offered? Two hundred, and said I'd be lucky to take that because I couldn't keep it and he'd make sure of it." She shrugged. "I told him to get his ass out the door."

"Hotel?"

"Yeah, better than the Wyoming up on the square. Great hotel, but only if the whole sporting district got shut down and turned into something else. You know where I was before I came up here? Dodge City, Kansas. You know what Front Street had on it? The saloons, the Longbranch, the sporting places? You know what the wheat farmers did to Front Street? They stamped it out. They erased it from memory. They made Dodge the most respectable and dry town in the whole state. They turned Front Street into ice cream parlors and hat shops. Dodge City, for crying out loud, Cotton!"

"And that's what they're doing here," I said.

"Sort of. Stokes wants this place, and he's working on it, and he's got a few ways and means that scare me. How do you get rid of Sally Sweet? Maybe you think up a few old charges and get me arrested. He come to you with those, yet? It's coming, Cotton. Or maybe he'll find some flaw in the title here, the papers I got saying this here place is mine and paid up. He's coming, Cotton, and he'll phony something up. You'll see."

"He'll have to get past me, Sally. You're legal and I don't intend to let anything get in your way. You've got rights and you've got property here, and if you're pressured, you tell me, Sally. Don't hide it from me."

She sighed. "You want me? You can have me anytime, for free, Cotton."

"You're twice my age, Sally."

"Rub it in, will you? Fine friend you are."

"I think I'm going to talk with Lawyer Stokes. He's going to learn something about the sheriff. He's going to learn that I don't budge."

She looked a little harassed. "I swear to God, Cotton, I don't know what's coming at me. I know they want me out, and the excuse is that I'm an old whore, but there's more going on here. They want a five-thousand-dollar hotel for free, or almost free, and they'll do anything to get it, because the owner's vulnerable and they can cook up anything they want and throw it at me." She stared out the window. "I sure as hell don't know what it is, and I hate the waiting. If they're going to screw me out of my property, I'd like to know how."

"I'll find out, Sally. I ain't gonna let this happen. You just hang on, and let me rattle Lawyer Stokes's teeth a little, and then I'll have some news for you."

"Maybe you should just be real quiet, Cotton."

"My ma used to say, if you see something bad going on and you don't do anything about it, then you share the blame. I'm going to do what I can, Sally."

She sat there, fear in her eyes, and I knew this whole thing was like a case of dynamite about to blow.

CHAPTER TWENTY-THREE

There was only one way to deal with Lawyer Stokes, and that was head-on, so I marched up Wyoming Street to the man's office and barged in. Lawyer Stokes looked a little pained, but rallied swiftly and adjusted his waistcoat to restore dignity.

I didn't much care for the man. The lawyer was so skinny that an ounce of fat would have bulged like a cancer on him. He burned off his entire supply of energy scheming how to improve his fortunes. There wasn't enough law work in Doubtful to feed half a lawyer, but Stokes managed to wax prosperous with great speed. Now he peered up from rimless spectacles at me, letting annoyance play over his thin lips and twitchy cheeks.

"Yes, what is it, Pickens?"

"You're picking on Sally Sweet, and you're going to quit it right now."

"Picking on Sally?" Stokes removed his spectacles and polished them and replaced them carefully, his skinny lips forming unspoken thoughts.

"Sheriff, she's an undesirable, engaged in criminal activity, and I am doing my utmost to get her to remove herself from Puma County. My sole problem is a sheriff who declines to enforce the law and clean up vice in our community."

"She's operating a boardinghouse. She sent her girls packing when the law took hold. She's as legal as she can be."

Stokes removed his spectacles once more, breathed on them, and wiped them clean using the sleeve of his long johns, which were peeking through under his shirtsleeve.

"Sheriff, if you don't mind my saying so, you are thick-skulled and witless, if not just plain stupid. In fact, I don't know how you got past first grade. You made it all the way to fifth grade, but that was only because of the kindness of your teacher, who willfully passed you through second, third, and fourth before you met your Waterloo in fifth. I don't quite know how you became sheriff, but it has been an ordeal for Puma County officials to get you to enforce the plain law, the law right there on the books."

"Well, my ma, she always said I'm quick with my trigger finger."

Stokes studied the cleaned lenses and placed his spectacles on his face, adjusting them slightly down the nose, which was his preferred mode of viewing the world.

"Sally Sweet as you call her, also known as Denver Sally before going underground, is continuing to ply her trade on her own. That she sent her girls away matters not a whit. She welcomes boarders and well, offers services. It's as plain as the wart on your nose, and just as annoying."

"I haven't seen it. You got proof?"

"Proof? You mean a witness? Who needs it? There is ample circumstantial evidence. She operates an alleged residence for males and flourishes there, and her reputation speaks loudly in this community. I haven't the slightest doubt that she is engaged in her nefarious trade, and if she were brought before any judge in Wyoming the verdict would be clear."

"You sure know a lot more than I know. I know she's hardly got any business yet. People quit coming to Doubtful since all them laws got on the books. She's mostly waiting for things to pick up."

"Sheriff, are you one of her customers? Is that it?"

"Well, she did tell me she'd rent cheaper than Belle, but I like old Belle, so I didn't move over there."

"Sally offered rent and other services?"

"Yep, rent and breakfast and supper."

"Some fine dining in her suite, I imagine."

"No, just some good potatoes and gravy and meat loaf on Tuesdays."

"You will arrest her and charge her with operating a house of ill repute. I will bring you the papers and you will proceed."

"You got any evidence?"

"Why, what you just told me."

"I don't get it, Stokes. And I'm not hauling her in until there's some reason for it."

"I see. Dereliction of duty. An actionable offense. Maybe I'll charge you. Send Sheriff Pickens up the river, is that it?"

"You quit picking on Sally. You heard me. You quit picking on her. You quit trying to buy her place for nothing. You're trying to pick up some property that's worth more than any other building in Doubtful. And if you cheat her any way, maybe you'll be the one in my jailhouse."

Stokes stared at me, ice building in his gray face, and I knew the man had gone from adversary to dangerous enemy.

But, oddly, Stokes changed the subject. "You're neglecting the Crossing. There's a wicked little makeshift town ballooning there. And putting vice onto river scows doesn't cut the mustard. I've researched it. County lines extend to the middle of any streambed that forms a boundary. Go do something about it."

"Give me some paper and I will."

"You don't need paper. You need to stop the

vice . . . if you're capable of it, which I doubt. Or if you've not been bought, which entertains my doubts."

Lawyer Stokes arose suddenly. "You've wasted enough of my time. I don't relish explaining things to a fare-thee-well. It would be helpful if we had a diligent sheriff with half an education at the minimum."

"Yep, I know it would, but they made me the man," I said. "I enforce the laws, until I'm out."

"Better sooner than later," Stokes said.

So, Stokes had some business for me out of town. I headed across the square, looking for Rusty, and found him swabbing out the jail cells with a mop.

"Looks like I got to go to the Crossing to do a little business," I said. "County attorney says there's wild and wicked stuff happening there, and that the county line runs to the middle of the Platte River. So, I'll be gone a day or two, and you'll be the law in lawless Doubtful, Wyoming."

"Sounds exciting," Rusty said.

"Lawyer Stokes has got something up his sleeve. About ten minutes after I'm outa here, he's going to show up with some paper, and that paper will be a warrant for Sally Sweet, and he'll want you to bring her in and charge her with running a house of ill repute."

"He still after her?"

"He doesn't care about her. He wants that

building. It'd make the best hotel in Doubtful. She put a lot into it, about five thousand, and he wants to cop it for nothing. The first step is to get her fined and out, and then he'll maneuver it into his paws, maybe for back taxes or something like that."

"So, what am I going to do?"

"Nothing, Rusty. You just leave her alone. She's not running a house of ill repute. She's mostly trying to keep her own property with a boarding-house operation. Just leave her alone."

"Don't serve her? Don't bring her in?"

"More than that. Keep him and the supervisors off her back."

"You sure she's not selling it?"

"No, not sure. But there's got to be some evidence, some reason, for making the pinch, and they won't be on the warrants."

"So I defy the county attorney?"

"Just delay. I'll do the defying when I get back. All you need is some sick leave, something like that. The way things are going, you'll probably be sheriff in a few days."

Rusty grinned. "That's what I like about you, Cotton."

I headed back to Belle's, got my slicker and a few overnight items, and headed for Turk's Livery Barn. Maybe Critter would like a trip, but maybe he wouldn't. You never knew about Critter, but a knee in his belly usually got him to thinking about his sins. Critter was a horse that needed to repent every Sunday.

As soon as I slid into that cold dark barn, Critter whickered

"I guess you want to get out of here," I said.

Critter snorted and nickered and sawed his head up and down.

"You look friendly today. I'll saddle you in the aisle," I said, unhooking the stall gate.

Critter didn't move.

"Come on out of there, you miserable beast."

But Critter moved to the head of the stall, refusing to back out.

"All right then, I'll come in for you."

I edged along a stall wall, and Critter exploded. A hoof narrowly missed me, crashing into the plank and leaving splinters in it.

"You're dog food," I said, sliding the bit between Critter's yellow teeth. In a moment, I backed Critter out and began brushing Critter in the aisle.

"High time you got out of town," Turk said. "If you'd quit arresting people I'd have some business."

"Pretty quiet in Doubtful, but there's some action at the Crossing."

"Invite them to town," Turk said. "This place is a bore."

Critter decided to bite Turk, who dodged the teeth.

"Sell him to the canners," Turk said.

"I thought I'd sell him to the county supervisors," I said, tightening up the girth.

I loaded my gear onto the saddle and tied it down, and led Critter into winter daylight. Critter humped and danced. I climbed aboard and felt myself being tossed around a while, and then Critter sighed, happily, and awaited directions.

"Need a couple of packhorses to carry bodies?" Turk asked.

"The supervisors wouldn't pay you," I said, and touched my boot heel to Critter's flank. The rank horse burst into a trot, and I settled him into a fast walk that would put me at the Crossing at dusk.

It was that time of year when nature is bleakest, with rotting snow and dirty heaps of slush, with naked trees and mean winds, with mire on the trails slowing travel and mud sticking to everything. But I was elated to get out, and Critter's mood matched mine, and we headed south along the mucky trail that would take us to the Crossing.

It was, actually, that time of year when mortals traveled least. So it was a solitary ride that March day, sometimes fast on frozen ground, sometimes slow and sloppy. I missed supper but slid into the Crossing after dark. It had grown dramatically, a

whole city that had mushroomed up beginning
even before Puma County shut down and blew
out the candles. But here were lights galore,
lights in every window. I saw no livery or hostler
and was glad I'd brought a feedbag of oats for
Critter. There were plenty of saddle horses in
view, mostly tied to long hitch rails along the riverbank. There were more bunkhouses than before,
with a lamp shining in most, and I also spotted a
few pens, where horses could be kept safely for
the night. But all the new log buildings on the
Puma County riverbank were nothing but
shadows compared to what I saw on the river, tied
to the shore with hawsers wrapped around snub-
bing posts. At the time of my previous trip, there
was one floating saloon, but now there were
three floating palaces, all of them built on large
scows, or flatboats, and accessed with gangplanks
from the riverbank. The saloon was still there, a
long room atop the scow, and it looked crowded.
Tied next to it was a gambling parlor, which also
served booze, brightly lit. The third, and plainer,
riverboat was darker and cruder, and had a red
lamp burning at the door. So at least some of the
gals had set up shop here, thirty miles from
Doubtful, in cramped quarters stretching in a
line on a big scow. There looked to be a small
kitchen or dining area at the rear end of the
scow, but no other amenities. I couldn't even see
how the rooms were heated. Maybe they weren't.

Stove pipes rose from the saloon and gambling parlor, emitting thin white threads of wood smoke into the dusk.

No one had noticed me arrive. I studied the layout closely. There was still a flatboat used for crossing the river, guided by a cable anchored on both banks of the North Platte. It was big enough to carry a wagon and team and some passengers. On the Puma County side, a virtual city had sprung up, mostly bunks and corrals, and one beanery with a tired-looking old cripple standing in the lamplight.

I probed through the dark, simply curious about what lay on the outskirts of this instant burg. What interested me most was new graves, but it was too dark, and I kept stumbling over cottonwood roots and gave up on that. The people who owned that property and operated the ferry, the Yumping Yimminys, were probably in the dark house, but no lamp was lit. I hiked along the riverbank, watching the mighty river, swollen from early thaws, roll by in starlight. It was a piece of water, and the county line ran down its middle. Them saloons and parlors were plainly in Puma County if that old turd of a lawyer was right. But who knows? I wished I could see the law saying the county lines split the rivers.

The scows bobbed in the inky waters, their great hawsers wrapped tight around the posts set deep into the bank. They sure weren't going anywhere. I saw someone from the gambler scow step out, head for the rear railing, and piss. That's how it was done around there. There'd be no water closets on board any of the scows, and a feller would need to head for an outhouse near the bunkhouses for relief if he needed to.

I didn't know who owned any of it. But it was time to serve the papers and start shutting the hidden city down. It sure wouldn't be easy.

CHAPTER TWENTY-FOUR

I took my time. No one noticed a stray stranger wandering about in the dusk. I peered through the small windows on the river scows but did not board them. Not yet. They were crowded. The makeshift sin town was doing a lot of business. I recognized some of the drovers in the saloon, men who had been coming to Doubtful. Some were wearing sidearms; most weren't. I spotted a couple of security men, both armed, keeping an eye on the crowd. In a place like this, they had to make their own peace, if that's what it might be called.

A crowd was lined up at the bar; more were sitting around tables at one end of the scow. The barkeep was familiar to me; he had poured at Mrs. Gladstone's Sampling Room before the Temperance ladies shut him down. A little smoke hung in the air; there wasn't much ventilation in there. Two chandeliers with kerosene lamps lit the floating saloon. The scow bobbed restlessly tugging on its rope tethers, which were ropes at the front and rear, snubbed to posts on the riverbank. A loose gangplank took customers to the riverbank.

I examined the middle scow, this one a gambling joint. Sure enough, the man behind the faro layout was Cronk, the gambler at the Sampling Room in times past. There were other tables in the cramped joint, each with a dealer. A tiny bar at one end served drinks to the drovers. A rear door led to a tiny deck, which served as the outhouse. Like the other scow, the gambling parlor was lit by two small chandeliers.

The third scow was darker, with only a single lamp at the single door. But there was a watchman there, and he wore a sidearm. The rooms were lit by small portholes, hardly a foot square, and curtained. There sure wasn't much light in there. A small deck at the rear served as an outhouse. There may have been four gals working in there; maybe more. Plus the madam, if there was one at all. Like the other scows, it bobbed on the river, tugging at its tethers.

Well, if the county line was somewhere out in the middle of the broad Platte, then these outfits were violating Puma County law, that was plain. I'd do something about it if I could. There were too many armed men to deal with, including whoever was in the old log house and in the bunkhouses that were available for customers. The best thing was to go unarmed. I slipped back to Critter, undid my gun belt, and slid the weapon into the roll I had tied behind the cantle. That would make the whole thing easier.

I pulled the steel circlet of office off my shirt and pinned it on my coat, just to make the visit official. I pretty much knew what I'd say, and hoped it would work.

I started at the third barge, the quiet one, walking up the gangplank where I was immediately waylaid by the security man.

"Two bucks, fella," the man said. "Then you wait your turn. You take whoever's freed up."

"You the owner?"

"No, that's someone else, and she ain't here."

"You tell her that Sheriff Pickens is giving her ten days to pull out, along with the girls and you."

"You the sheriff, are you? Sorry, pal, this ain't Puma County."

"Our county attorney says the line runs down the middle of the streambed. So it's Puma, and you'll shut down. I'll be returning in force. You won't want to deal with that."

"Horsepucky, Sheriff."

"I've given you the word. Ten days. April fifteen I'll be back."

"Go to hell, Sheriff. I ought to shoot you and throw you overboard."

"But you won't."

The guard didn't answer.

"Ten days, or this place gets busted up, and you won't like it."

"It's all horsepucky," the man said.

That was about what I expected. For them, the reality was a little sin-town and a lot of quick cash. Not some lone lawman helpless to crack down.

The next place was easier. I walked up the plank and onto the scow, and into Cronk's gambling den. The dealer had put some work into it. The cabin was enameled white, and there were some oil paintings of nudes on the walls, and he and his dealers were all wearing clean white shirts.

Cronk looked up from his game, and recognized me. "Sheriff?"

"Well, Cronk, fancy meeting you."

"Yeah, surprise, eh?"

The faro game halted, with six players listening. Every one of them was a drover from the ranches south of Doubtful. Two were armed. There were two poker games going at the round tables in the place.

"County line goes to the middle of the stream, Cronk. So this is Puma County. Got to shut you down."

"Bug off, Sheriff."

"You got ten days, Cronk. I'll be back with force to enforce it."

"Yeah, five scared merchants and the Temperance women."

"Don't underestimate the women, Cronk."

The gambler smiled, bit off the end of a small cigar, and lit it. "I never underestimate women. And I usually overestimate you. Don't know why. I'm probably overestimating you right now." He eyed me, studying my waist, and smiled. "You were smart. It would be real dumb to walk in here looking for a fight."

"That's what my ma always told me," I said. "Don't pick a fight with four-hundred-pound gorillas."

Cronk smiled and puffed. "I don't think we're leaving. And I don't think we'll head for the other side of the river. Not if all our customers got to take a ferry. So we'll stay. And you can bring the damndest posse you want, and you'll just end up with a mess of funerals. Sorry, Sheriff, this place won't melt away."

He pulled two cards out of the box, the soda and hock.

The cowboy visitors had absorbed it all, and word would soon get back to the ranches. I didn't know whether that was good or bad.

This barge was narrower than the others, and the tables were lined up in a single row. It didn't feel comfortable, either, and I wondered why cowboys would even bother to sit down in a small cabin on top of a wooden scow. The players were older men. I didn't see any wild and wooly young drovers among them. And unlike most any saloon, this place was a mausoleum, so quiet you could hear the clatter of chips being bet.

Sin City sure wasn't much of a place, with everything as temporary as could be built. It looked like it might blow away at any time, which is exactly what gave me some hope that I could shut it down without trouble. I didn't care one way or the other, but I'd do my duty.

I headed down the gangplank to the muddy shoreline, and headed downstream to the remaining boat, this one big and long. It was a large floating raft, a big collection of logs lying in the water, planked over and carrying a log cabin that housed the saloon. Rough-sawn lumber had been shaped into a saloon, and not a cent had been wasted on refinements, including whitewash or paint. Water slapped gently against the floating logs. The saloon rested lower than the other structures.

I studied the layout and managed to peer inside a bit, enough to see that this was the most popular of the three pleasure palaces. It was full of wild young cowboys, some dressed up in kerchiefs, and plenty of them wearing sidearms. One kid even had a pearly handled revolver hanging over his wooly chaps. A bright, bristling wild saloon, miles from the law, and as dangerous as a place could be for a lone lawman on an errand.

I saw several of the T-Bar boys in there, including Foxy and Weasel Jonas. George Roman, who ran the Lizard Lounge in Doubtful, was tending bar here. Well, that was maybe good. It meant that I wasn't dealing with a stranger. Roman was a tough customer, but he would listen and weigh what was being said.

I decided I'd cased the place enough and wandered up a wide gangplank to the bobbing deck, and into the saloon. I was spotted at once, and things quieted swiftly. There were plenty of eyes looking me over, and noting that I was not armed.

"Well, Roman, you've got yourself a new saloon," I said. "And the same old boys drinking it up."

Roman simply stared, as if I wasn't worth talking to.

"County Attorney Stokes tells me this is still Puma County; the line runs down the middle of the streambed. So you're not legal here."

"So?"

"So I'll give you ten days to shut this down and get out."

"And what happens then?"

"I'll show up and enforce the law."

Roman smiled slowly. "I'm sure you will, Pickens. And we'll start a cemetery. Who we gonna put in there? Maybe Stokes? Maybe Grosbeak? I tell you what. The first hole will be for Eve Grosbeak."

"You could move across the river, you know."

"No, I don't know. There's no trade over there. My trade's right here. And no one has to take a ferry to come here."

"Well, then, I have nothing more to say. April fifteen is the day, Roman."

"Sure, Cotton," he said.

"Hey, if it ain't the sheriff," said Wiley Wool, an Admiral Ranch hand. "How ya doing, old man?"

"I'm still sheriff, but just barely."

"You come to shut this outfit down, did you?"

"That's what I'm doing, Wiley."

"You're owned by the Temperance women, are you?"

"No, but if there's a law on the books, I've got to enforce it."

"Well, ain't that something? You come out here to pay us a visit, did you?"

I saw the way this was going and decided to back away. "I've done that. On my way, Wiley."

"Naw, I don't think so, Sheriff. You ain't on your way, not yet. Is he, fellers? Lookit him. He's still dry."

"Dry, is he?" said another. "Guess we've got to fix that. We got us a little welcoming ceremony here, Sheriff. Man can't come and drink with us till he's been initiated."

They were going to dunk me. I decided to take a few with me, and the nearest was Wiley. I plowed into Wiley, sending the man's drink flying, and pushed Wiley into the feller behind him, so they both staggered back. But when I went to grab a handful of Wiley's shirt and haul him to the water, half a dozen young bucks leaped up and howled down on me. I saw Roman's security man coming, too, and knew I wasn't going to stay dry for long. I swung and slugged, but soon some arms pinned me, and I found myself wrestling more muscle than I could deal with.

They were hooting. This was as good as it got for a bunch of liquored-up young bucks. I lunged, broke free, only to get chopped in the face and slugged in the throat, which caught the air and paralyzed me. And then it was over. They lifted me bodily, six of them, and carried me to the downriver end of the barge and pitched me off. I landed in the drink, feeling the thunderous cold of snow melt numb me instantly. The cowboys howled, watched me struggle as the river tore me away from the boat, and then they vanished inside.

I knew I had to get out, and do it fast, in wet clothing and wet boots. And then as I righted myself I struck bottom. I was in shallow water. Those barges hardly had any draft, and there was little more than a foot of water under them. Shaking, I waded gingerly toward the bank, gaining ground until I could clamber up the slippery slope and out. Water rivered out of my duds.

The bunkhouses were not far, and I needed

that heat instantly. But I headed for Critter first and led the wary horse toward the shelters, tied him to a rail there, and barged in. There were a couple of dozing cowboys in there, probably drunk. There was fire enough in the potbellied stove to keep the place warm. I tugged at my soaked boots, which didn't want to pull off, and finally succeeded. I drained water out of them and set them next to the stove, upside down. I pulled off the rest of my stuff. My long johns were soaked and cold, so I got out of them.

I sure as hell didn't have enough in my kit to wear, and it looked like I would be stuck there all night getting dried out. I headed out into the dark, terrifying Critter with my nakedness, and brought my bedroll in. There wasn't much in there, but I would have a pair of blankets and a slicker and a bunk and some heat. I draped my icy stuff around the potbellied stove as best I could, stuffed some slabs of cottonwood into the stove, wrapped myself in the blankets, and settled down on a hard bunk to get warm. I sure didn't know what to do about anything. At least I was out of the river, but not out of the woods.

CHAPTER TWENTY-FIVE

Something woke me a long time later. Moon-light spilled through the sole window. I studied the bunkhouse, not knowing why. There were probably half a dozen cowboys in there. The stove still radiated a little heat. I slid out of the bunk, felt my long johns, jeans, and shirt, and found them still damp, but icy. It would do. They would be cold on my flesh once I got out, but I had my slicker and bedroll to wrap myself in on the long ride home.

I clawed my way into the damp long johns and then donned the shirt and pulled up my jeans. The stuff was clammy and miserable. I eased my foot into a boot and found it icy. That was going to be the worst of it, but I slowly dragged it up until my foot slid into its usual pocket. Oddly, it didn't chill me. I got the other boot on, rolled up my blankets and tied them inside my slicker, and slipped into the night. Judging by the Big Dipper, which had rotated around to the east of the North Star, it wasn't far to dawn.

Critter, who had been tied to the rail all night and was feeling put out, bit me on the arm. I unwound the reins, led him away from the rail, and tied my bedroll behind the cantle. The horse was hungry. So was I. I studied the sin-town. It never slept, and even now a lamp burned in the saloon and another in the gambling parlor. A river breeze chilled me. It seemed to ride the current out of the mountains, bringing winter down to the valley where spring grass was rising. A hint of wood smoke caught in my nostrils, reminding me that there were half a dozen stoves operating there, one in each scow, others in the bunkhouse and the ferryman's house. I saw several horses, their ears high and gaze alert, studying me and Critter.

The river breeze was chilling me fast, turning my clammy clothes icy. I needed to do what needed doing and get out. I found my folded Barlow knife in my pocket. It would have to do. I walked gently toward the riverbank, fearful of arousing a dog, but nothing stirred. I eyed the log raft and two scows bobbing on the water, the occasional creak of the gangplanks the only sound. I tried lifting an edge of the gangplank and found it was loose. So were the others. Nothing attached them to the banks or the scows.

I studied the dark windows, wondering if I was being watched. Well, I thought, the risk was worth it. I pulled the Barlow knife open and quietly sawed through the downriver hawser of the saloon raft, leaving the raft still tethered by its upriver rope. The dull knife didn't cut through the hemp easily, but finally I severed it. I sawed through the downriver tether of the gambling parlor, and the downriver tether of the floating cathouse, and waited to see if that caused any notice. It did make the scows weave some, but no one sounded any alarm. I wondered whether there were poles aboard to steer the scows. None were visible on the decks. I set to work on the upriver hawser of the saloon raft, which was creaking from the new pressures on it. And when the knife severed about three-quarters of it, the rest gave way violently, with a snarl, and the black waters swiftly pulled the floating saloon away. I studied it just long enough to determine that it wasn't being driven into a riverbank but was heading into the main channel. I set to work on the gambling scow and set it free. Its rope snapped hard as it fell apart, lashing me and making a crack that sounded like a gun shot. But the scow slid into the night, rotating clear around, drifting sideways downstream. At the last I severed the rope holding the floating bordello, using a little skill this time, letting the last strands separate slowly and without a crack. The black waters pulled it free. Its gangplank splashed hard and thumped the side, and I was sure it woke up several people, but no one bloomed in the moonlight, shouting. The saloon was already out of sight. The gambling parlor was rounding a broad curve of the North Platte, centered in the main channel. The floating cathouse soon followed.

I studied the sleeping settlement known as the Crossing, where wood smoke layered the night air, and thought it was time to beat it out of there. The three scows were on their way to Nebraska, and no one on board had a way to stop them. It was sort of entertaining. I folded my Barlow knife and restored it to my damp pocket. Those fellers would be a little put out, but they'd asked for it. And I'd report to Lawyer Stokes that the Crossing was now as innocent as lamb's wool. Stokes would be irate that I hadn't arrested the whole lot and brought them in for trial. That's the way Stokes was. He was less interested in solving a problem than getting what he could out of it, such as fines and jail sentences and acclaim in all the right circles. Stokes was a true-born turd.

I collected Critter, who snarled at me, and I led the horse out of the Crossing and paused at a place that looked like it had a little fresh grass popping up. I let Critter graze a while, knowing he was mad at me for not taking the bit out of his mouth, which made eating real messy. But it didn't matter. I sat on a slope, watching the distant settlement leak wood smoke, wondering if they'd give chase. They would know who loosed the barges, and knew where I was going. I heard a distant gunshot from downriver and realized someone onboard a scow was trying to signal the settlement. If the shots woke anyone, there'd be a scramble downriver to catch up and try to lasso the barges and drag them back. But even though there was a crackle of shots from downriver, no one in the settlement stirred. That was just fine.

I robbed Critter of the rest of his breakfast and headed back to Doubtful, with a blanket wrapped around me to ward off the deep chill of my damp clothing. The funny thing was, I believed my success wouldn't cheer anyone in town. It didn't bring in any fines, which would disappoint the supervisors. It would thwart Lawyer Stokes's plan to fire me and get a new and more obedient sheriff. I decided the best thing would be not to say a word. I'd keep my little triumph to myself. Maybe share it with Rusty. If anyone asked, I'd tell them I had given them ten days' notice.

I rode slowly out of the Platte River valley, and heard no more than the night breezes, while Critter picked up his feet and put himself into a jog, eager to dig his snout into some oats. Daylight arrived when I was still ten miles from town, and I enjoyed riding through the sweet quiet of dawn, watching the sun ascend upon the vast reaches of Puma County, illumine the snow-clad peaks of the Medicine range, paint them in gold, and climb higher. It would be a fine spring day. I reached Doubtful about ten, gave Critter an extra bait of oats and plenty of hay, while Turk watched disapprovingly, and combed out the sweaty hide under the saddle blanket.

"You find anything out there?" Turk asked.

"Regular hellhole. So nice I pretty near gave up my badge and moved in. More fun than around here," I said.

"Maybe I should move the livery barn out there. I've lost money ever since them Temperance women took over the town."

"You'd have a right smart trade at the Crossing, Turk."

"You clean out all them criminals?"

"I told them they had to vamoose in ten days."

"And what did that get you?"

"A dunking in the river."

Turk grinned slowly. "Cotton Pickens, you're a hell of a sheriff," he said.

I knew the story would be all over Doubtful in about one hour, and thought that was pretty good. It was a regular knee-slapper.

I walked over to the sheriff office. At first I thought Rusty was out of there, but then I found him asleep in one of the cells. Just why Rusty always slept in the smelliest cell I couldn't say. Maybe he liked the smell of rancid puke.

Rusty awoke with a start and rubbed his eyes. "You clean out all those sinners and make Puma County pure once again?"

"They got ten days to give up their wicked ways, Rusty."

Rusty grinned. "I'm thinking of applying for town constable of the Crossing."

"They don't need one, Rusty. They got about six toughs watching out. I couldn't find a cemetery, but that probably means that the river's it. Kill a man, send the body downriver."

"That's called a victimless crime. No victim, see?"

"What happened here?"

"Just like you said, Stokes arrived with some paper an hour after you rode out, and told me to throw Sally Sweet into the jug. I asked him what for, and he said never you mind, some legal mumbo jumbo, and I said I'd think about it, and he jabbered a while and stormed out threatening to send me to the state pen. That's where it stands."

"That was good, Rusty."

"Well, he gave me a lecture about virtue, which I endured, but just barely."

I smiled. It was good to be back in Doubtful, where every woman was a virgin, and every man was, too. I was tired, but I had to report, and decided to start with Stokes.

I walked into Stokes's lair and found the man reviewing his accounts. Stokes looked up, studied me, and grimaced.

"Back so soon? No doubt you failed."

"There's a little settlement there, all right. Three scows or rafts. A few people we know. I told them they had ten days to shut down or I'd come in with force and do it for them."

"You didn't round them up? You didn't act? You didn't shut them down?"

"No, sir. I visited each scow and told them they were in Puma County. George Roman's got the saloon. He had the Lizard Lounge here. Cronk, Mrs. Gladstone's gambler, was operating a gambling outfit. A faro game and two poker tables—and a pocket bar. That's all his scow could hold. I don't know who operates the bordello. Absentee. A rough customer keeping house for the owner."

"Let me get this straight, Pickens. You witnessed crime operating freely in Puma County and didn't shut it down?"

"No, sir, I didn't. There were a lot of them, and one of me. And most of their house thugs were armed, and plenty of the drovers were, too."

"So you caved in, spoke some polite words, and scurried back to Doubtful."

"No, sir, I gave them ten days to shut down or I would do it for them."

"And what happened then?"

"They threw me in the river, Mr. Stokes."

"Ah, some sheriff you are, Cotton Pickens. You let a mob of hooligans best you. I'm sure they're laughing."

I sighed. I hardly knew how to explain it. "Mr. Stokes, sir, this isn't a dime novel. In a dime novel, the sheriff pulls out his two six-guns and blasts away, and the other gents start shooting back, missing the sheriff, of course, or creasing his flesh, and pretty soon the dime novel sheriff's got them all defeated, with bodies here and there, and the rest with their hands high, ready to be marched back to town and thrown in jail. And then somehow he herds fifty people back to town and locks them up. Trouble is, Mr. Stokes, that's not how it is in real life. I might have sprayed a few bullets, five in all, killed a few men, maybe some that wasn't causing trouble, and then I'd be hit by about twenty men in there, and you'd never see my body because it would be tumbling down the North Platte River."

"That doesn't excuse your cowardice and incompetence, Sheriff. I think there'll be some changes in the wind, as soon as I report all this to the supervisors. Now you've alerted them out there at the Crossing, and it'll be twice as hard to bring them to justice. You will cost us lives, Pickens."

"I guess you want a dime novel sheriff. Shoots fast, kills a lot, and never gets hit. Faster than anyone, and smarter than anyone. That it?"

The county attorney licked his dry lips. "You're exaggerating, of course. What we need is a competent sheriff who's not a coward and has better than a fifth-grade education, and can think straight. And we don't have one. And soon we're going to get one. Do you understand?"

"Guess I do," I said. "But until you pull my badge, I'm still in office and I still got a job to do."

CHAPTER TWENTY-SIX

I wanted to visit Sally Sweet and get the story, so I started down Wyoming Street. The town sure was peaceful. Spring was in the air. But I hardly got a block before Mayor George Waller accosted me.

"I'm real glad I spotted you, Sheriff. We did it."

"Did what?"

"Funded the town. New source of income. The city fathers, namely me and Hubert Sanders and George Maxwell, enacted the ordinance. No spitting in public. Two-dollar fine, rising to five dollars for repeats. And you're our salvation, Cotton. You go out now, soon as it's published, and haul people in for spitting. Two dollars apiece."

"I hate to pinch people for laying a gob on the street, George. Why don't you hire a town constable?"

"Because that costs money, and you're the best

man for the job. You could get ten dollars a week out of Turk. He spits like there's no tomorrow."

"You sure the city's so broke?"

"We're in debt, Sheriff. No fees from the saloons, no table fees from gamblers, no license fees from the parlor houses, no fines from the girls in them. The county supervisors wiped out our city budget."

"Well, I think I'll pass. I got county laws to enforce, not city ones."

"You're being stubborn, Cotton. We're not incorporated, and you're the only law we got."

"Well, you go print up a card I can give to people when I catch them firing a gob, saying it's your law, not mine."

"Oh, no, we want you to be the brave front for our non-spit way of life."

"You just want to get yourself reelected, that's all."

"That too, Cotton."

"I ain't gonna do it. But I'll deputize one of them Temperance ladies and let her do it. She can arrest me if she catches me. Say the word, and I'll deputize Eve Grosbeak and Manilla Twining as sheriff deputies in charge of spitting."

"Hell's bells," said Mayor Waller. "That would start a revolution. I've been hearing rumors. There's a mess of cowboys planning to vote in the June elections, and they're talking about throwing everyone out and putting in people who'd repeal all those new laws."

"It all started when women got the right to vote," I said. "You can't get anywhere until you repeal that and get them back into the kitchen."

"You're right, Sheriff. The world's going to hell fast. We've got to stop it. It's like dandelions. Give 'em an inch and they'll take a yard."

"If we want change around here, we've got to take away the women's vote," I said. "I don't know how to do that. Maybe a poll tax. They ain't got a dime."

"You know, all those cowboys are thinking the same thing. I talked to Big Nose George and Spitting Sam the other day, when they was loading up a wagon with flour. They said it's hopeless. Doubtful's worse than a funeral parlor. They've got to outlaw female voting in Puma County or else everyone'll pull out."

"I sure don't know how to do it, but the first thing is to toss out them county supervisors who got wives always telling them how to vote. Then, get some fellers to run. I mean, fellers the women wouldn't think of supporting. And we'll all get behind them."

"Sheriff, you're onto something. We got to get rid of Amos Grosbeak—he's the worst, and Twining and Thimble, almost as bad. None of 'em can be redeemed because they got mean wives that run 'em. Never underestimate what a wife can do to a man, Sheriff."

"Well, that's what it comes to. Elect women and first thing you've got is anti-spitting laws."

Waller went his way. It sure was a satisfying conversation, and I was glad to get a little opinion from people on the street. I hawked up a good gob and spat at a pile of horse apples that were still warm and had a few early flies buzzing around. I'd spit all I wanted until they published the new law, and maybe I'd spit some more after that. I wondered what Doubtful, Wyoming, was coming to. There was more freedom in Rochester, New York, than in all of Wyoming.

The first thing I noticed when I got to Sally Sweet's boardinghouse was that she was flying some flag or other, a fancy one with a lot of gold thread in it, and some shields on it, and some black letters in Latin or something or other. Who could say? But it sure was a fancy flag, and there was a little crown embroidered on top, making it look real important.

I entered her door, setting off the cowbells, and Sally emerged at once from her suite, wearing a silky kimono. And then right behind was a dapper little fellow with a pencil mustache with daggers of black hair in both directions, all waxed and looking ready to stab. He had a robe on, too, and darned if it wasn't the same silky design as the flag fluttering out front.

"Cotton, I'm so thrilled to see you," she said. "Meet my husband."

"Husband?"

"Absolutely, Cotton. I'm a countess. Meet Count Cernix von Stromberger, Count of Upper Silesia and Baron of Lesser Latvia."

"You got married, Sally?"

"Last night. We consummated it first, and then went to the judge and he tied it up for us. That Axel Nippers, he sure knows how to read a marriage ceremony fast. We were in and out of there faster than Cernix could say I do." She eyed her man. "Cernix, darling, meet our dear sheriff, Cotton Pickens."

"Just fine, just fine," the count said.

"How did this happen? Did you know each other for long?" I asked.

"No, I stopped by, looking for a free room, and she accommodated me. A palace revolution in Upper Silesia put a strain on my finances. We took a liking to each other at once. I had a title and no money, and she had a fancy boarding-house and a yearning for a title. So Sally Sweet became the Countess von Stromberger."

"Oh, my, Lawyer Stokes is fit to be tied," she said. "Do come in and let us brew you some Bulgarian tea."

"What's Bulgarian tea?" I asked.

"I don't know. Cernix brought it, but it puts a person in a very special mood, doesn't it Cernix?"

"It does. It removes pain and improves the libido."

"Whoopee," said Sally. "You have enough libido for a month."

"What's libido?" I asked.

"You poor dear. You'll find out some day," she said. "I don't think you have a lick of it."

"Well, my ma always said I make up for it."

She started some water heating, and we settled in her kitchen. The count was a restless fellow, itching and bouncing.

"I tell you what, Sheriff," he said. "It's a sad world when a man can't even enjoy a sip of wine. I told my chickadee here, Doubtful needs reform. It needs a parliament. It needs a duke. If Doubtful were to appoint me, I'd be most happy to legislate some new laws, more generous and humane than the ones your wretched hen-pecked supervisors have imposed on the weary world."

"They go along with their wives, all right," I said. "But the wives are real nice ladies. They're trying to get me married off, without any luck. Mrs. Grosbeak's got a mess of peacocks in her yard, and it's a trial just to get from the gate to her door without being half bit to death."

"What you need is a revolution," the count

said. "A little stiletto work. A boot to the skinny behind."

"Cernix is leading up to something," Sally said.

"I am. It's time for reform in Doubtful. It's time to throw off the yoke. It's time to send the Women's Temperance Union packing. It's time for you, my dear sheriff, to run for high office on a generous platform."

"Me?"

"You're exactly the right man for the job."

"All I want is sheriff."

"And arrest people for spitting in the street? I heard about that."

"Well, I'd probably just dodge that a little."

"No, young man, you can't dodge it. It's a slippery slope. First it's saloons. Then it's gambling and cathouses. Then it's spitting. Then it's smoking. Then it's enjoying a stroll on Sundays. Then it's—who knows where it'll stop, eh? Tyranny in skirts. You've got to do something, show some public spirit. You're the man of the hour, and destiny's calling you."

I could hardly imagine running for office. Sally served up some of that brew, and it tasted a little bitter but put me in a fine mood.

"In Lower Silesia, we elevate women to sainthood, and that takes care of it," Cernix said. "You've got to know how to handle a woman, and that's something you need to learn, boy."

It sure was a pleasant visit. I learned that Count

von Stromberger had run afoul of an obscure ordinance outlawing carrier pigeons, and before it was settled he had spent a half million kroner defending his right to raise carrier pigeons and also fighting cocks. It so ruined him that he fled to the New World, looking for opportunity, and now he had found it.

"Well, I got to get back on duty, Count, and you can get back to your libidos," I said.

"That was exactly the right thing to say, boy. You think about it. You've got to run for office to spare this county additional grief. You'll be the salvation of Puma County and its suffering people. You put together a slate, and run together, so you'll have a majority on the board of supervisors. The countess and I, we'll help you any way we can."

"That sure sounds real fine," I said.

But once I got into the fresh air of spring, I knew I'd stick with my job. I liked being sheriff. I didn't always like the rules I had to enforce, but I sure liked being the law in Puma County. People on the street waved, or tipped their hat, or nodded, and everyone in the whole county knew me. So by the time I got back to my office that spring afternoon, I'd decided not to run, even if it was sort of pleasant to think that someone wanted me on the county board.

"Where you been?" asked Rusty. "It's sure sleepy around here."

"I've been meeting Sally Sweet's new husband, Count Cernix von Stromberger."

"She married that crook?"

"What about it?"

"He's on half the Wanted dodgers in the West."

"Well, he's pretty fine, and he's rescued Sally from Lawyer Stokes, and maybe I'll just keep an open mind about him."

Rusty grinned. "Sure, Cotton. Enforce the law without fear or favor."

Rusty sure made me mad.

Two or three peaceful days slid by in Doubtful, with grass coming up and tulips getting ready to bloom and daffodils defying the night frosts and shouting that warmth was on its way. And then Supervisor Amos Grosbeak called me in. I hurried up to the man's spacious office, thinking there would be trouble.

"You planning to go out to the Crossing and shut it down, like you said?" Grosbeak asked.

"Well, I'm fixing on it. I'll need to recruit a posse. I'll get you and the other supervisors and the businessmen in town, and Doc Harrison, and we'll ride over there and put the place out of business."

"Well, ah, you probably won't need a posse. Certainly not a large one. I've heard a strange thing. Came in by wire. Three scows loaded with criminals got cut loose of the Crossing and floated down the North Platte River, helpless to stop because they hadn't so much as a pole to steer with. The story has it that they yelled at people along the way, but no one knew how to rope the scows. This went on until they crossed the Nebraska line, and the next anyone knew, the scows had gotten to North Platte, a town pretty much operated by Buffalo Bill Cody, and this time the howls of the criminals were heard on shore, and a bunch of Cody's troupe lassoed the scows and brought them in. Well, Sheriff, there was immediate celebration. The scows supplied exactly what North Platte was lacking, and North Platte had cash in its pockets, so the debased criminals on the scows were making ten times more each hour than they earned in a day at the Crossing."

He scowled at me.

"Now how could that be? You know anything about that?"

"Someone cut 'em loose," I said. "Ain't that a hurrah?"

"You botched the job. You should have arrested them and brought them in for violating Puma County law," Grosbeak said. "Now they're being rewarded for a life of vice. Sometimes, Pickens, I think you were born without brains."

"It's not true," I said. "I got a few."

CHAPTER TWENTY-SEVEN

The three county supervisors occupied their usual seats in the Puma County courtroom, and Lawyer Stokes was hovering like a tarantula off to one side, dressed this day in funereal black. It sure looked like a hanging party to me, and that was exactly what it was.

Amos Grosbeak did the talking, since he was the top dog among the supervisors. It was he who had summoned me and Deputy Rusty Irons to this meeting.

"I'll get straight to it, Pickens. We're discharging you and your deputy. As of today, you are no longer sheriff of Puma County, and your deputy is no longer in your employ or the county employ."

I wasn't surprised. "You mind telling me why?"

"Dereliction of duty. Time after time, you have failed to enforce the laws duly enacted by this county and this board of supervisors. Most recently you failed to enforce the law at the Crossing, where vice flourishes unimpeded. You went there and did nothing and let the criminal element escape."

"Well, they ain't in Puma County anymore."

"No thanks to you. You might be a good man with a revolver, but you've been entirely ineffectual in law enforcement. It was unanimously decided, by recorded vote, to discharge you and your deputy." He turned to his fellow supervisors. "Is that not correct, gentlemen?"

Reggie Thimble nodded. So did Lester Twining.

"Let it be put on the record that all supervisors agreed. Now then, Pickens, we are disallowing your travel costs to the Crossing, since you failed in your duty, and we are assessing your salary the administrative costs of discharging you, which means we are deducting eleven dollars from your April salary, which means that you and the county of Puma are dead even."

"No pay for April."

"Certainly you received pay, but the expenses you have imposed on us because of your derelictions are equal to the pay. Therefore, we are done with you. Please surrender your badge and the jail key to us forthwith, and remove any personal items from the County Office."

"You got a new man hired?"

"Three new men, solid and true, and devoted to the law and the county. If a celebrated shootist such as yourself is of no worth to us, then maybe a few Paul Bunyons would be an improvement. We've hired the woodcutters and sawmill man Lemuel Clegg, who will be our new sheriff, and his boys Barter and Cash, who will be his deputies. We look forward to vigorous law enforcement. They are in complete accord with the law, and they assure us they will enforce any law we enact, without fear or favor. We believe Doubtful and Puma County will benefit from their peaceful, quiet, strong natures."

"Them Cleggs are good men. I only hope they don't get shot, since muscle don't do a lot of good when it comes to guns."

"That will be enough of your insolence, Pickens." Grosbeak rapped the gavel and held out his hand. I unpinned my badge, and so did Rusty.

"It's the usual screw," I said.

That met with a rap of the gavel.

"We got all three of them for only two dollars more than the pair of you," Grosbeak said. "The county will save money."

"They gonna enforce the city's new spitting law?"

"They will enforce all the law without fear or favor. The Cleggs are manly and oozing with virtue, and I wish we had thought to employ them in this most noble calling long ago. It would have spared us a lot of grief."

He eyed me with vast distaste.

I walked out of there feeling a little peeved, but also relieved. Now I wouldn't have to enforce a mess of laws I didn't much approve of. I'd lasted longer than the other sheriffs the supervisors had appointed.

"How about you?" I asked Rusty.

Rusty worked up a good gob and fired it at the street, but no one caught him en flagrant delicto.

Me and Rusty didn't have much personal stuff to remove from the office. Just an ancient sweater and a few spare stockings with holes in the toes and worn-out heels.

"What you gonna do?" Rusty asked.

"Spend my last nickels on some chili at Barney's Beanery, quit Belle's Boardinghouse, and then get Critter out of Turk's barn and go somewhere."

"Yeah, but where?"

"It's spring, and the mountains are looking real good to me."

"I don't know what to do, either. It's like we've got something hanging over us, and we need to free ourselves from it."

"The only thing hanging over me is a mess of rules I don't want. Minute I step out of Puma County I'll be fine."

"Me, I'm red-haired and prone to fighting. Cotton, the trouble with you is you ain't got red hair. If you had red hair, no one would call you thick-skulled."

"You want a fight, do you, Rusty? I know how to pick one if you're of a mind."

"I always like a fight, Cotton."

"You speaking serious, or just blowing farts?"

"When have I ever backed away from one?"

"I guess I'll leave Critter in Turk's Livery Barn. You and me, Rusty, are running for office."

"We're what?"

"How are we gonna fix up Puma County if those three peckerheads, Grosbeak, Twining, and Thimble, are in office, causing all the trouble they can? Do you think anyone's opposed to them? Not as I've heard. There's an election coming right up. Should we just let them go back in and cause worse trouble?"

"There's three of them and two of us, Cotton."

"I'll get Big Nose George Botts to run with us. He's not got kindly feelings toward the supervisors."

"You think we can do her?"

"You got any better ideas?"

"You ever run for anything, Cotton? I mean, don't we have to file forms and do stuff?"

"We'll get it straightened out. Maybe Sally Sweet, I mean whatever her name is now, she can help us out."

"Do you really think we should?"

"We're desperate. Puma County's on the rocks."

"Do supervisors get a salary?"

"Aha, now you're talking," I said.

"But we've got to win, Cotton. How do we win against all those rich men?"

"Beats me, Rusty."

"And what are you gonna say? I mean, you got to be for something and against something."

"That's not so hard. We're against all them new laws and want to pull them up by the roots and get back to the way it was."

"And what are we for, Cotton?"

"Getting the women out of there. This whole mess started with women voting. We got to repeal that. We'll say that it's not right, and women make good cooks and mothers, but they should let men alone. We're the true men in Puma County. We're the ones to run the place. How does that sound?"

"Yeah, but they got voting rights in the state constitution, Cotton."

"Well, all we have to do is keep it out of the county. They can't vote for county supervisors. They can vote for the governor, but not for county supervisors. We'll pass that when we get in."

"You think that'll work?"

"Beats not having a job, Rusty."

"But what'll we call ourselves? We need a name. We need something catching."

"The Puma Peckerheads. My ma always said a good joke wins the day."

"That doesn't seem real funny to me, Cotton. I think we should be the Anti-Woman Party. That says it all, and no mistake."

"Suit yourself, Rusty."

That's how it started. Pretty quick after the supervisors discharged me and Rusty, we got our dander up. There would be a hot contest for the Puma County supervisor board in June. Just about the first thing I did was ride out to the Admiral Ranch to get Big Nose George to run for office, but George said he'd rather be burned at the stake by Joan of Arc, so that was that. Me and Rusty decided the only other likely winner would be Cernix von Stromberger. That was a name and a half.

It was sure odd, not being sheriff. The people of Doubtful didn't know it yet, and greeted me as if I was still wearing the badge. But me and Rusty hiked down Wyoming Street to the old sporting district, where the only occupied building belonged to Sally Sweet.

Cernix greeted us cheerfully. "Ah, the wayfarers of Doubtful. Come to arrest Sally, I suppose."

"No, sir, we ain't lawmen anymore."

That set back the count. "You don't say. What happened?"

"The supervisors decided I ain't doing my job, so they fired me and Rusty here, and they'll put a few lumbermen in."

Sally heard the last, having emerged from her downstairs suite in a shimmery dressing gown. "What's this? You're out?"

"Yes, ma'am, Grosbeak finally had his way with us, and we're just regular citizens now."

"That spell trouble for me and Cernix?"

"It could real bad, ma'am."

"You want some booze?" She smiled. "Now that you aren't sheriff?"

Rusty waved a hand. "I don't know about him, but I'll take one and a refill."

"She's got a three-year hoard," the count said. "It's not enough. Dry spells last seven years. That's the biblical dry spell."

But Rusty was following Sally into her boudoir, where she had a stash. "Here," she said, handing him a bottle of Old Orchard.

Rusty sighed and moaned, and began working the cork loose.

"I don't suppose you know what you're going to do," Cernix said.

"Well, that's what we came to talk about. Me and Rusty, we've decided on something real big. And we've got some real big stuff for you, Count." I paused for effect. I wasn't above being theatrical. In fact I paused until Sally and Rusty appeared, each with an inch of amber stuff in a tumbler. Rusty was looking almost happy, at least for a redhead.

"We're running for office. We're running against the supervisors. We're going to push repeal. And we're going to push getting women out of politics."

"That's the best idea I've heard. The trouble began when we got the vote," Sally said.

"Well, me and Rusty, we thought it over real

hard. If women didn't get the vote in Wyoming, that Temperance Union wouldn't have gotten any power, and if women weren't pushing to shut down your sporting house, it wouldn't have happened, and if women hadn't pushed for Sunday laws shutting everything down, we'd still be able to go to Barney's Beanery on Sundays, and if women hadn't deprived Doubtful of its revenue, there'd be no spitting laws for peace officers to enforce. So we're running against it. First thing, we'll repeal all that stuff."

"Who's the third candidate? There's three supervisors," the count asked.

"You."

"Me? But I'm titled."

"You're a resident by marriage, and that's all it takes."

"What will I say?"

"That you're Count Cernix von Stromberger, married to Denver Sally, and it's time to throw the bastards out."

The count gazed at the blue sky outside, and at Rusty sipping real hard, and at me. "I'm in," he said. "Now, have you formed a party?"

"Well, me and Rusty don't see eye to eye here. I want to call us the Puma Peckerheads and Rusty wants to call us the Anti-Woman Party. Maybe you could chime in."

"You're the Puma Peckerheads," Sally said. "It has just the right ring."

Cernix nodded. "The Peckerheads we are."

"I never got into politics before," I said. "It's sort of a pissing contest, ain't it?"

"More like a gunfight, except it's words, not bullets," Rusty said.

"Not just spraying words around hoping to hit something," Cernix said. "You'll want to shoot words accurately, hit the target every time, and not ever miss. You'll want to choose your words carefully, because the wrong word'll come back and hit you."

"I'd rather be a gunfighter," I said.

"Here's all it takes. You just tell it true. You just talk about what the supervisors did to this county, and you'll win," Sally said.

We sat around her table sipping her booze and planning our campaign. The next day, the three of us went to the county clerk and got recorded as candidates. That's all it took; word raced through Doubtful like lightning, and men gathered in knots on street corners to talk about it. I was pretty scared. I'd rather go after an armed criminal with my revolver than get into one of these spitting contests, but I was committed. Me and my running mates were going to undo a lot of trouble in Puma County.

CHAPTER TWENTY-EIGHT

Truth to tell, I couldn't stay at Belle's boarding-house anymore. I had no income. So I knocked on Belle's door and told her I was quitting the place.

"But Cotton, you can't do this to me. You're my most honored guest."

"Well, I can't rub two nickels together, Belle, so I'm outa here."

"Where are you going?"

"Well, ah, I've been offered a place."

"Where, Cotton?"

"Sally says she'll take me until I become county supervisor and can pay her back."

"And what if you don't win?"

"I guess Puma County will see the last of me."

She looked sort of melancholy. "You could stay here if you want. A woman needs a little attention now and then. You could make me happy just be dropping by and giving your old friend a nice little hug or two, or maybe a few more."

"Well, I couldn't do that for rent, Belle. It ain't right."

"It's so hard for a refined woman to meet the right men in Doubtful," she said. "There are plenty of men, but so uncouth. I'm so tired of uncouth males I could almost scream."

"Well, Belle, when you get the mistletoe up next Christmas, just let me know and I'll give you a real uncouth hug, the kind you might enjoy."

"You're a brute, Cotton Pickens."

"My ma never told me I was that. She said I was a lot of things, but brute is a new one."

Women sure were strange. She acted like she was put out. I loaded up my gear, which wasn't much, and carried it down Wyoming Street to Sally's, and put it in the room she had given me. I knew the room, all right. Its last occupant had been Chiquita Swivelhips, the Argentine Bombshell. She made a lot of money but then she took sick and Doc Harrison couldn't cure her.

It was a nice room, with a well-stained blue-striped mattress on the bed, and a mirror on the wall with pictures of saints poked into the frame. I felt right at home. I had wondered about saints for a long time, but had never met any. Now I had a mirror festooned with them, and they might give me some notions.

I settled my razor and shaving mug on the commode, and headed downstairs.

"I'm in, Sally. You keep tabs now, and when I'm elected I'll pay you back. If I can't pay you back, I'll give you Critter. He needs a new boss."

"If you're elected, you won't need to pay me back. I'll be in business again, Cotton."

"Well, I've got one vote, anyway," I said.

It was time to get out and campaign, and it was a good day for it, with the late March sun shrinking the dirty snow heaped here and there. Doubtful was having a festive day, with women out shopping and children caroming around like billiard balls. There were a few ranch wagons parked on Wyoming Street, which meant the outlying ranches were stocking up on beans and flour and coffee. I had no plan other than to introduce myself, ask for people to vote for the Puma Peckerheads, and thank them for their interest. Truth to tell, the whole business scared the crap out of me. I'd rather fight twenty hooligans armed with brass knuckles and knouts than go out and greet people. I hadn't given a thought about what to say, either, except I was against women voting.

Well, it'd be something to learn. I sure didn't know how to stop strangers on the street and ask them to vote for me, but I steeled myself. I wished Rusty Irons was with me, or maybe Count Cernix, but they weren't around, and I'd have to weather the ordeal by my lonesome.

I thought I'd try out a man, first. I understood men a lot better. In fact, the young gent loading bags of barley into a ranch wagon was a man I knew, King Glad, from the Admiral Ranch. I had rescued King from real trouble once.

"Howdy, King," I said.

The young rancher paused after settling a fifty-pound bag of barley into his spring wagon. "It's the sheriff," King said.

"No, I got evicted. Lem Clegg, he's the sheriff now."

"I hadn't heard. Lem's a good man."

"King, I'm running for county supervisor. Me and the count and Rusty Irons. We're gonna repeal all this bad stuff that's come down the chute. We're gonna license saloons and all again, so your drovers can have a good time in Doubtful. And we're in favor of keeping women away from the ballot box."

King Glad paused, his gray eyes surveying me and his expression solemn. "Sorry, Cotton, I'm a ranching man now, and I've put my wild times behind me—for good reason. If you try that platform out on my sister Queen, she'll shoot you proper. If anyone tries to keep her from voting, she'll blow his cajones to smithereens."

"Yeah, well, nice to see you, King. Give my best to Queen."

That didn't go so well, but there were a lot of good folks in Doubtful just itching to repeal all these new notions.

I saw another fellow I knew, Ole Petersen, a wheat farmer who was plowing up an entire section and putting it into winter wheat. Ole was loading some repaired harness into his wagon. Jim Scuttles, the harness maker, had been working on it.

"Ole, it's good to see you," I said.

"What have I done? Don't accuse me. I hardly even get to Doubtful."

"Ole, I'm running for county supervisor. We need reform in Doubtful. It's gone the wrong direction. A man can't come to Doubtful anymore and have a good time."

Petersen glared. "The last thing I want is a good time. The last thing I want for others is a good time. We should all work and struggle and get ahead and be good to our children. That's why I came here, to give something to my children."

"Ah, well, there's lots of people who get real worn out herding cattle, and plowing fields, and they'd like some pleasant company in Doubtful. A vote for me will make sure that everyone's happy."

"Happiness is the holy grail of fools," Petersen said. "What they should do is tear down every building on Saloon Row, cover it all up with good earth, plant grass, and make a park of it, and destroy the memory of it."

"I see, well, nice to visit with you, Ole."

I wasn't liking the campaign so far. Maybe Rusty would have better ways to win votes.

Ah, but there was Mrs. Drago, wife of the town's well-digger. She was dragging her unruly carrot-haired boy, Charley, with her. Charley looked like he'd rather be fishing.

"It's you, Sheriff," she said with a smile.

"Oh, I'm not the sheriff anymore, Gwendolyn. I got, ah, forcibly resigned from the high office, and now I'm a politician."

"What a pity," she said.

"I'm running for county supervisor, along with two others. We're the Puma Peckerheads, as we named ourselves, and the Peckerheads want to defeat the mean bunch in there now."

"Well, I like the name, Peckerheads. It has a poetic sound to it."

"We're in favor of bringing happiness to Doubtful," I said. "We've got to drive the Temperance Union clear out of town, and let the men gather in their favorite saloons once again."

"Gathering? Is that what you call it? I call it fighting and getting drunk and spending the money that their families need for food and clothing."

"Well, lots of ranchers are happiest when they can come in, buy things, and have a drink before they leave Doubtful. And the Peckerheads are for that."

She slugged the whiny boy. "What else are you for?" she asked.

"Repeal of women's voting. Everything went downhill the day they got their nose into the tent."

"I believe you are referring to camels. I don't think women wish to be compared to camels, Sheriff."

Well, some women look just like a camel, Mrs. Drago."

"I wonder if you'd name a few, Mr. Pickens."

"Oh, I think camels are real nice looking. Manilla Twining, she makes a wonderful camel, don't you think?"

"What I think, Mr. Pickens, is that men should be disfranchised, and women should have the vote exclusively. Then the world would be a better place. Good day."

I tipped my hat to her as she dragged the brat along by the ear.

It sure wasn't going the way I'd planned. But I'd hardly started, and with each encounter I could refine my approach, and after a while I'd be as smooth as a Tammany Politician. At least I had learned a few things. I had thought that pretty near everyone in Puma County was opposed to the Temperance reforms, but I was learning that a lot of citizens favored them, and favored shutting down all the life in the sporting district. The very thought of it made me ache. Maybe getting fired was the best thing that ever happened to me.

I was thinking about a bowl of soup at Barney's Beanery when I encountered Eve Grosbeak and Manilla Twining themselves. I figured I was in for it, and I couldn't just run down the nearest alley, which was between the Emporium and the Drover's Rest. There they came, dressed for springtime in big hats with lots of artificial flowers on them, and looking like they owned the whole county. I decided just to root my feet into the ground and stand there like a solid oak and let them wash by me.

But it didn't work that way. They swooped down on me, full of good cheer.

"Why, child, it's good to see you. I hope you're staying washed," Manilla said.

"We heard you've been relieved of office," Eve said. "Amos could talk of nothing else all day. Are you enjoying it?"

"I'm, ah, entering politics, ma'am."

"Why, so we've heard! That's wonderful. It helps divide the vote."

"Ah, I don't quite follow you, ma'am."

"Call me Eve, sweetheart," she said. "Manilla and I have filed for office. We're running against our husbands. They're too timid, and pussy-whipped, and we're going to kick them out and take over. We've got more reforms in mind, and we'll make sure they are enacted."

"You're running against your husbands?"

"Poor dears. They aren't very effectual, you know, and everyone says we've got them under our thumb, which is semi-true. It doesn't help their campaigns when everyone says they're just pussy-whipped. And now you've come along, just as we'd hoped, and you'll divide the male vote, and we'll be elected."

"You mean you're glad I'm running?"

"You bet, dearie," said Manilla. "You'll get the reactionary vote. It would have gone to our husbands, but now with you in the race, all the males in town will divide between the Peckerheads and the Grosbeak clique. And we'll walk in."

I was feeling mighty proud, having finally gotten some approval. "I'm just rarin' to go, ma'am. I'm running on a Repeal Suffrage platform, and that's getting people lined up who never voted before. Why, nearly every ranch hand in the county's planning on voting for us."

"Cotton, dear, make sure you wash your socks regularly," Manilla said. "It's something you need to do."

They sashayed down the street while I watched their behinds sway. It was a pleasant way to spend a minute or two. But this whole thing was getting too complex for me. Now it was a three-way race, and those gals were running against their own husbands. Not a bad deal. Maybe I should be in favor of Female Suffrage. It sure was something to think about.

I had hardly gotten fifty feet when along came the new sheriff, Lemuel Clegg, and one of his boys. Probably Barter. And the pair had shiny badges on their chests. Lem Clegg was built like a barrel, and all of it was muscle from felling logs and sawing them up. His boy was an even larger barrel, and even stronger. I envied them. Being built like prize bulls would help them in their job. A minor tap of a Clegg fist would send an adversary flying. The Cleggs were about ten times heftier and tougher than any cowboy that ever sat a horse, and had biceps that set women to swooning.

"There you are. We've been looking for you, Cotton," Lem said.

"It's good to see a good man wearing the badge," I said.

"Well, ya, but we got a complaint about you. You've been harassing people, and old Grosbeak, he says politicking on the streets is disturbing the peace, so you gotta stop."

"I was just greeting people, Lem."

"Well, the supervisors, they say to make you quit or haul you in and fine you."

"Fine me?"

"Two dollars for disturbing the peace. You

gotta quit bothering people and just mind your own business on the streets of Doubtful."

"Oh, I get it. And does that apply to other folks, too?"

"It applies to everyone running for office, Cotton."

"Like them two gals over there, who are running against the supervisors?"

"Them two? Running for office? It sure does. First women I've ever seen running for office." He turned to his boy. "You ever seen the like, Cash?"

"Blamed if I've ever seen one do it," Cash said.

"Well, they've violating the law right and left, disturbing the peace every which way, Lem."

"I haven't got it all read up yet, Cotton, but if you say so, I'll go nip them."

"Nip 'em both and throw them in the jug for a while, and then let them post two-dollar bail, Lemuel. Them gals are sure disturbing the peace around here."

"We'll do that, Cotton, and thanks for the tip. We got to keep the streets peaceful."

CHAPTER TWENTY-NINE

The envelope arrived by private messenger early in the morning, just when me, Rusty, and Cernix were sitting around, sipping java and waiting for Sally to finish making breakfast. Cernix answered the door, took the envelope, and watched the boy scurry off.

"It's addressed to Messrs Cernix von Stromberger, Cotton Pickens, and Rusty Irons," he said. "Shall I read it?"

"I think maybe so," I said, relieved to escape that chore.

The count unfolded some fancy paper from the blue-tinted envelope, while Sally threw more stove wood into the firebox, fried eggs, boiled oatmeal, set the table, started more coffee, laid out strips of side pork on the grille, scrubbed and wiped last evening's dinner plates, sliced and cooked toast, put out some butter, put out some marmalade, and refilled the salt shaker.

Cernix examined the sheet and cleared his throat. "It's from the Women's Temperance Union of Puma County, and it's signed by Eve Grosbeak, president. I'll just read along here, and see what it's about."

"Probably complaining about us being unfair," I said.

"No, that's not it. It says, 'Gentlemen, The Women's Temperance Union will sponsor a series of debates among the candidates for the office of county superintendent. The purpose of the debates is to acquaint voters and other citizens with the views of the candidates so they may make informed choices at the polls. The first of these will be May 1, on the Courthouse Square, weather permitting, or in the courtroom if the weather is not clement. Each debate will discuss issues of interest to citizens of Puma County. One is Woman Suffrage, the second is Prohibition of Spirits, the third is the suppression of vice and houses of ill repute in the county, and the fourth is for each candidate to express his or her plans for the future of Puma County.

"'We have arranged the debates in this fashion. On May 1, at ten in the morning, the candidates Mr. Cotton Pickens, Mr. Amos Grosbeak, and Mrs. Eve Grosbeak, will debate. On May 7, at ten, candidates Count Cernix von Stromberger, Mr. Lester Twining, and Mrs. Manilla Twining will debate. On May 14, also at ten, Mr. Rusty Irons,

Mr. Reggie Thimble, and Mrs. Gladys Thimble shall exchange views. Mr. Hubert Sanders, of the Puma Stockmen's Bank, will moderate. We look forward to seeing you.'"

"Yoicks!" said I.

"It's nothing. We shall defeat them handily," said Cernix.

Sally was muttering something as she dished out eggs and bacon, loaded bowls with oatmeal, slapped toast on the table, clapped a plate of butter next to the toast, and started more eggs because I always wanted five.

But I couldn't eat. I stared dumbfounded at the steaming food, paralyzed. I eyed the other two candidates, who were toying with their breakfasts. I finally set my fork down and stared helplessly at the window.

"Well?" asked Sally, whose forehead glistened with the morning's labor.

"Maybe I should quit. I never wanted to be a supervisor anyway."

"You're worrying about the debate? It's easy. Just talk about whatever comes to mind," said the count. "Just enjoy yourself, and be aware they haven't brains enough to put in a shoebox."

"Who hasn't?" asked Sally.

"The whole collective lot except for us."

"I can't just get up there and jabber away. That's worse than getting executed by a firing squad," I said.

"Nah, it's fine. Just remember words are bullets, and you got to fire them faster than the rest," said Rusty.

But I wasn't buying it. "I'll get cremated," I said.

"Where's your spine, Cotton Pickens?" Sally asked. "I thought you were a real man, but now I'm not so sure."

That did it. "All right, but it's like someone pinned a bull's-eye on my chest," I said. "And I don't want to be a supervisor that bad. I don't speak ideas so hot."

"Sure you do," Cernix said. "What you need to do is talk about your dreams. Just ignore what the rest are jawing about, and talk about your dreams. Don't even say what you'll do in office. Talk about a county where friends can gather in a saloon and have a good time being friendly, and a cowboy can come to town and enjoy the bright lights instead of being stuck out on some ranch with nothing but cows for pals. Talk about that. Talk about a county where everyone's free to do what he wants, without all these rules they're thinking up. You want to persuade people? Talk about freedom. You want to be free to do whatever you feel like doing, and you want the same for everyone else. That's what I'm going to say. I'll be glad to debate Mrs. Twining. I'll drive her back into her gopher hole."

I dabbled with my eggs, ate the bread except

for the crusts, and scorned the marmalade because it was for sissies.

Rusty, he was just wolfing down chow and grinning. But he was red-haired, and that meant he was spoiling for a fight, and it didn't matter whether it was female dragons or county commissioners. He'd step right in, all right, and leave a few bloody noses. And there was something else about Rusty. He'd spray out a few compliments, charm the ladies, smile at his opponents, and walk away with a victory. I envied him. But my ma always said redheads were the lucky ones.

But the very thought of getting up there on the courthouse steps and addressing all them people on the square, it just made me faint. I'd rather be at my own hanging.

It just sort of hung over me after that. I walked over to the Courthouse Square and eyed it. Now it looked different, like it was enemy turf, or maybe they'd be building a big scaffold for me there, with a noose and a trapdoor, and were all just waiting for me to show up and start jabbering while I stood on the trapdoor. It was like if I failed to carry the day, they'd just spring the trapdoor, and I'd be history.

All I could do was sweat a little, try to greet people, avoid Lem Clegg or his boys, who were looking for excuses to nab me, and hope I'd survive. I wasn't very sure of it. But one thing was clear. I had no choice. If I wanted to win the election, I'd have to debate the Grosbeaks.

Over the next few days, I couldn't eat and lost five pounds, and tried to think up what I would say, but my mind would simply start buzzing, like a saw cutting a log, and then I'd give up and think that me and Critter could just blow town and let the rest take care of itself.

And then it got worse. I wasn't sure I was right anymore. Maybe women should vote. Maybe all the saloons should be shut down. Maybe all the cathouses should be sealed up forever. Maybe I wasn't thinking straight now. So doubts began to gnaw at me along with all the rest. I got no help from Sally or Cernix or Rusty. I was getting so tense I spent twenty minutes in the outhouse each day, instead of three. I wondered why I didn't just collect Critter and ride out and never return.

Nonetheless, May 1 rolled around, and it was going to be a pleasant spring day, and the debate would be in the square, with the speakers on the courthouse steps. I studied the arrangement, looking for an excuse to escape, but I couldn't think of anything. At Barney's Beanery they cheered me along: "Just like a hanging party, Cotton. You'll be fine but for a busted neck."

"Thanks," I said, checking it to make sure.

I remembered what the Temperance women were saying about my clothing, and managed to get my union suit washed, along with my stockings, and even got some grease rubbed into my scruffy boots so they didn't look too bad. By ten o'clock I was resigned to my doom and met with the others on the platform. A goodly crowd had collected. No one in Doubtful had ever heard a debate before, and that sure excited some interest. It wasn't so much a debate as letting each candidate have his speak, but that was okay, too. I'd let the lawyers do the arguing.

I looked pretty clean, but I wasn't up to Amos Grosbeak, who wore a dark three-piece suit, with a cravat and a gold watch fob. Shiny shoes completed his ensemble. And I wasn't up to Eve Grosbeak, either, who wore a dark suit that buttoned clear up to her neck, with a wide-brimmed hat to keep the sun off. I wished I hadn't worn my stained old hat, battered and friendly and just right for a warm sunny day, but it was too late.

The moderator, the banker Hubert Sanders, looked sporty in a brown tweed suit and a polka-dot bow tie. He had fine sideburns and a little jutting Vandyke beard, along with fine mustachios, which make him look formidable when he was turning down a loan application.

I was glad there was a spring breeze, which kept black circles from growing under my armpits. I peered out upon the sea of faces and saw nothing but good cheer. Lots of women out there. Not many children, thank heaven. Over yonder was

Sheriff Clegg and his boy deputies, keeping order for this amazing event. There was a little speaking stand set up there, and someone told me it was called a lectern, and a fellow could get behind it, feel safe, hammer a fist into it, and read from notes. But I had no notes. I'd just try to tell it the way I saw it.

At a minute or two after ten, Sanders studied his gold pocket watch, tucked it back in, and rapped for attention.

"Good morning, good morning," he said. "What a fine day for a debate. I'm so glad you good folks have come forth to listen to our candidates talk about Puma County, and the issues now before us."

I finally saw Cernix and Rusty at the back of the crowd, but Sally was nowhere in sight, which may have been a wise move. Sanders talked a minute about the Women's Temperance Union and how it sponsored this public-spirited event, and then he got down to business.

"Now, I've decided to conduct our debate in this fashion. Ladies first. And then Age before Beauty. That means we'll hear from the lovely Eve Grosbeak first, and then her fine husband Amos, the incumbent, and lastly, our fine former sheriff and protector, Mr. Cotton Pickens."

I desperately needed to take a leak and pondered a way to get to the outhouses behind the courthouse, but it was too late. I'd stand cross-legged and hope the others weren't too windy. Maybe I could unload some coffee from behind that lectern if it got real bad. There might be a puddle, but no one would figure it out.

"Now, our first topic this golden morning will be women's suffrage, and we're including it because it is an issue in the supervisor campaign. One of the candidates wishes to repeal the vote for women, at least in Puma County, as I understand it, and if I err here, he will clarify his view in due course. Now, without further ado, I am honored to present Eve Grosbeak, candidate for the office of Puma County supervisor."

Eve stepped right up, looking pert and snappy, and there was a lot of polite applause scattered through the crowd. Truth to tell, no one had ever seen a female candidate for any public office before, and it was sort of scary. There had been Cleopatra back in Egypt somewheres, but that was ancient history, and since then you couldn't find anyone anywhere, except maybe Queen Elizabeth or some of them other royals. But in the good old US of A, she was pure strangeness. She drew some papers from her handbag, placed some pince-nez on her nose, smiled, and plunged in.

"I'm sure I'm a great oddity to you, my dear people, but you'll see that I am truly the wave of the future not just in Wyoming, but clear across our fair and beautiful republic," she said.

It seemed to me that she had already captured the entire crowd, even before she got cranked up, and she wouldn't even need to launch a stem-winder of a talk to walk away with the whole she-bang. Women had all the advantages. All they had to do was smile, like she was, and they'd get whatever they wanted. I vowed I wouldn't smile a bit when I talked, and I'd show them what a stern and unsmiling man meant to Doubtful, Wyoming.

CHAPTER THIRTY

But Eve Grosbeak wasn't smiling. Instead, she surveyed all those faces, caught the attention of all those people who had come to see something unheard of: a woman running for office. She turned quietly to me.

"I will talk about woman suffrage," she began, "because it was made an issue in this campaign. One of the candidates wishes to repeal the right for women to vote granted in the Wyoming constitution, or at least nullify it in Puma County. He is a fine man, and was a fine sheriff.

"But I am puzzled, Mr. Pickens. In what ways do you feel we are unequal to men, and unqualified to vote for candidates? I hope you will tell us. Do you feel we are less intelligent? If so, explain how that is the case. Do you think we have less spine and resolution than males? If so, please explain. Do you feel we are too sheltered, that the world is too harsh and cruel for our tender eyes to behold? Do tell us if this is your view. Is it simply because you are a traditionalist and want nothing new, and shy from progress? Tell that to us, too. Do you suppose we are less moral or ethical, and this counts against us? Give us your opinion of that. I know that every man, woman, and child before us wishes to know."

Then, surprisingly, she abandoned the podium. I was digging in for a long-winded diatribe. What woman didn't talk twice too much? But there she was, smiling gently and settling in her seat.

"Well, now, that was short and sweet," said the banker. "Next is Mr. Amos Grosbeak, the incumbent."

Eve's husband proceeded gently to the podium, looking uncomfortable in his best suit, best cravat, starched white shirt, polished high-top shoes, and new shave gotten at Brubaker's Tonsorial Parlor.

"Well now, esteemed citizens, dear wife, cherished friends, esteemed colleagues, admired voters, honored guests, and thoughtful listeners. I won't spend much time here. Mostly I wish to stand on my record, for progress, but measured progress, avoiding extremes, making each step forward sound and financially responsible. My opponents are saying, privately, that I have succumbed to the pressures of my active and political mate, but I will flatly deny that. I am no more henpecked than a bull moose. I listen to what she says, but draw my own conclusions in the bosom of my soul. And since I am standing on my record, there is no more to say, and I surrender this podium to the next esteemed candidate."

"Well, well, the Grosbeaks have scarcely consumed five minutes," Hubert Sanders said. "And without further ado, may I give you Mr. Cotton Pickens."

I would rather have ridden a bucking bronc, but I was stuck, and at least I had one or two allies out there to clap.

I got behind that thing they called a lectern and studied the bunch, discovering a few flea-bitten smiles, which heartened me. It sure was a fine May day, with puffball clouds sailing merrily through the blue heavens.

I knew what I wanted to say, but the words came slow and poorly, so I couldn't get my thoughts together very well.

"Well, thanks a heap," I said to all those swells in their fancy duds

"I guess I've got some questions to answer. Truth to tell, the ladies are fine with me, and a lot smarter than I'll ever be. My ma, she was right smart, and there wasn't nothing in the world she didn't know about. That's not my problem with this at all."

Some of that crowd were grinning, as if waiting for me to make a damned fool of myself. "Here's what happens when the women get the vote," I said. "Freedom disappears. That's the long and short of it. Everything in the world is fine until they start telling us it ain't fine anymore. A man's got a right to do anything he wants, including ruin himself, if he chooses. He's got a right to walk into a saloon and order a drink and enjoy his friends. He's got a right to get into a fight and bust bottles over the heads of the rest, and they've got a right to bust his nose and bloody him up.

"If a man's got an itch, he's got a right to go get it scratched. If a man's got the need, he has a right to go fix his need wherever there are gals eager to fix him up. It's getting so a man can't breathe anymore. A man's almost got to have permission to walk through town. A man can't even lay a gob on the walkways. A man's getting more and more hog-tied and bound up and muffled and cuffed. A man can't even yell, or hoot, or tree a town. A man, well, you got the idea. This all happened after the women got the vote. They call it reform, but all it is, it's oppressing men and keeping men from being free. Any man wanting to do just what he pleases in life, any man wanting to prove he's a man, he's gonna oppose suffrage because that's where it all starts. Let them vote and the next thing they've got a Temperance society and they're shutting down the saloons and shutting everything else down, and life sure gets boring. They come on and on and on, thinking of what next to control, and pretty soon we'll all be their slaves. They got men hog-tied and henpecked and pussy-whipped and lassoed. It's like a man getting his beard shaved off even when he wants to keep it and grow it and make it the biggest beard in the county. So that's my platform. A man needs to be a man."

There was a scatter of applause, but not much. I sat down, waiting to see what came next. I thought it was a pretty good talk I had given, and it got right to the heart of the matter. A man needed some spitting room.

"Well, young feller, that was eloquent. But I confess I don't feel hog-tied and lassoed," said the moderator, Hubert Sanders. "Maybe I'm missing something."

The next round involved the enactment of prohibition in Puma County, and once again, Eve Grosbeak was the first to speak.

"When there is evil in a community, we seek to cut it out. Where there is desperation and darkness, we seek to bring hope and light," she said. "We sought to bring hope to the drunkard's family, to spare children and wives the beatings of men made into brutes by spirits. We sought to put food on the tables of families and keep drunks from spending in saloons what was needed by women and children.

"We sought to keep men who imbibed too much from killing or maiming one another, or shooting up the town, or wounding innocents. We sought to return the drunkard to the bosom of society, where he might again be welcomed by his loved ones and his colleagues. We sought by shutting down the gin mills to reduce the arrests and fines and trials and jailings of men made mad by spirits.

"We sought to subdue men who become monsters when imbibing, causing all manner of hurts on others. We sought to end the fears permeating Doubtful whenever liquored-up cowboys from the ranches go on a rampage, threatening the lives and honor of the gentlefolk here. We sought to end the exploitation of cowboys by card sharks operating in the saloons, cleaning liquored-up ranch men of every cent they earned.

"We sought to throw out of the county the conniving, scheming, cruel operators of dives and hellholes, whose only purpose is to extract everything they can get from cowboys, including their saddles, horses, and anything else they might in their stupor leave unguarded.

"My dear friends, here in Doubtful, we have peace and safety. We have comfort. Liquor and guns don't mix, and now we have a small paradise where we all can live without violence or tragedy . . . Let me tell you from the bottom of my soul, dear friends, prohibition is the best gift that Puma County ever received."

She settled quietly in her seat. I sensed that there were some, all male, who would like to object, but knew they were outsmarted.

"Well, Mrs. Grosbeak, that was eloquent and moving," said the moderator. "Now we'll hear from the incumbent, Amos Grosbeak."

Amos got up, adjusted his cravat, and eyed the crowd. "Why, I'll stand on my record. Crimes of violence have declined, the town is safer, and all is quiet in Doubtful. While I yearn for a little sip once in a while, I think it is wise public policy to keep Doubtful dry. That's all I need to say."

"Now, then, Mr. Pickens, it's your turn," said the moderator.

"Oh, I can see how this here is running," I said. "Mostly all that bad stuff, it's an exaggeration. Men just like a nice saloon to get together and chew the fat and enjoy life. Trouble with a dry county is there's nothing to do. I'm for freedom. A man should be free to do what he pleases. A man should be free to run the sort of shop he wants. That's all there is to it. You either have freedom or you start oppressing folks. And I'm for letting people have their way. That's all that needs saying."

This time I got a fine round of applause, but I sure didn't see any women clapping.

Hubert Sanders began clearing his throat and

acting nervous. He finally collected himself and began the next phase of the debate.

"Now, I've got to confess that I've never seen a public discussion of this little item, and it's something I'd rather not see, but here it is, and these brave women sponsoring this event have got it here for the candidates to talk about. I guess you all know what I'm talking about. But we'll proceed, but if this gets out of hand, why I'll ask the candidates to cease. And of course, all you sweet mothers, and fathers, too, you may wish to steer your children away. Little ears can be big funnels, and of course we honor innocence in children for as long as possible. So, without further ado, I'll turn your attention to Eve Grosbeak, and we'll just see how this goes."

Eve paused at the lectern, gazing serenely at the crowd. No one left, and everyone was curious about how this would play out.

"I'm not going to talk about good and evil. I'm not going to talk about morals. I'm not going to refer to religion. I'm going to talk about something entirely different, the suffering and degradation and torment of those who have been forced into a brutal business, one that exploits its victims and sends them to an early grave in a pauper's corner of a cemetery.

"I'm not talking about wicked women and men, but victims. I'm talking about the poor women who are driven from their childhood homes by abusive fathers and have nowhere to go but this bleak life. I'm talking about women fleeing mean husbands, cruel families, or places with exaggerated ideas of right and wrong. I'm talking about desperate girls, who would not otherwise enter the life of an inmate of a bawdy house but for the sheer cruelty of circumstance.

"They are victims, made sick, made melancholy, made suicidal, made hopeless, made addicted, by the life they have fallen into. We, the Temperance women of Doubtful, are all proud that we have talked the supervisors into ending this awful, bleak slavery, this misery, in our fair county. We have closed these grim places. We have sent the exploiters who made money from this misery away from Puma County forever.

"We have eradicated evil in our midst, simply by enacting laws prohibiting it. What more is there to say? Along with closing the saloons, closing the houses of ill repute is our proudest achievement. I'm running on that achievement. There is work yet to do to make Doubtful a sanctuary of good marriage, the peaceful relationship of the sexes, and an island of respect for man or woman that we all can enjoy. Let us continue to fight vice and misery, which leads only to an early grave. I stand proudly before you, knowing that we have brought sunshine into the lives of many women and men, too, in our county."

She smiled gently and returned to her seat. The crowd was very silent. More puffball clouds raced across the firmament. I sure didn't know what to say. I thought a lot of those girls liked the trade, but how could I even mention it? There were some gals, wild as March winds, who'd sure hate to give up the life. And they should be free to do so.

As expected, old Amos Grosbeak seconded his wife and said he was running on his record, and thought the world was better because there were real sweet ladies in it.

"And now we'll hear from Mr. Pickens," said Hubert Sanders. "Where do you stand, sir?"

"This here's a private matter, and the county's got no business poking its nose in. I think it's none of anyone's business. My motto is, *'If there's an itch, there needs to be someone to scratch it.'*"

Well, that was all that needed saying, so I returned to my seat.

Old Sanders, he thanked the crowd and said to come next week to hear the next debates, and pretty soon the crowd drifted off. No one came to me with a handshake or a slap on the back, but there sure were a mess of people smiling and shaking old Grosbeak's paw, and a mess more, mostly womenfolk, who'd gathered around Eve

Grosbeak, and the women were all chattering away so fast it was plain unlikely anyone heard anyone else.

I slid out of there, entirely alone, and no one even noticed my passage. So that's how it was to run for office, I thought.

CHAPTER THIRTY-ONE

I was blue. I'd hardly ever been blue before, and the feeling was so strange it didn't seem to belong to me. The world was changing. This thing called civilization was sneaking in, day by day, and along with it all sorts of people and laws telling me I couldn't do this and couldn't do that, and I'd better learn to live with it.

None of the small crew at Sally's boarding-house could cheer me up. Sally smiled and told me I needed to move to the Far East. Rusty told me I'd be fine if I got my badge back and could start arresting people for spitting on side-walks. Count Cernix said that if Puma County switched to a parliamentary monarchy, things would go better.

But that didn't help me one bit. Up until re-cently I had been free as the wind and could do whatever I damned well felt like doing. Now there were naysayers on every corner, people who'd got out of grade school and done some high school, too. There were meetings and committees and bunches of people intending to do good. All this hit me right in the gut. Rusty said he felt it, too, but he wanted to hold out as long as he could. But that didn't sit well with me. I still thought it was all woman inspired. The world was just fine until all these women starting messing around with it, and now what was left? I couldn't even belly up to a bar and buy a drink.

I couldn't figure out who was right or wrong, and all I knew was that a melancholia had crept into me, and I spent my days in a dour mood, avoiding company. Maybe there were other frontiers I could escape to, now that this one was sliding into a quiet, settled life. But the country was running out of frontiers.

I mourned, because it was like watching a funeral of something I loved. The wild freedom was dying. One morning I headed for Turk's Livery Barn and eyed Critter.

"Guess we'll get the hell out of town," I said.

I must have sounded pretty blue, because Critter just nodded, sighed, and nickered. Critter was behaving in ways unheard of. He didn't try to kick me or jam me into the stall wall or bite my arm, and he didn't even load up his lungs with air to make it harder for me to draw the cinch tight. That nag just allowed it all to happen, as if Critter were becoming civilized himself, instead of behaving like the rank bronc he really was. It sure puzzled me. I thought I'd sell Critter if he kept going downhill and buy myself a rank horse.

"You owe me for a week's board," Turk said.

"I'll pay it when I'm elected."

"From what I hear, you'll never get a county salary again."

"Well, take it from all the money I saved you by not pinching you for public spitting."

Turk wheezed and spat. "World's coming to an end," he said. "If a man can't spit, there's no reason to live."

"That's how I feel."

"I need some Chinamen and an opium parlor," Turk said. "There ain't anything else interesting about Doubtful."

"Nearest one's in Laramie," I said. "The university professors keep her going."

I mounted, and Critter didn't even hump or buck. He just stood there and dropped apples, and then we rode out of town. I didn't know or care where I was going; I just wanted to go where there was less settlement. I was suffocating in Doubtful. Maybe I belonged in a bunkhouse instead of in a town like Doubtful that was growing quieter and more orderly every day. Maybe all I needed was some cowboys around me to start feeling fine again.

I rode north, vaguely thinking I'd go toward some familiar buttes, where a long spur gave me a panoramic view I cherished of wild, unsettled country. Just get out and look at the open world. Look at the Rockies to the west and the Medicine Bows across the plain. Maybe that would put my thoughts on the right track. When there was too much civilization around, mountains were the cure, and open country the healing.

A few years ago there were no roads at all through this rough prairie country, but soon there were trails, mostly wrought by ranch people going somewhere, and now there were regular turnpikes, sometimes impassable but mostly clean and hard. This May day there were mudholes, but that didn't slow Critter down. He was tired of civilization, too. Maybe he was looking for a bodacious mare, I thought. It was the time of year when males started hunting for females.

A sharp wind gusted now and then, driving grit into my face, but that's how Wyoming was. I got several miles out of Doubtful, but it didn't do me any good. Instead of feeling freed from civilization, it was like being on the end of a fishing line, where all the laws of Puma County could reel me back in. But I continued anyway, mostly because Critter was having such a fine time.

It got to be noon, but there was nothing to eat. I hadn't packed a lunch. I'd just wanted to get out of town and stay out. So I decided to ride and starve and face into the west wind, and feel the sun starting to burn my wintered flesh. And that was fine. I was sick of boardwalks and mercantiles and banks and women with parasols.

Up ahead were riders, lots of them, in a settled trot and coming my way. So I reined in Critter and waited. There sure were a mess of them, maybe twenty, and they were heading toward town. Sure enough, it turned out to be pretty near the whole roster of the Admiral Ranch, and Big Nose George Botts was in the lead. I knew half of these fellers, and they were a hairy and wild bunch when they felt like it.

"Well, if it ain't the sheriff," said Big Nose.

"Sheriff's Lem Clegg now, Big Nose."

"Yeah, I heard. Him and his deputies, they've got to learn to ride a horse. They can't be the law and run around in a wagon."

"Well, the whole place is civilized now. Who needs a horse, Big Nose?"

The foreman of the Admiral Ranch frowned, pulled a bag of tobacco from his pocket, rolled a cigarette, and lit it.

"Hear you got pussy-whipped," he said.

"It sure wasn't a pretty sight, Big Nose."

"You're not much of an excuse for a county superintendent."

"You took the thought outa my head."

"But we're going to put you in anyway," Big Nose said. "You're better than nothing. We've had enough of this crappola and we're going to stop it. You may be a swayback old nag full of fistulas and farts, but we're riding you to the finish line."

"That's real friendly of you."

"You know what this is? A voter party. We're going in to get ourselves registered to vote. And so is every man on every ranch. And you'll get our vote, even if you don't deserve it. I'll tell you something else. There's two men for every woman in this county, and we'll see to it that every loose male from the south end of Puma to the north, and maybe beyond a little, gets run into Doubtful to vote, and if he don't vote the right way, he's going to disappear from Puma County and float down the river." He turned to his crew. "Tell this poor excuse for a candidate it's the gospel truth."

"It sure is, Cotton," said Smiley Thistlethwaite, a notorious womanizer and reformed outlaw.

"Yeah, Pickens, we'll make our X for you, even if you're a piece of dog turd," said Alvin Miller, who was packing two pearl-handled Peacemakers and had a scattergun hanging in a scabbard.

"The way we see it, Pickens, is that we're going to put you in office, along with your worthless deputy and that strange idiot from across the seas, and then you'll owe us a few things, like repealing a few laws."

"Like the dry laws?"

"That and a lot more, Pickens. You're going to get your ass in office, and you're going to repeal the whole thing, and you're going to send engraved invitations to every saloon man that got drove out to set up shop and enjoy life and expect a good trade again. You got that?"

"I got it, Big Nose."

"And if you welsh on us, Pickens, we'll string you up so high you'll have time to recite three prayers before your neck snaps."

"I got it, Big Nose."

"All right, then. We're going in to register. And so's everyone else. We've been talking back and forth on the spreads, and we're sending every man in the county in to get fixed up to vote. I tell you, Pickens, it's been an ordeal since January. We can hardly keep drovers on the range. Half the outfits can't hire enough men because word's out about Puma County. If this keeps up, half the ranchers are going to quit. The first thing any new hire asks is whether there's a saloon somewhere. But the sheep outfits aren't so bad off. They tell me they're doing fine, as long as there's some ewes around. But we ain't saying that publicly, are we, boys?"

He spurred his horse and the whole bunch rode past, looking pleased with themselves. Life sure was interesting.

I touched my heels to Critter, and the horse swung into an easy jog, heading straight to the buttes. I'd been on this journey a few times. So, maybe the three of us Peckerheads would win after all. At first I thought that was mighty fine, but it kind of worried me. If I actually got into office, and actually tried to repeal all them laws, what would happen? It might be real bad in town.

I rode another mile to the turnoff and headed west along a familiar trail that would take me straight to the buttes. There were three buttes, and one was easily accessible along a dirt trail that had been used for ages by animals and also by humans seeking to see what lay ahead. The buttes figured in some of the local lore. They were useful to war parties intent on ambush, useful to ranchers looking for lost cattle, useful to the occasional sightseer, like me, who wanted only to see the free world. Some spring storms were brewing fast as I headed west, and from the buttes I could watch the squalls march across the vast open land, towering clouds with blue-black bellies slanting rain into the empty land. Once I had sat on Critter halfway up the butte when a storm engulfed Doubtful while sun shone everywhere else.

When I came to the barbed-wire fence I could scarcely imagine what it was doing there. Three strands of wire ran arrow-straight north and south, the wires stapled to juniper posts, which was the only irregular thing about the fence. But there was no pine forest nearby, and the sometimes twisted juniper had been put to good use.

But there was no gate. The wires lay across the

trail I had used as long as I had been in Puma County. Me and Critter were on the Admiral Ranch; I wasn't sure what lay beyond it, but it probably belonged to Thaddeus Throckmorton, who had been collecting sections of land and was now apparently enclosing them. And blocking an ancient trail. I thought wildly of cutting the wire and continuing onward, but I reined Critter around and started back, my planned sojourn out in the wilds suddenly transformed.

Fencing was rare, but it was coming along, and some day the open range would be under wire. But it sure did annoy me. The world was changing out in the country as well as in the towns, and this wasn't much different. I'd been stopped by a fence, my will thwarted. In town the new laws were thwarting a lot of cowboys who wanted a drink. I didn't know what to make of it, but it wasn't my world anymore, and the worst thing was, I knew it would never return to the old days of the unsettled world. I had ridden all this way to escape melancholy, and now my desolation was all the worse.

CHAPTER THIRTY-TWO

That three-strand fence running straight down a section line out on the plains shocked me worse than anything that had ever happened to me. I rode Critter home, hardly aware of where I was going. It felt like being sentenced to jail the rest of my life.

I pulled into Turk's Livery Barn late in the day, unsaddled and brushed Critter, and fed him a bit of hay while Turk glowered.

"I hope you know you're running up a big tab," Turk said.

"Yeah, well, maybe you can take Critter off my hands. There's no place to ride anymore."

"No place to ride, is there? No place to go on a horse? No wonder the supervisors got rid of you, Pickens."

"It's all over," I said. "Everything died."

"What you need is a good woman, Pickens."

"That's like going to jail," I said.

"You have my condolences, Pickens."

I ignored him, closed the stall gate, stared at Critter a while. A mean horse and no fences was better than a fenced world and a little wife. I wanted to head for the sheriff office, but it wasn't mine anymore. I finally headed for Leonard Silver's Hardware Emporium and found what I was looking for. A back room was stacked with rolls of barbed wire, floor to ceiling. There was more wire in there than I had seen in a lifetime.

"You looking for wire, Pickens?"

"Didn't know there was any in Puma County."

"We got lots of it, any type. You want two strand, three strand? You want two-barb, that's cheapest, or four? You want staples? We got several sizes. Some fellows want real long staples to hang the wire on, whiles other gents want to cut corners a bit."

"You been selling a lot?"

"It's been walking out the door all spring, Pickens. Thaddeus Throckmorton's got most of his ranch fenced, and he's not alone. I figure I'm selling a mile of fence a day from here. Two, three years, all the ranches will be fenced in. Oh, there'll still be some open range, some big roundups, but it's gonna disappear pretty quick now.

"By the time you're middle-aged, Pickens, it'll all be fenced. They won't hardly need any cowboys anymore. Just one or two to haul feed or drive the cattle into the pens. Once they fence, they can grow crops without having stray stock trample it down and eat it up. And then the next big thing, irrigation. Pretty quick, you'll see a lot of big outfits putting in dams across creeks, or building pump houses and running water through irrigation ditches to the pastures or grain fields they want to water. It's the future, Cotton."

"I got born too late," I said.

"Oh, there's more coming. Once things get fenced up proper, there'll be lots of breeding up. The old common cattle, they'll gradually get sold off to the butchers. There'll be good-blooded bulls brought in, to breed up the herds, put more meat on each animal. That takes fencing, you see. Can't have runty bulls crowding in and leaving their mark on a herd. And they'll start breeding up the cows, too, so they're more fertile and grow quicker. Not so many barren cows anymore. And that takes fencing so ranchers can control who mounts what.

"Can't have some low-class, dumb, half-educated bull around, messing with nice, refined, sweet-natured cows. You get the picture, Cotton? You looking for some wire? Gonna fence some pasture for Critter? Now if I was you, I'd fence in Critter, six feet of barbed wire, just to keep neighbors from getting upset with you. Who'd want a mare bred by that outlaw?"

"No, just curious," I said, fleeing the gloomy

rear room where rolls of barbed metal awaited buyers.

That left me even worse off. No wonder me and Critter lived in a sort of truce. We were brothers.

I headed back to Sally's boardinghouse and found Rusty and Count Cernix and Sally sipping cold coffee.

"You're back earlier than you thought," Rusty said.

"Ran into a fence."

"Why didn't you go through it?"

"No gate. Just fence."

"Can they do that?"

"It's done, Rusty. The world's changing. Leonard Silver told me he's selling enough wire each day to build a mile of fence. It ain't ever going to be the same."

"How's a lawman supposed to chase outlaws if there's fence everywhere?"

"I guess they think there won't be any outlaws anymore."

"You're looking pretty blue, Cotton," Sally said.

"Oh, I'll get by, somehow."

"Cotton, you're really in sad shape. I know how to fix that," she said.

"Leave me be," I said.

"I can brighten your day," Rusty said. "There's been a mess of cowboys at the courthouse fixing to vote."

"Yeah, I ran into Big Nose and his bunch. He says every cowboy in Puma County's vowed to get registered and vote. He says they're going to elect us, no matter what, and we should get busy and repeal all them new laws so they can start whooping it up around here again."

"Well, maybe they'll pull it off," Rusty said.

That didn't cheer me. I'd seen the future, and I didn't fit anywhere in it.

"Cotton, what you need to do is become a politician," Count Cernix said. "Just promise to cut spending, dole out favors, and get us into a war now and then so everyone profits."

"Go to hell," I said.

I wasn't sure what was gnawing at me, but it was making me impossible to live with, even among my friends and allies.

"What are we supposed to say? Bring on the past? Repeal the future? I just saw the future. It's a barbed-wire fence across an old trail."

"I liked you better when you were sheriff," Sally said.

A few days later the next debate rolled around, this time between Count Cernix von Stromberger, Lester Twining, and Manilla Twining. Again it was a fine May day, and a crowd collected at Courthouse Square to hear the candidates. Hubert Sanders again moderated, and Manilla led off.

"My argument for woman suffrage is that men

shouldn't vote at all," she began. "Men are the prisoners of their passions, whereas women maintain a cool and objective approach to all the issues of the day. That is why men get into war, while women keep the peace. If men didn't vote, we could be living in a world without bloodshed and battles and all the false glory of killing one another in the name of some cause or other. All one needs to do is make sure that women vote, women dominate each government, and women edit the press and the magazines, and you will see a revolutionary change in the way human life is conducted."

She went on like that a while, and I thought it was pretty good. Maybe men shouldn't vote or hold office or edit newspapers or any of that stuff.

Next up was Count Cernix, and he offered a little different perspective. He said female monarchs were top notch when it came to beheading rivals and fighting wars. During the French Revolution who were in the front row during all the guillotining? Women, knitting away, while enjoying the way that eyes blinked and lips moved when the executioners held up the severed heads of the victims. And of course, he went on, who could compete with Catherine the Great of Russia, or Elizabeth of England, when it came to intrigue and blood?

That sure entertained me. I thought maybe I'd

like to have a few guillotines available in Puma County.

Hubert Sanders next invited Twining, the incumbent supervisor, to speak to the cheering throng. Lester was a retiring sort, not at all comfortable in front of people, and yet a man radiating dignity. I scarcely knew him, because the supervisors all spoke through the voice of Amos Grosbeak, who had a gift of gab. But here was Lester, who nervously adjusted his cravat, eyed the transparent blue sky, and plunged in.

"Ladies and gentlemen," he began, "I am running on my record, and I think I can give you a very good account of what I've achieved, simply by inviting our fine new sheriff, Lemuel Clegg, to the podium here, to answer a few questions."

He waved, and sure enough, Lem Clegg lumbered up there, about as wide and muscular as he was tall, his whole body shaped by his lumberman's skills. But he wasn't a lumberman now; he was the county lawman, and the little badge on his plaid shirt shone in the glowing sunlight.

"Lemuel, you took office shortly after the county closed down all the saloons, houses of ill repute, gambling parlors, and so forth, and prohibited the sale of spiritous drink in the entire county. Could you answer the following please?"

The sheriff nodded.

"Since you took over as sheriff, how many murders have occurred in Puma County?"

"None, sir."

"How many assaults against males?"

"None, sir."

"How many assaults upon women?"

"None, sir."

"How many robberies?"

"None, sir."

"How many burglaries?"

"None, sir."

"How many times have you charged and jailed a prisoner since you came into office, sir?"

"Just one. I got him for spitting in public, and he got himself fined and left an hour later."

"And how many jail meals has the county served prisoners since you took over?"

"None, sir."

"And how many complaints have you heard; people reporting a crime or a fight or trouble?"

"Well, there was that boy beating up a dog, sir. I stopped him."

"Anything else?"

Clegg shook his head.

"That's my record as incumbent, and I'll stand on it," Twining said.

"Fine, fine, thank you, Supervisor Twining," said Sanders. "And now, once again, the esteemed new citizen of the republic of Wyoming, Count Cernix von Stromberger," he said.

I had to give the count credit. As he made his way toward the lectern, he smiled, bowed almost to the ground, lifted his wide-brimmed straw hat, saluted the crowd, and finally settled quietly behind the lectern.

"I imagine I am the first titled person most of you have ever seen," he said.

"And hopefully the last," someone shouted.

"Well, I agree with your sentiments. We are progressing toward democracy. Now I am running on the sin ticket, and I'll tell you why. It's the way to save money. The entire budget of Puma County and the fair and sweet city of Doubtful can be raised with various sin taxes, quietly applied. So I am offering you an argument that goes straight to your purse."

I could see that the count had his audience caught and hog-tied.

The count sighed, smiled, and said quietly, "It's fine to have expert witnesses, such as we've just enjoyed. Sheriff Clegg made an impressive argument. But my witnesses will not be experts, they will be yourselves. You yourselves will answer my questions, and you yourselves will come to your own verdicts, and you yourselves will let those verdicts guide you as you vote for county supervisors in a few days."

He smiled and began, almost casually. "You who own real estate in Puma County, how much have you paid in tax assessments upon your holdings until this year?" He waited patiently and then pounced. "None! Because there were no property taxes. The entire county budget was raised by other means!"

He let that sink in and then pounced again. "Now then, all of you who hold real estate in the splendid town of Doubtful, Wyoming, how much were you assessed in taxes upon your homes and businesses and yards and lots?" Again, he paused. "Nothing, right? There were no taxes, because the city's entire operations were funded elsewhere, and no burden was placed on you."

I looked around. Count Cernix was sure making his point, and all those faces turned his way registered it.

"My friends and fellow citizens—yes, I am a naturalized American—the entire burden of government in Puma County was indeed paid by someone. By saloon owners who bought licenses, and gamblers who bought table licenses, and the operators of bawdyhouses, who paid licenses not annually, but quarterly, and the inmates who paid monthly, creating a fine revenue flow. Let me point something out to you. All this burden placed on dubious enterprises had the economic effect of discouraging such enterprises. They were heavily taxed and licensed, which discouraged their growth and kept them carefully confined to one small corner of our beautiful city. So my argument is, take advantage of human nature. Take advantage of those whose appetites require these anodynes. Remove the prohibitions, but let the fees and licenses form their own barriers, and you will have a city without the burden of property taxes, and a city that has turned certain appetites into an engine of bright and shining prosperity."

I wasn't so sure about all that. It sounded a little made up. But it sure had started that mess of people to thinking.

The debate dragged on for a while more, and then Sanders called it quits.

Sally rushed up to the count. "You clever man, you turned the tide," she said.

I thought that maybe the count had done just that. There was one more debate left, between Rusty Irons and Reggie and Gladys Thimble, and after that it would be time for Puma County to elect its supervisors.

CHAPTER THIRTY-THREE

The last of those debates sponsored by the Temperance women rolled around too fast, as far as I was concerned. I didn't like any of it. I preferred to settle arguments with a whack on the head with my billy club and some cooling off in my jail. But that was the past. Doubtful, Wyoming, was marching into a brave new world, and the frontier was vanishing almost day by day.

This one occurred on an overcast spring day with some sharp-edged air pushing through out of the north. Maybe that was good. Anything to shut the mouths of politicians was good. I hadn't any notion what my former deputy, Rusty Irons, was going to blabber about up there in front of the world, so I'd just have to wait and see. I realized that me and Rusty hadn't talked much about all this stuff. We had been too busy keeping the lid on Doubtful during the wild times to think much about what was good and what wasn't.

The best thing Rusty had going for him was a head of red hair, and also a sunny nature. He sure could take some boneheaded cowboy and get the feller to laughing all the way to the jail. That was Rusty for you. He was the quickest feller with a gun if that was needed, which it wasn't anymore, but Rusty's real genius was just being sociable. He enforced the law of Puma County just by gabbing happily with most everyone, by issuing little warnings, by slapping some old rogue on the back and steering him to his horse. So I sure was curious about what Rusty was going to do up there.

Rusty probably would have easy prey. Gladys Thimble was scarcely known, and not a likely candidate for supervisor. She was one of the ladies with an enormous bust and a skinnier south side, while her husband had a narrow top and a middle that expanded like a pear. I thought that was fitting. If the two of them ever got to hugging, they would fit together like a jigsaw puzzle. Her man, Reggie Thimble, had been in office forever and had gotten fat, and some said he'd gotten fat devouring public funds a little too easily, but no one ever proved anything. Gladys didn't have much to say up there; she sort of trilled like a clarinet and allowed as how it was time to put women into office and get all the problems of the world solved in a hurry.

Reggie, he made a different sort of appearance. He was a talker, on and on and on, and pretty quick he got himself on all sides of every issue. He talked about his sentimental attachment for saloons, and how they were comfortable clubs for men to enjoy themselves, and he talked about drunkards and how they ruined families, and he talked about how great it was to be young and full of wild oats that needed sowing, and how great it was to settle down and get hitched and start a family in a safe world. It sure was a performance, all right, and by the end of it he had persuaded those listeners who managed to stick with him for twenty minutes that he was on their side. They all heard what they wanted to hear from his lips, and sort of forgot that he'd said anything else.

I marveled. That feller Thimble was a shooter of words, and he shot more forty-five-caliber words with plenty of powder behind them than any other politician I had ever heard. He had thousands more words than Rusty Irons would ever have, and he fired them all that cloudy morning.

Last on the agenda was Rusty Irons, slim, dressed in ordinary work clothes and not fancied up, mostly because he couldn't afford any better. Now the thing to know about Rusty is that he can talk anyone out of anything. He could talk an old maid out of her maidenhood. But he can also talk anyone into doing something. He can talk an old scrooge into donating to the home for unwed mothers. He can talk cowboys into going to church. He can talk churchwomen into visiting a sporting house. When I was sheriff, I depended on Rusty's gift of gab to get more done than six deputies who were good with shotguns.

So Rusty got up there and sort of scratched his red hair, and told us all that he loved women. "I love women in all sizes and shapes, from little ones to old ladies. I grew up in a household full of sisters, and it just comes natural to me to have a mess of sweet, happy, busy women around, looking after things. That sure was a fine household, because all them girls, they just whipped out meals, ran the carpet sweeper over the floors, and mothered the new babies coming along. I just wish there were a lot more women in the world, and especially in Doubtful where there's about two males for every female, and nothing comes out even. I always figured, when a place has a woman for every man, then that's about right; and when there's a man for every woman, that's what keeps women happy."

I couldn't imagine where Rusty was going with all that, but it didn't matter. Rusty was a spellbinder.

"Now, until there's equality of the sexes in Doubtful, things just ain't right for either the women or the men around town," he said. "When there's a dance, there's six young fellows for every eligible girl, but their mamas are telling them these six fellows aren't proper to dance with because they're cowboys, and they're not going to treat a gal right, and settle down and earn some money and have a family and all that. Now that just ain't right. It's bad enough that there are so few nice ladies compared to all the drovers and ranchers in Puma County; it's worse because the mamas of these girls are telling them not to get hooked up with a cowboy or even worse, a sheepherder. No telling what a sheepherder will do if he's desperate."

I was sort of sliding away. I didn't want to be around when the mob stormed the courthouse stairs and threw Rusty off the nearest cliff.

"Well," Rusty said, "if I'm elected, I'll do my best to make all our randy young men comfortable. I'll try to even up the men and women in Puma County. I'll import women. We'll get it all evened out some way or another, so long as you elect me, Rusty Irons, and my old pals, Cotton Pickens and the Count Cernix from wherever the place is."

Well, that was it. Old Rusty, he just smiled and bowed and lifted his sweat-stained Stetson high, and waved it a few times, and then shook hands all around and meandered off the courthouse steps.

"Well, friends, that concludes the debate between all the candidates for county superintendent," said Hubert Sanders, sounding bankerish. "We'll see you at the polls on the sixth day of June. The polls are at the schoolhouse," he said.

I was feeling dumber than usual. I didn't know what Rusty was talking about. But Rusty immediately had a few cowboys around him, and then a flotilla of the town's single girls, some of them all dressed up in summer whites, even if they were pushing the season a little. You'd think that Rusty was a vaudeville star, the way they were making cow eyes at him. Trouble was, there weren't six single girls of the right age in all of Doubtful. That was the whole trouble with the town. With the saloons shut down, and the sporting houses boarded up, and even the gambling tables chased out, and not more than six women in Doubtful pining for a husband, things were pretty unhappy for all the young and unmarried males around there. There wasn't anything to do but cause as much trouble as possible.

That old election day rolled around bright and sunny, but some clouds over the distant mountains suggested there might be some thundershowers or hail late in the day. The schoolhouse polling place was to open at eight, so me and Rusty and the count all got down there early, thinking to vote for ourselves. But there was a line of cowboys a block long. There were cowboys from every ranch within forty or fifty miles. They looked like they meant business, and they were ahead of all the locals, who eyed the line and went back home, thinking to vote later when the cowboys got done.

There were horses tied to every post and fence. There were people staring, startled to see so many drovers and ranchers. But I discovered trouble, too. Up near the schoolhouse, Sheriff Lemuel Clegg and his boys were arguing with some cowboys from the T-Bar Ranch.

"You boys, you're wearing sidearms in town, and that's against the rules. And you can't go into a polling place with that hardware. So you just go hang them gun belts on your saddles and wait in line proper," Clegg was saying.

"You gonna make me, Clegg?" muttered Weasel Jonas.

"You're going to follow the rules, and you're not going to vote until you pull off the belt."

Jonas laughed. "Guess you're gonna have to pull it off of me yourself, lumberjack."

I knew how it was building. Maybe a quarter of the cowboys in that line were wearing sidearms, almost as if they were deliberately provoking trouble. There was plenty of resentment out on the ranches, and now it was coming alive on this election morning.

Trouble was, I was a candidate. I shouldn't be getting into a confrontation with voters. Or maybe I should. Clegg needed help.

"Weasel, you unload that belt, and the rest of

you, too. You don't go armed into a polling place. I want your vote, and you'll not be able to vote for me if you fellers don't follow the rules."

But Weasel was just grinning. "You gonna make me, Pickens?"

Clegg didn't like it. "I can handle this, Pickens Don't mess with my business. Stand back. Me and my boys will see it done right."

"Sure, sure, Clegg," said Weasel, who was enjoying himself.

It was eight and the poll workers were opening the door and letting the line move forward.

The first cowboys weren't armed, and they stepped inside, but then Weasel was next, and Clegg stopped him. "Weasel, I'm not going to ask again."

Weasel started laughing, and in the middle of it swung a haymaker at Clegg. It hit the sheriff in the shoulder and bounced off. The lumberman hadn't even wobbled. Clegg just stood there, his hand out, demanding the gun belt. He sighed. "Hate to do this, cowboy," he said.

He lifted Weasel up by his shirt and lowered him as if he were a pile driver.

Weasel's friends barreled in to help, but Clegg's boys simply lifted the T-Bar men as if they were feathers and crumpled them into the earth. One of the cowboys went for his gun, but Cash Clegg's foot landed on the man's arm and the man howled in pain.

I had never seen such muscle as I witnessed in the Cleggs. And they weren't half trying. Several more cowboys sailed in, the joy of a good fight written on their faces, and they got nowhere. The Cleggs were rooted like fat oaks to the ground. A Clegg fist connected with a cowboy jaw or nose now and then, and the cattle industry succumbed.

"Look at that!" said Rusty. "It's sailboats against the ironclads."

"What's an ironclad?" I asked.

"An iron-sheathed warship," the count said. "Cannonballs bounce off it, just as fists bounce off these Clegg boys."

I itched to get into it, but knew it would go against me in the voting, so I just watched, acutely aware that Puma County's new sheriff and deputies were handling the brawl better than I could.

The brawl ended as suddenly as it started.

"We're here to vote," someone yelled. "Hang up the guns."

It was King Glad, the young master of the Admiral Ranch, imposing order not only on his outfit but all the rest.

Strangely, the drovers obeyed. They unbuckled their gun belts, hung them over saddle horns, and returned to the line, which now was working quietly through the polling place. There were plenty of cowboys who couldn't read, but they'd been instructed where to scratch their X, and talked about it in the line.

The effect of these amassed cowboys was to scare off the other voters, and I didn't see a woman in the voting line. But that would change. Sure enough, after a couple hundred cowboys had voted and ridden off, some of the town people ventured out, including all those women in the Women's Temperance Union.

They smiled at me, and I smiled back, and the sheriff and his boys stared sternly.

After the poll closed, the votes were counted, and Cotton Pickens, Rusty Irons, and Cernix von Stromberger found themselves the incoming Puma County supervisors.

CHAPTER THIRTY-FOUR

I desperately wished I had lost the election. I felt like a cow stuck in mud. I had no more idea of how to be a county supervisor than I had about taking a wife. I could hardly read those blasted documents.

Maybe there was some way out. I headed for Lawyer Stokes's office, thinking to pry myself loose.

"You sure that election was fair and square? Shouldn't it be challenged?" I asked.

Lawyer Stokes stared upward at me through his rimless spectacles, his lips pursed. "You aren't the only one," he said. "But the fact is, you and your dismaying colleagues were elected by wide margins. We thought to challenge all those cowboys, since half of them aren't bona fide residents of Puma County, but the sad reality is that you were elected by a lot of people in Doubtful who were publicly saying they support all the new morality laws but privately voted for you fellows running on the sin platform."

"You mean a lot of people, like businessmen, they want the old days back?"

Stokes sighed. "It's a benighted town, my young friend. So go forth and do your worst."

"But why? Why all those votes for us?"

"Money. The morality laws cost the county and the city their income. All those licenses, fees, fines, paid for two governments. And both the city and the county were fixing to install property taxes until you gents came along promoting vice."

"Well, ain't that something?" I said. "You'd think everyone would be happy now."

"I assure you, your victory is the source of deep pain, Mr. Pickens. It is a woeful retreat from progress and safety and comfort."

I pondered that. There sure were a lot of bossy people wanting to tell other people how to run their lives. Bunch of bossy Temperance people telling other people not to touch spirits. Bunch of bossy moralizers saying to shut down the sporting houses and deny some poor old cowboy a little pleasure. Bunch of bossy folks telling other people not to lay a dime on a faro bet. Bunch of bossy churchgoers wanting to close down all business on Sundays. Bunch of bossy snobs telling other people not to spit. I thought the busybodies who wanted to tell others how to live and take away their liberties outnumbered the people who just wanted to live and let live.

Well, me and Rusty and the count could repeal all those miserable laws, and maybe then I'd resign. Maybe we could fire the sheriff and his boys, and have the supervisors appoint me and Rusty to the sheriff office again. I liked keeping the lid on Doubtful; that was what I really wanted to do.

When we finally took office in mid-June I thought maybe there'd be a mob of people pressuring me not to repeal all those do-gooder laws, but no one showed up. Lawyer Stokes, acting as county attorney, led us through the process. We had to submit the repeal bills, subject them to public hearings, and then vote them up or down.

I sort of enjoyed being a big shot. They were calling me Sir and Mister. I'd never had a Mister in front of Cotton or Pickens in my life. It sort of invested me with some weight, so I got to tipping my stained Stetson at the ladies, and letting the boy at the tonsorial parlor put a little wax on my boots. And now that I was on salary I took a bath once a month, kept my two union suits washed, and even invested in a white shirt. I discovered I didn't need to wear a cravat; there was a thing called a string tie that would do just fine, so I took to wearing that and a clean shirt.

Funny thing, even those Temperance women were smiling at me. Maybe that was because they could still vote. That was the only part of my program that got shot down. Me and Rusty and the count could do nothing about woman suffrage except try to change the Wyoming constitution, and that was beyond us. Lawyer Stokes told us we couldn't nullify suffrage in Puma County; the county wasn't a separate little nation, seceding from the state. So I learned to live with it, even if women voting was plainly an affront to nature and an evil in its own right.

At the July supervisor meeting no one showed up at the hearings, so we voted to repeal all those laws. On August 1, after publication of the repeal laws, the town of Doubtful and the County of Puma would be wide open, and soon enough there'd be rip-roaring saloons, wild cathouses, gambling parlors, and plenty of good times seven days a week. Word sure got out fast. The story got told in Laramie and Cheyenne, Denver and Fort Collins, and even in North Platte, Nebraska.

The merchants were smiling again. In a little while, the rush would be on. The saloon men would sweep in, buy up those saloons now in the hands of speculators, and madams would arrive with whole wagonloads of women, and the gamblers in their black suits and stovepipe hats would settle in, license a table or two, and set up shop. And just as soon as the booze started flowing and the chips rattled on tables, and new decks of faro cards got cracked open, and the girls got settled in their little rooms, the cowboys would ride in, whoop it up, and blow all that pent-up pocket change they'd been sitting on.

August 1 sure was a hot summer day, the kind that reminded people of hell, and the merchants were licking their chops. So were the supervisors, and Mayor Waller, who desperately needed something more than public spitting fines to keep the city in cash. The city clerk and the county clerk were all primed to issue licenses. It was all set up so that some saloon man coming into town could be up and running within the hour. Mayor Waller had even pre-signed a dozen licenses so as not to waste a second. There were bets on the tables around town as to how fast it would take a saloon man to set up shop and start the booze flowing.

But there wasn't any migration to Doubtful that day, so people ascribed it to word not getting out, and sat back to wait for the onslaught through the week or the month.

Back at Sally's I got curious about Sally's plans.

"You gonna open up again, Sally? Bring in some girls?"

"Hell no," she said, slapping some oatmeal in front of me. "I'm done with that."

"How come?"

Sally glared at me. "I'm a countess. How many gals get to be a countess? All my life I wanted to be a countess, so why should I run a whorehouse?"

Well, there was a new argument.

"Nothing keeping you from both," I said. "You could run Countess Sally's and call it the fanciest blue-blooded cathouse in Wyoming."

"Eat your oatmeal and mind your business," she said.

"Now if you'd let me rule over Puma County, we'd do that," Count Cernix said. "But being a count doesn't fit in with running a bawdyhouse."

That puzzled me.

And still, no one arrived in Doubtful to set up shop. I walked along the forlorn wrecks of Saloon Row, with their broken windows staring balefully at me, and the rats scurrying around in decaying rooms.

Then at last there were two applications for licenses. The Elks, one of those brotherhoods that were getting formed all over the West, applied for a bar license for their clubhouse. And so did the Moose, a rival outfit with a lot of the town's businessmen in it. But the third, the Odd Fellows, much the most popular of those outfits all over Wyoming and the West, still abstained.

So the brotherhoods got their clubs and bars up and running, and invited the cowboys off the ranches to sign up as members. A few did. Big Nose George and Smiley Thistlethwaite became Elks, and Weasel Jonas joined the Moose, and a dozen more cowboys took out membership in one outfit or another. The Elks bought the place next to Sally's and fixed it up, and pretty soon a feller could have a peaceful drink with his friends in a peaceful saloon run by one of the brotherhoods. But no madams showed up, and a feller had to go clear down to Laramie for a little hoochy-coochy.

Sally had a few cowboys come knocking at her door, but she just got mad at them and told them she was a countess and to mind their business unless they wanted to rent a respectable room from a respectable noblewoman.

Meanwhile the county treasurer was howling, and so was Mayor Waller. Puma County was flat-out busted and its checks were no good, and it would be up to the new supervisors to do something about it, immediately, before the county collapsed and state officials swarmed in and imposed their will on Puma County. The big rush to open up a sin business never happened. Times had changed. Wild old Doubtful was a thing of the past. The world belonged to farmers and preachers and politicians whose idea of progress was to apply nitrous oxide to all citizens so they could fall into painless slumber.

I could hardly imagine it. Somehow, everything was changed. Wyoming was becoming civilized. If a man wanted wild times, the only place left was El Paso or Tucson. All the rest of the West was a big yawn. Poor old Sheriff Lemuel Clegg and his boys had nothing to do. There were entire weeks when nothing criminal happened in

Doubtful, and the worst crime anyone had heard of was when some rascal boys tied tin cans on the tail of a billy goat and the enraged goat ran into the middle of a Temperance Ladies picnic and butted Eve Grosbeak in the rear, sending her flying into Manilla Winding as they were sipping sarsaparilla. The rotten boy was remanded to his father, who whipped him with a riding crop, but only once because he thought the boy had done Doubtful a favor.

So the Cleggs hadn't a thing to do but blot up county wages and loaf around, keeping order by sending dogs home. It sure was a strange new world for me. And it was about to get worse.

Sam Peppingwell, the Puma County treasurer, said the county was plumb out of cash and nothing coming in. The money from the sin business didn't materialize. And therefore he couldn't pay the supervisors their salaries, much less anyone else the county owed money to, including himself. So the supervisors had better be quick about enacting a tax, or all hell would bust loose.

Well, that wasn't good news.

"What're we gonna do?" I asked my colleagues while downing Sally's oatmeal.

"Tax real estate. What else?" Rusty said.

"Ten cents an acre for ranches, five dollars a city lot," said the count.

"Anyone got any better ideas?" I asked.

"Yeah, wear your sidearms to the next meeting," Rusty said.

I thought Rusty Irons was right.

Sure enough, when I, Supervisor Pickens, put the new taxes on the agenda, it sure caused a ruckus. In fact, the whole town of Doubtful got up on its haunches and howled. When the bills got published in the *Advertiser*, which didn't want to do it because it hadn't been paid for county advertising, it set off pretty near a riot around town, and there were plenty of fellers muttering something or other about stringing up the supervisors to the nearest hanging tree and letting them drop.

I got to visiting some of the people around Doubtful, and every man and every woman was plumb set against the new taxes, and that included any tax at any price. And I hadn't even heard from the ranchers yet.

Sheriff Lemuel Clegg came over to the supervisors' offices about then and said that if they didn't get paid by the next day, they'd quit; they'd sure not work for nothing, and they hadn't seen a pay envelope for two months.

"Lemuel, we're working on it," I replied. "It's gonna take a bit of time, but we'll get some revenue going here pretty quick."

"Not if they hang you first, Cotton. And I'll let them do it, too. You haven't paid us a nickel in so long that you deserve to swing."

"I'm glad I deserve something or other," I said. "My ma always wondered what I deserved, and I always told her I deserved new boots."

"Twenty-four hours, Cotton. You pay us our wage by this time tomorrow, or Puma County's got no sheriff and no deputies. Hear me?"

"I always knew I'd get that job back," I said.

CHAPTER THIRTY-FIVE

Well, all of that hit Doubtful, Wyoming, like one of those sudden thunderstorms out of the Medicine Bow Mountains that dump tons of hail on a town even in midsummer. The roses don't survive. Word got around that the supervisors were going to impose taxes on real property, and right away, I thought I'd be more comfortable standing in the path of a tornado.

The first thing that happened was that the Cleggs all quit, bitter about not getting paid, and headed back to their lumbering operation. The supervisors hustled to the courthouse, accepted my resignation, appointed Countess Sally Sweet von Stromberger as the new supervisor, and then the three of them voted to make me sheriff once again.

I was sort of pleased to get out of being a supervisor; I wasn't cut out for that. I'd leave politics to the cobras and rattlers and boa constrictors of the world. It was easier to face thugs with knives and guns than to face glad-handers. So I put on the badge, and I put on my gun belt and my old Peacemaker, and headed for the jail, where I got hold of the jail keys and emptied the Cleggs' pisspots, which they left uncleaned as a sort of retaliation for not getting a pay envelope. I was alone in there, without a deputy, facing the worst storm in Doubtful's brief history.

By then it wasn't just the Cleggs who weren't getting paid. It was everyone the county owed, and they were mad as hornets, even as the rest of the citizens were mad as bees about taxes and the cowboys were mad as wasps because there weren't any saloons just for them. So there were two mobs waiting to hang the supervisors, and I didn't know which bunch was the angriest.

The showdown would come that afternoon, starting at one. That's when the emergency session of the supervisors was scheduled. I decided the best way of cooling things was just to do some walking. Let them see the badge, and let them see that my old, half-forgotten gun belt was back on. Let them ask how I came to be sheriff, and I would tell them. Let them blister me with accusations, and I'd tell them to talk to the supervisors. So that's what I did. The people of Doubtful hardly noticed I was sheriff; what they wanted was a dead halt to any taxation. They were damned if they would submit to tyranny, and they'd hang any supervisors who might try to tax them. That was pretty rough talk, and I realized a lot of it was coming from those I'd thought of as friends. And they weren't just angry; they were threatening. If there were taxes, those responsible for them would hang.

Indeed, a few people, even Mayor George Waller, were pushing and shoving, jabbing fingers into my chest, ranting and howling. I just smiled and said I'd see them in the courthouse, and to come unarmed because no one with a gun was going to walk in. I would not be responsible for a massacre, which is how it was looking to me just then.

Well, by one o'clock a mob had gathered at the courthouse, and that bunch was ominously quiet. Maybe that was a good sign. No one was brawling. I spotted businessmen like George Waller and Belle, my former landlady, and Len Silver, and Hubert Sanders, and also the postmaster, Alphonse Smythe. Turk stood there, looking sour. The former supervisors were standing there, and also their wives, and One-Eyed Harry First, who ran Barney's Beanery. They sure were looking stern. There were plenty of others there, forty or fifty in all, but they could all jam in if people were willing to stand. Rusty and the von Strombergers were already in, so they wouldn't be harassed going in. The one thing I didn't see was people from the outlying ranches. Maybe they hadn't gotten the word. It took a while for news to ripple outward from the county seat. So what I had feared the most, an influx of armed and militant ranchers, wasn't in the cards. But all that could change in an instant.

At about one, I opened the door of the courtroom and let them in, and they came peaceably enough. I couldn't tell who was carrying a concealed weapon, but at least these city people weren't wearing iron at their sides, and that said something. Maybe, just maybe, this would all come off.

They filled the room and stood around the walls, and when the hour arrived, Rusty Irons, the chairman, rapped with his gavel for order, but he didn't need to. This room was quieter than a century-old tomb.

Rusty, always ingratiating, smiled toothsomely at the mob and welcomed them, and explained that the Cleggs had quit because they hadn't been paid, and I had taken their place and Sally had been elected the new supervisor by the others.

"Yeah, and you're taxing us to death," snapped One-Eyed Harry.

"Yes, and you're sticking the people in town with the bill, while the ranchers got off free," said the usually dignified Hubert Sanders.

"And the city's not getting any share of it," said the mayor.

"It's not even remotely fair or equitable," said the postmaster.

When Rusty tried to find out what would be acceptable and fair, it turned out that nothing would be. The only intelligent request came from Belle, who said there should be one rate for improved town lots and another for unimproved.

"Guess that makes sense," Rusty said.

"Two bits a lot unimproved, four bits for an improved," she insisted.

"That'd hardly pay to keep the county going, Belle," Rusty said.

"Then quit trying to screw city people and go where it counts. All those rich ranchers with big herds eating free grass on free land. Tax them. They're getting away with robbery."

"If they don't own land, what should we tax?" the count asked.

"I don't know and don't care. Tax children. The more they've got the more they should pay. It's schools, isn't it? Pay per brat. Five dollars a brat a year."

It went on like that, everyone trying to cut the tax or shift it to someone else, and no one getting anywhere. I listened real sharp. I didn't see any bulging breast pockets, but you never knew, and it was my job to keep the whole meeting from blowing up.

The whole thing droned on, everyone yelling about fairness. The supervisors mostly just shut up; the real fight was between all those people wanting to stick someone, anyone, with the taxes.

"I'll tell you this," Turk was saying. "There's no way on earth that you're gonna stick me with a tax. There's no way I'll pay. Especially since the county owes me money. You try to take my property from me and it's over my dead body. You try taxing away what I've earned by hard work, and I'll move out. I'll leave this damned county behind. I'll leave the livery barn to rot because I'll go where people care about business and a property owner has some respect. You hear me? Give me liberty or give me death. That's what the colonists said, and that's what I'm saying."

That was quite a speech, and it set off a howl. No one disputed him, and everyone joined him. "Go ahead, tax me and tax my bank," Sanders said. "I won't be here to assist your robbery. I'll be long gone from this accursed county."

That's how it went. One by one they stood up, said they wouldn't pay a nickel, swore that the proposed taxes were unfair, and said they'd move out, turn the place back to the devil. That sure was some rhetoric, and they sounded like they meant it.

"And don't tell us the county needs money," George Maxwell, the funeral parlor man, said. "We know that. You register deeds, keep the peace, operate a court, maintain roads, and all the rest. We know that. But it's not right, not fair, to tax Doubtful when the whole cost should be shared by Puma County. So I join the rest. Not one cent will I pay, not now, not ever."

He sat down, and suddenly no one had any more to say.

"You fellers all done?" Rusty asked.

No one responded.

He turned to the other supervisors. "Guess we'll have to vote. Hope you fellers have got your armor on."

"I think you ought to tidy up the language a bit, gents," said Lawyer Stokes. For once he was smiling, because he was among the unpaid employees of Puma County.

They hashed it out: Property tax for that year, beginning January 1, would be a dollar for unimproved city lots, two dollars for improved, a dollar for agricultural homesteads, and ten cents an acre for patented range. Other rural holdings would be a dollar.

"The ranchers get off cheap," Stokes said. "They're mostly using free public land."

All of this was swiftly put to a vote, and it was so recorded, and the last dour citizen of Doubtful abandoned the courthouse to go weep over the loss of a dollar or two of his annual income. That was a real blow in a town as poor as Doubtful. But the deed was done, and new tax laws were sent off to the printer.

Somehow Doubtful had escaped a disaster. I

sensed that it wasn't over. The town sat like a butterfly on a wooden case of DuPont Hercules dynamite. I thought the next few weeks would be pretty tough, and I'd have to keep a careful eye on the supervisors. There had been plenty of threats, and there were people wandering town who thought that taxing them to keep the county afloat was a criminal act. Rusty could probably take care of himself, but the count and countess were another matter entirely. The count was a foreigner, and his wife an ex-madam, and it sure would be easy for a disgruntled citizen to put the blame on them.

Times had changed. The frontier was disappearing fast. The good citizens of Doubtful seemed to grasp that. When they ejected the establishments that catered to randy, rowdy, thirsty cowboys, they also cut off the revenue that the town and county had depended on. And at last the grumbling citizens came to understand that. If you were going to have a government to keep you safe and protect your property and school your children, you were going to place a tax burden on people. It was all a little boring for me. I could bust heads and explode caps with the best of them, but this was the new world settling into place.

The printers got the tax ordinances published. The county clerks got busy with assessments, and after a while all those tax notices sailed out from one end of Puma County to the other.

I felt pretty fine about having my badge back on my chest. Mayor Waller wasn't demanding that I arrest people for spitting. No supervisor was insisting that I ride out into the county to catch hideaway roadhouses serving up redeye. So all that was fine. A little money was trickling in. The county treasurer got some cash off to the Cleggs and began paying other overdue bills. Some people, including Eve Grosbeak and Manilla Twining, had proudly paid their property taxes within hours of the time they got their tax notices. And by the end of the next day, plenty of Doubtful's citizens had gone over to the courthouse and shelled out. So Puma County was back in business, and pretty soon it would get around to paying me a salary, too. In a week or two, the outlying ranches would pay up, mostly likely when they sent a spring wagon in for supplies. It was all going to work out just fine.

But then, when it looked like the trouble was over, that case of Hercules blew, and the butterfly never knew what hit it.

CHAPTER THIRTY-SIX

A river of riders flowed into Doubtful, obscure men in dark hats wearing dark bandannas to cover dark intentions. They arrived after sundown, in the last after light of a summer's day, and divided themselves according to some plan not yet revealed. They rode good horses and rode them well, and were men familiar with saddles and livestock. Most were armed with revolvers, but there were some with scatterguns, and a few carried sheathed rifles, intended for special purposes. Some of the men led pack mules burdened with mysterious and bulky things carried in panniers. This invasion had the look and feel of an army, a dark cavalry, but its mission was known only to itself.

Sleepy Doubtful was mostly in bed, though a few family people were enjoying the last light while sitting in porch swings, while the women were rinsing lemonade glasses or turning down wicks in the kitchen. The citizens of Doubtful were scarcely aware of the horsemen, or the apocalypse settling silently over them, and would scarcely know that by morning they would find themselves in a new world.

The night riders were divided into contingents, each with a task, and each was led by a veteran Puma County rancher. Each platoon contained employees of several ranches, and none of these smaller groups consisted entirely of men from one outfit. That was considered unwise in a time when cooperation, not rivalry, would be crucial to the success of the mission.

King Glad, the young master of the Admiral Ranch, had one of the most critical tasks, and he rode quietly, at a determined walk, to Courthouse Square. He had the ever-reliable Big Nose George and Smiley Thistlethwaite with him, but also Weasel Jonas and others from the T-Bar. Andrew Cockleburr, who had one of the outlying spreads and raised nothing but shorthorns, was in charge of the south road and the telegraph line down to Laramie. He had Jesse Tilton and Wiley Wool with him, and a host of others. Rocco Benifice, the wily old mustanger over on the west side of the county, and his crew would guard the west road. Consuelo "Bully" Bowler, the bilingual operator of the vast Bowler holdings, and his crew, which included Carter Bell and Plug Parsons, were assigned to the main street and business district of Doubtful. Thaddeus Throckmorton, the irritable slaver who claimed the whole northern half of Puma County as his range, but had patented only a few thousand acres around watering holes, had been assigned the most important task of all, which would soon unfold at Countess Sally's boardinghouse and elsewhere among the residential areas of Doubtful. Alvin Ream, a small-time rancher to the east, was given the roadblocks to the east and north. Spitting Sam, a foreman now for the Blue Horizon Cattle Company, owned out of state, had the vital task of coordinating and communicating. His men, all skilled runners and as good on foot as in the saddle, were poised to deliver messages among the various platoons. There were, in all, nearly three hundred masked and armed men flowing like an inky river into Doubtful that summer night.

Act One was simple. Andrew Cockleburr's men climbed a telegraph pole south of Doubtful and clipped the wire. That would prevent information from leaving or reaching Doubtful's two terminals, one of them in the *Advertiser* and the other in the office of County Attorney Stokes. Cockleburr's men then set up a roadblock, a log and brush barrier across a narrow stretch of canyon, and stationed themselves on both sides of it. At that point Spitting Sam's messenger raced into town with the news, which would begin Act Two, which was to be directed by King

Glad. Swiftly his men broke into the locked and darkened sheriff office, lit a lamp, commandeered all keys, including one of the jail sets and a courthouse set. They secured all arms and ammunition in the jail, examined desk drawers for hidden weapons, and then stationed an armed contingent in the sheriff office while the rest headed for the courthouse. There they entered easily, occupied the various offices, including those of the judge, the clerk and recorder, the treasurer, and registrar of deeds. They quickly found the official seal of the County of Puma and confiscated it. Then they posted armed men at the doors of the courthouse, and in the various chambers, and thus occupied the seat of government.

So far, all of this had happened in deep silence, as Doubtful drowsed into a summer night. Spitting Sam's messengers then headed for mustachioed Thaddeus Throckmorton, the most formidable leader and the one who had the most critical task. He and his crew of rebels were quietly surrounding Sally's boardinghouse, where I, as well and the entire Puma County Board of Supervisors, resided. But there were also men fanning out into the dark residential streets, where parties of four or five riders gathered patiently at the homes of county officials, who would be quietly awakened and herded into the jail cells for a while.

It was a peaceful summer night. At least so far. Whether it remained that way would depend more on the conduct of a certain Cotton Pickens, namely me, and the supervisors than anything else. There was an agreed-on scenario carefully worked out in a barbecue beef-and-beans meeting a few days earlier at the Admiral Ranch. If the supervisors followed it, the tax revolt would end peacefully. If not, there might be revolution, bodies strung from nooses, and death by gunshot. And there might not even be a Puma County, or a county seat named Doubtful.

Throckmorton nodded to his picked men. They paused at the stairs outside of Sally's.

"You know what room Pickens is in?" he asked softly.

"The Argentine Bombshell one," some cowboy whispered.

"I'd rather have my gun ready for her," another said.

"She sure was a lot prettier," someone muttered.

"And where Rusty Irons is?"

"Yeah. He's got French Splendour's old bed."

"Good. And the count and countess are in the downstairs suite, right?"

"You betcha."

"All right, men, do your duty," Throckmorton said.

The parties fanned through the boarding-house. The ones about to plunge into Sally and

Cernix's boudoir waited for the rest to get into place. Throckmorton heard soft footfall for a while, and then quiet. He and Shorty and Smart Will stood at the door of the Argentine Bombshell, the wildest and wickedest lady in old Doubtful. It was a new Doubtful now, and everything had changed.

Throckmorton nodded. The men tried the door, found it unlocked, and slid in. Moments later I discovered a cold steel barrel pressed into my mouth and another pressed against my chest. Shorty lit a lamp.

"Pickens, why are you wearing a union suit on a summer night?" Throckmorton said.

Coming out of deep early sleep, I eyed the three.

"It needs to be washed, Pickens. It's yellow around the fly," the rancher said. "Your ma didn't raise you proper."

I wasn't concentrating on that. The steel pressed into me occupied all my thoughts. I eyed my own gun belt on the ladder-back chair, but Shorty lifted it away. Smart Will slid a hand under the pillow, looking for artillery that wasn't there. I eased back and waited.

There were thumps and voices elsewhere in the building. The revolution had begun.

In a few minutes me and the three supervisors had been gathered in the kitchen, where a single kerosene lamp cast yellow light into the shadows.

The glint of blue steel surrounded the officials of Puma County, steel that wagged and waved in the lamplight, steel in the hands of masked men.

The count and countess wore robes and were looking huffy. Rusty Irons sat in his underdrawers, nothing else, his hairless chest bronze in the low light. I wore a union suit head to toe, once white but now a pastiche of gray shades.

"Guess you're treeing the town," I said.

"No, Sheriff. This is not about wild cowboys having some sport. Times have changed. The county is settled. This could be a revolution—depending on what happens," Throckmorton said.

"You mean it ain't a dime novel," I said.

"It's as far from western fiction as it gets," the ringleader said.

"Well, in a dime novel I'd whip out a hidden gun and blast you all to hell," I said. "My ma, she always said—"

"We're tired of hearing about your ma, Cotton," Rusty said.

"What is the meaning of this? I wish to return to my bed," Sally said.

"It's a tax revolution. You will repeal your new Puma County taxes—or be overthrown."

"Overthrown is it? You get out of here, all of you, starting with you, Throckmorton."

"I think you should know, madam, and gentlemen, that certain things have happened. There are three hundred men gathered here. Several of these groups guard the roads. No traffic arrives or leaves. One of those groups has cut the telegraph line connecting the town to Laramie. Other groups have occupied the sheriff's office and jail, and every room of the courthouse. The weapons in the jail have been secured, along with keys. Still other groups patrol the business district, and still other groups are poised at the homes of all county officials, clerks, the treasurer, and so on, ready to capture them. There are others who are preparing a hanging tree. Too bad we have no guillotines, but nooses will do. You will find your necks in the nooses unless you do exactly as instructed. And I wish to remind you, as your sheriff is fond of saying, this is not a dime novel, and these are not cowboys treeing a town. This is a revolution, and it may overthrow the government of this county."

"I guess you got to tell me what a revolution is," I said.

Throckmorton ignored me.

"It'll last about two days," Cernix declared. "About the time it takes for the militia or federal troops to arrive."

"Meanwhile, your body will be swinging from a noose, along with the bodies of the rest of you," Throckmorton said.

"What good will that do you? Legislation done under duress has no weight; it'd last a few days. Man up, fellow, and take your little boys home."

"Count, I'm afraid you don't quite get what's happening here. It's not just duress; it's much more. And I'm done with your whining. Here's what you will do. You will dress and we will escort you to the courthouse, you, too, sheriff. You will call an emergency meeting of the supervisors, and you will repeal the tax law. Our men have the county seal; we will make it official. We will tear up the assessments and you will be set free."

"I absolutely refuse to abide by this coercion, and I will not vote for any law while night riders are a threat," Cernix declared.

I thought that was real brave.

"I won't vote; I absolutely refuse to take part in your charade," Sally said.

Rusty was keeping his mouth shut.

"You may wish to save lives, then," Throckmorton said. "The nooses are not just for you; they are for every official in the county: Stokes, all the rest. We've got ten nooses ready for your necks. It's up to you whether the rest of the government hangs. You can save their lives. They're not even responsible, just people fulfilling the laws you make. But they're about to die, leave behind widows and orphans, thanks to you. Unless you stop it."

"What the hell are you doing this for?" Rusty asked. "It's just taxes."

"It's our life blood, and you will not bleed us. We settled this county. We fought hard to keep it.

We beat off nesters and Indians. We fought for water. This is our land, and this is our livelihood, and no heavy-handed government on earth is going to bleed us. There are three hundred good men ready to defend our rights. We are the masters of our destiny, we embrace liberty, we will operate as we choose, and we will not pay one red cent."

"There's hardly twenty of you actually have a ranch. The rest are just in it for fun."

"Enough. You'll find out what they're in it for. Take your choice. Get dressed and we will take you to the courthouse and you'll legislate—or not. If not, we'll take you to the hanging tree and we won't be dithering, either. You will live for less than one hour from this moment."

Cernix stood, formidable in a blue robe. "Take me to the noose. I will not abide this."

Sally, trembling, stood also. "Wherever he goes, I go. Whatever he believes, I call my own."

Rusty, he just smiled.

I sure didn't know what to do. I felt about as helpless as a titmouse. This sure was no dime novel. So I just kept my mouth shut.

There was a long pause, deep silence in that kitchen, and then Throckmorton himself broke it. "Take them, and if they resist, drag them. We'll get on with it," he said.

Chapter Thirty-seven

I sure wasn't feeling much like a sheriff. Those fellows were serious, and they were going to do whatever they had to do, and they were organized to do it, and were prepared to face the consequences.

"All right," said Throckmorton, "you have one last chance: we can go to the courthouse or the hanging tree."

"What do you expect to gain from this?" Cernix asked.

"A new county government. I've already been elected the provisional chairman. The other provos, as we call them, will remain secret."

"And the state militia will never show up," Sally snapped.

"No, they won't. The state's officers are bought and sold like apples."

"And the cavalry's not riding in," Cernix said, scorn in his tone.

Throckmorton smiled. "The cavalry we might worry about."

That sure entertained me. A column of blue-clad cavalry was the only thing on earth these revolutionaries feared. It was true the cavalry had a little magic. Over in Silas Magee's haberdashery the snappy cavalry officer's uniform in the window had drawn customers for as long as I could remember. Magee always bragged that he'd been a cavalry officer, but no one could ever prove it.

It sure was dark. There was a long pause, and then Throckmorton spoke quietly. "Let's get on with it. The whole thing must be done before dawn."

The cowboy revolutionaries prodded the count and countess, Rusty, and me, outside and into the summer's night. It was utterly silent in Doubtful, where citizens slumbered peacefully. A sliver of a moon did nothing to allay the deep dark. I wandered along barefoot, in my stained white union suit; Rusty in his white underdrawers; the von Strombergers in their robes. The destination became plain after a bit. Southeast of town, on the creek, rose a massive cottonwood with burly, sheltering limbs, as noble a tree as ever grew in Puma County. Twenty or thirty cowboys stood around the tree. There were ten nooses strung from a single splendid limb, lit only by a single lantern. The cowboys were all masked, but I figured I would know plenty of those faces if the masks came off. Rusty would know them, too.

When we arrived, not much happened at first. We simply settled on the ground and fought mean and hungry mosquitoes. The revolutionaries were waiting for something, and I finally figured it was the rest of the county officials. Throckmorton had said the whole batch would be strung up if the tax laws weren't repealed. That meant waking all those people and dragging them to the hanging tree. The revolutionaries were sure well organized.

"You still know how to play the bugle, Rusty?" I asked. "You could play 'Taps.'"

Rusty glared at me and hunkered down inside of himself.

"I always liked them cavalry commands, Attack, Boots and Saddles, all that."

"No cavalry's gonna show up, Cotton," Rusty said.

"Never know," I said. "Cavalry shows up most any time."

Rusty stared at me.

The count and countess sat quietly. They had a special burden on them. Their decisions were affecting the fate of several lives. But the count just glared proudly at his captors. The seconds and minutes clicked on, and finally some men showed up dragging Lawyer Stokes in a nightshirt. He looked pale, if not terrified, his hair disheveled and his gaze piteous. Collecting the rest was apparently proving to be difficult, but I didn't doubt it was going to get done. It still was not far past midnight, and there was another four hours to dawn.

I couldn't sit still anymore. "You fellers mind if I head into the bushes? This here's making me needful," I said.

Oddly, my captors laughed. Throckmorton jerked a thumb. "Keep an eye on him," he said. I rose slowly and headed for the riverbank where willow brush grew thick, and as soon as the lamplight had dimmed, I stripped my union suit off and arranged it in the brush to look like I was sitting, my back to the lamp, the suit faintly visible to the crowd. Then I pulled up river mud and clapped it over me, especially my shoulders and neck, and my cheeks, too. I hoped the shine of dripping water wouldn't catch lamplight.

Then I simply stepped into the creek, hoping not to snag my feet on deadfall or sharp rocks, and headed upstream, toward Doubtful. I thought I might have only one minute, so I moved as fast as possible, feeling the uneven riverbed under me, but making progress, and then the blessed darkness covered me entirely. I was naked and it was after midnight, and I could enjoy the sliver moon.

Behind me I heard shouts and knew the ruse had been discovered, but darkness is infinite, and it extends three hundred and sixty degrees and embraces both sides of a creek, and catches up everything in its murk.

I knew Doubtful would be bristling with sentries and patrols because this coup had been well planned. I also knew, because Throckmorton had blabbed a little, that some of the cowboys were patrolling Wyoming Street's business district, which is where Magee's haberdashery was, and where I needed to go. I hoped Rusty would act but doubted that he would. But Rusty was no dummy; he'd eyed me sharply at the hanging tree.

It sure felt strange wandering around buck naked, and I hoped Eve Grosbeak wasn't nearby, but there wasn't anyone to see me anyway. The town slumbered. I got into town and past the old sporting district and the tumble-down saloons, and kept a sharp eye out. I didn't see any cowboys around, and suspected the revolutionaries had all gotten scttlcd in Barney's Beanery since there wasn't anything to do.

Still, I edged from shadow to shadow, never sure of anything, and when I got to the block with Magee's store in it, I studied extra hard. I wasn't sure how I'd get in, but I'd find a way. I hated to break glass, though; I was barefoot and the noise might stir up the sentries.

I worked around to the alley. Something, probably a shard of glass, bit my foot. I couldn't see the ground, and alleys were not the place to go barefoot, but I had no choice. At the rear of the haberdashery I felt around for a key on a nail. Half the merchants in town kept one stashed in such places. It sure was no easy task, and the clock was ticking and lives hung in balance, but I kept feeling around, aching for that key, but I didn't find one. I fumbled around, found the door handle, turned it—and felt the unlocked door give away. I sure hoped Magee wouldn't mind if I borrowed the stuff in the window. I remembered to close the creaking door behind me. Then I worked forward, past shelves of fragrant woolens and cottons and linens, past glassed counters full of cravats and bowler hats and suspenders and leg garters.

And there it was in the window, the mannequin wearing the blue uniform of the United States cavalry. I only could hope the damned thing would fit.

It did, well enough. I got the tunic and coat and trousers off the dummy and got myself into them, glad I was a medium and the cavalry outfit was a medium. I got into the blue pants with the stripes down the side, the shirt, the jacket. The boots, that was another matter. I pulled and yanked but I was out of luck there. Maybe I could ride barefoot. I got the kepi on my head and buckled the fancy sword in its sheath. There wasn't anything else; no revolvers to wave. But the sword might do if there was a bit of moonlight. Then I saw the cavalry bugle at the foot of the dummy, and I was glad of that. I didn't know how to blow it, but Rusty did, and maybe Rusty would find a way, if Rusty was still alive.

I wished I could light a lamp and see how I looked in a mirror. My ma always told me to enlist, and I never did, but for an hour or two I'd get to be a cavalry officer and make holy hell around Doubtful.

I sure wondered about stepping out into the alley. That sword sheath would shine and clank. The bugle would catch starlight. But there wasn't any choice, and there wasn't any moon to speak of, so I did.

Sure enough, the revolutionaries had collected at Barney's Beanery and were brewing up some java in there. I hastened across Wyoming Street and down the block, and reached Turk's Livery Barn. I plunged inside, into a wall of utter blackness, and felt my way along to Critter's stall. Critter nickered. That was unheard of, and I was extra wary as I opened the gate and stepped in. My bare feet immediately plunged into warm horse apples, which were a comfort, as any barefoot farm boy knew.

"All right, I'm going to do this in the dark, and if you mess with me I'll cut your ears off,"

I said.

"Don't cut mine off," Rusty said.

"Rusty!"

"Oh, that was fun, Cotton, except there's people fixing to get hanged."

"Saddle up something, and tell me."

"What do I hear clanking?"

"I am now a cavalry officer, thanks to Magee. Here's a bugle for you."

"Ah, it all comes clear," Rusty said. "When you slipped out, they sure were having a fit. It took a couple of minutes, maybe even five, because that old union suit was plain there in the lamplight, and it just didn't occur to them you'd left the suit behind. About then, the next bunch of county officials showed up in their underwear, and that was a real good moment for me to get out, and I did. They haven't got all the county officials yet, but we got no time at all."

"You're good for some bugling?"

"Like a rutting elk, Cotton."

"All right then, it's the cavalry going at 'em."

We finished saddling in the livery barn aisle, mostly working in the dark, and Critter obliged, trying only twice to rip off my hands with his buck teeth.

"Cut it out," I snapped.

"We got any guns around?" Rusty asked.

"There's a few lariats hanging around here. Take one if you can feel it out."

"Anything else?"

"I've got one hell of a sword," I said, "and you have one hell of a bugle. You know the calls?"

"Most of 'em. I've got Boots and Saddles down, and I know Forward, Rally on the Chief, Gallop, Charge, and Commence Firing."

"All right, you're the artillery, then," I said.

I led Critter into the night and then mounted, and waited patiently for Critter to quit his humping and complaining. Then we rode out, our horses clopping loudly in the street. There were still dozens of revolutionaries around, in the courthouse, the jail, the business district, and gangs of them were dragging county officials out of their homes. But the clop of horses evoked no challenge, and it didn't take long for us to pass the sporting district and turn off the roads toward the creek bottom half a mile distant.

"You know how we're gonna do this, Cotton?"

"Sure, we're going to ride right in."

"And I hit them over the head with the bugle?"

"That'll do," I said.

Up ahead there was turmoil, and now half a dozen lanterns lit the giant cottonwood and the crowd at its feet. There were shrieks and sobs, but the masked revolutionaries were slowly getting the Puma County officials ready, putting them all on horses, sliding nooses over the necks and tightening them, and getting the horses lined out. In a minute or two there'd be some sort of yell, a mess of cowboys would slap the rumps of the death-horses, which would plow forward and the nooses would pull the county people off the nags and leave them twisting in the night breezes. It sure wasn't a very pretty sight, all the masked men getting things set up. But Throckmorton sat quietly in his saddle, his face alone unmasked, observing the show.

It was too far ahead for me to see who was up and ready and who wasn't. I couldn't tell Count von Stromberger from Lawyer Stokes. I couldn't see where Sally was. I only knew that in moments, an entire government would be massacred, and all for a few cents an acre of taxation.

"You fixing to go?" Rusty asked.

"You know the call for Charge? Let her rip," I said.

Rusty lifted the horn to his lips: *Da-dah, da-dah, da-dah, da-dah, dee-dah, dee-dah, dee-dah, dee-dah; da-dah, da-dah, da-dah, da-dah, dee-dah, dee-dah, dee-dah, dee-dah . . .*

And he and me kicked our horses into a gallop.

CHAPTER THIRTY-EIGHT

That bugle sure stirred up things at the hanging tree. After a little confusion, those lamps were snuffed, and all that remained was an eerie half-light, a foretaste of the dawn that was coming in a while. It had taken them a long time to collect the county officials.

Rusty knew his bugle was the only real weapon he and I had, so he kept on blatting away, the notes keen in the night air. Gallop, Commence Firing, Rally on the Chief. That old bugle sang in the night, and every veteran among the cowboys knew those songs and knew what was coming, and pretty quick there was an uproar around there.

I sensed, more than saw, that the revolutionaries were fleeing for their lives, climbing on panicked horses, skedaddling on foot, getting out, anywhere, somewhere. Me and Rusty hammered forward, our mounts at a lumbering gallop, Rusty easy in the saddle, tooting away.

It was a good thing there wasn't any light, or they would see that Rusty was wearing only his underdrawers. Rusty sensed it, too, and pulled up just beyond what starlight afforded, and began noodling out more bugle calls while I plunged straight into the camp. I pulled that handsome saber out of its sheath and began waving it around, flashing the air with it as I roared in. But the last of the cowboys had fled, howling, into the night. I emitted a rebel yell that might well have carried clear back to Doubtful and headed straight toward the line of panicked horses carrying the county government on their backs. Most of the doomed had not yet had their hands tied, and were hanging onto the hanging ropes or nooses even as the horses plunged out from under them.

I could see just enough to tell that these people might be hanged after all, so I rode in hard, and with giant sweeps of my saber I severed rope, letting struggling men tumble to earth. I saw my blade slice Sally's rope, and the count's, and saw that Lawyer Stokes was struggling, hanging on to the rope for dear life. I thought about it for a moment and decided even Lawyer Stokes needed saving, and sliced the rope in two. Stokes landed in a heap, howling with indignation. I wasn't so sure the county treasurer should be rescued, but my better nature conquered my instincts, and I sliced the man free. The horses skidded out from under and trotted away.

I could just make out the count and countess yanking the noose away from their necks, and frenzied officials wrestling with their own strangulation. But there was no time for more. It was getting almost light, and the ruse would likely be uncovered, and the revolutionaries would swarm back in and end the whole charade.

"Get out of here; get to safety," I yelled at the count.

"Safety, you say. Are you daft? Give me a horse! We're going to whip those scoundrels."

Rusty still hung just out of sight in the murk, bugling Boots and Saddles.

"Where he goes, I go," Sally yelled.

"Get the rest to safety," I yelled.

But Count Cernix was stalking the horses intended to hang them, caught two, brought them in, and hunted around.

"There were some rifles lying here," he said, kicked around, and then yelled happily.

"Got a repeater and a scattergun. All right there, Sheriff, off we go."

"I'll join you," yelled Stokes. The man found a horse and mounted.

A bit more light revealed the county officials

knotted about, freeing themselves from their nooses.

"Get to safety," I yelled. "The town's full of cowboys. Maybe two hundred in there."

"We'll rout them out," Cernix said.

"Courthouse, Wyoming Street, and all roads out."

"We'll fix them. Time to roll."

"Off we go," Cernix howled, and the howl sent a shiver through me. That man had been in war.

It had grown quiet. There was no telling where the cowboys had gone. I hoped they had gone straight to their ranches.

"Rusty, cut that damned bugling," I said.

"My lips ain't what they should be," he said. "Count, you mind lending me that scattergun? If there's some fighting in town, it'd be handy."

"It's yours," the count said.

The cavalry command rode toward town even as the eastern horizon began to show a line of light blue. I waved the saber around, just to flash some light toward observing eyes. There sure wasn't much of an army behind me, but it'd have to do.

"My dear sir, have you any plans?" Cernix asked.

"Maybe you got some," I replied.

"The jail and the courthouse. The citadel of government. The heart and soul of Puma County. Fly the flag."

"Which first?"

"The jail," Cernix said. "It might yield treasures. But then the courthouse. We're going to fly the flag by the dawn's early light, what so proudly we hailed in the twilight's last gleaming."

I had never figured out what all those words meant, but that was fine. They'd hammer the jail and snatch the courthouse.

"Likely snipers along Wyoming Street," I said. "Swarmed with them before."

"Up the bloody alley, then," Cernix said. "Scare the daylights out of 'em."

"Mr. Pickens, have you a plan?" Stokes asked.

"I'm thinking daylight's gonna end our game. So we've gotta do her on the sly. I might be dressed like cavalry, but my boots are at Sally's and daylight will show bare feet, and Rusty's pants, and the rest of you. Say, there, Stokes, can you tell me my rank?"

Lawyer Stokes edged his mount closer and smiled. "You're a lieutenant colonel, Sheriff."

"That's enough to command a regiment," Count Cernix said. "Very good, sir, we are a regiment."

"I'm thinking, let's sneak in, no bugle, nothing to wake up the world."

"Done!" said Cernix.

"Mr. Sheriff, I'd like the honor of storming the courthouse. I would like it on my résumé that I led the charge, and was first into the citadel."

"You got her," I said.

"Very well, dear friends, and now, into the breach," Cernix said.

We stormed the alley, clopping up three blocks, past the business district, and finally onto Courthouse Square, where the only resistance came from a flock of subversive pigeons.

"Rusty and me, we'll take the jail. We've been there. The rest, you capture the courthouse. We've got the shotgun, you've got the rifle."

"Farewell, dear friends, and may we meet again," Cernix whispered, and he and Sally and Lawyer Stokes headed their mounts across the square, while some magpies began squawking.

At the sheriff office, the door hung open. But I took no chances. Me and Rusty slid along to the side and then swung into the dark aperture, Rusty's shotgun ready and my saber drawn.

The place was empty. It had been abandoned in a hurry. There was no one in the cells. There weren't any keys visible, and no arms, but that would all get squared away. Then Rusty spotted the keys on the wooden floor. And soon we found some shotguns stashed under a cell bunk.

Me and Rusty smiled at each other.

"Better help those fellers at the courthouse," I said. "We've got the jail in our pocket."

The sky was bluing now, and the promise of a fine summer's day was at hand. A bird trilled. The city of Doubtful scarcely knew what the night had brought. Me and Rusty slipped cautiously into the courthouse, saw no one, and I thought it might be smart not to surprise anyone equipped with a rifle, so we began shouting and pretty quick found the rest in the courtroom.

Stokes was hunting for something, which proved to be a Wyoming flag, and this he carried to a staff that projected off the front of the courthouse. He opened the window, ran the flag out, and saluted smartly. It fluttered there in the dawn light, caught by the first rays of the sun.

"It was a great honor," he announced. "We have conquered the seat of government. We have driven the foe out. We have restored order. We have rescued Puma County from sedition and rebellion. We have pledged our lives, our fortunes, and our sacred honor.

"We subdued the hosts of darkness. We defeated the armies of the night, armies meant to do great harm to the placid and honorable citizens of the county. We have curbed insurrection, fought against insuperable odds, against an insidious enemy, a fiendish cabal of malignant subversives, whose purpose was to deprive this state and these citizens of a just and good government. And all this was done by the perpetrators for the sake of a small, inconsequential, tax on their holdings, which in their unscrupulous and hollow minds, they conceived as an evil to be extirpated by violent means.

"Gentlemen, lady, we have carried the day, and

may it live forever in the annals of this city, this county, this noble state, and this glorious nation. I am proud to be a part of it. If my own small contribution to this great restoration is someday honored with a bronze statue on the square, I shall be more than rewarded. I shall be humbled. May my children and grandchildren pause at that statue and whisper, 'This was his finest hour.'"

With that, he sat down and wiped tears from his eyes. I felt the same things he did; every person present had felt the breath of death on him only hours before. This was no dime novel; this was bitter reality, which almost swept us all into our graves.

"Guess you fellers ought to get along home," I said. "Me and Rusty have a lot to do. There's roadblocks to look at, and a telegraph wire to patch together, and all. Count, there's a mess of county officials off somewheres, and I'd like you to track them down. I'd also like you to get ahold of the businessmen around here and get a militia together. No telling whether this here rebellion's over or not."

"At your service, sir," Count Cernix said.

"Rusty and me, we'll come with you to the boardinghouse. I'd like some boots and Rusty would like anything to cover his pretty near bare-naked carcass."

We locked up the courthouse and the sheriff

office, and slipped back to the boardinghouse, where we found some of the rest, who had intuitively come there for news or safety. The count swiftly took over.

I was feeling mighty peculiar about wearing that uniform, so I ditched it and got into my regular stuff, with the sheriff badge pinned on my shirt and my feet in my scuffed boots, and that felt much better. I'd get that uniform back to Magee real quick, and tell him how it all worked out.

I was tired. We all were. We had been up all night. It wasn't over, either. Who could say what Throckmorton was even now conjuring up?

"Guess we better check things out," I said to Rusty, and we rode quietly south, where we found nothing, twisted the telegraph wires back together, and then checked the east, north, and west roads out of town.

"You can see where they were hanging around. Look at the prints. Look at the horse apples. But it all came to nothing."

I nodded. I was wearing out fast, and I could see that Rusty was asleep on his feet. I had one more thing to do, which was to get the uniform back to Magee, along with an explanation. I hoped the haberdasher wouldn't mind.

But by the time we got back to Courthouse Square, we found a crowd. All the relatives of the county employees had been talking, and now there were plenty of folks wondering what had happened. But Lawyer Stokes was filling them in.

"We defeated them, with courage and grace, with intelligence and audacity. We faced doom and responded, and drove the vandals out of our precincts. I am proud of the modest role I played, as the Scourge of the Rebellion, flailing away at dark design, chastising evil, encouraging our troops, heartening those whose necks were in the noose. Yes, friends, I am proud. See that flag flying proudly from the courthouse? I raised it this morning. With my own two hands, I defied gunshot and death and ran that flag out the staff, where now it resides, the legitimate emblem of our fair state. Yes, friends, I led the charge into that very building, against all odds, and now you see the result. Good order, peace, and safety."

"Holy cow," said I. "It's General Stokes."

"I'm going to bed," said Rusty. "Lieutenant Colonel, you gonna dismiss me?"

"He wants your seat, Rusty. He's running for office."

"Fine, I'll resign and you can make me your deputy again."

"You can bugle that around town, Rusty. Make it Rally on the Chief."

CHAPTER THIRTY-NINE

It sure was a hot day to ride, but me and Rusty hoped to make the best of it. With any kind of luck, the holdouts would surrender and peace would come to Puma County. I had a mess of warrants in my saddlebag. The perpetrators of the tax revolt had been charged with ten counts of attempted murder, insurrection, kidnapping, and a few more items. Lawyer Stokes had gotten busy and had the paperwork done in record time, which was to say, a week after the great midnight revolt.

And now Sheriff Pickens and Deputy Irons were en route to arrest the whole lot and haul them in. That was going to be entertaining. Word had filtered into Doubtful that the whole bunch was holed up on Throckmorton's ranch, and they had seceded from the United States and declared themselves the Shorthorn Republic.

The boundaries of this new entity stretched across the north side of Puma County and extended to the Montana line, which made it a fancy piece of real estate.

I had my old Peacemaker with me, and Rusty a short-barreled scattergun in a sheath, but we didn't know what sort of army the new Shorthorn Republic had recruited to defend its borders. Word had drifted back to town about all this, especially their new motto: *"Give me liberty or give me death."* The Shorthorn Republic had made a flag, too, with a prairie rattler on it and the legend, DON'T TREAD ON ME. I didn't quite know how the new republic embraced the ranches of all six of the perpetrators, but maybe some sort of land swap had been worked out. But word was that most of the whole midnight army was up there, around a hundred cowboys and their bosses, just itching for a chance to teach anyone a lesson.

"You think they're legal?" Rusty asked.

"Ask any Indian," I said. "They tried it a few times."

"I guess they ain't. You got any notion what's gonna happen when we get there?"

"We take our prisoners back; we get shot down; we get took hostage, or we join 'em."

"You're a card, Pickens."

"I wish my ma and pa had given me another name. Who wants to be Cotton Pickens?"

"I've heard that before," Rusty said. "Man up.

Face life. You're stuck with a bad name. Get over it. Let's go get ourselves killed."

It sure was going to be a scorcher. Not even the magpies protested as we rode by. And the lizards hardly bothered to skitter off the trail. We paused halfway up the county, sucking warm water from our canteens and pissing on some prickly pear. Then we boarded our horses and continued. Critter was in a sullen mood, irate at having to haul a hundred fifty pounds on a blistering day, and he was looking for opportunities to bite me, but all he'd nailed so far was my boot toe.

"Sorry, you're stuck," I said.

We arrived at Throckmorton's front gate early in the afternoon, and sure enough, all those warnings were true. There were breastworks thrown up on both sides. Two flags flew. One, a white bed sheet painted with axle grease, said SHORTHORN REPUBLIC, and the other was a red woman's skirt with that DON'T TREAD ON ME emblazoned, with the rattlesnake coiled at the crotch. There wasn't a breath of air, so the flags hung limp and impotent like a man at the end of a honeymoon.

There were a few cowboys behind the breastworks, and they had rifles.

"Who goes there?" yelled one gent.

"Pickens and Irons," I yelled.

"This is the Shorthorn Republic. You got a passport?"

"What's that?"

"It's a paper thing issued by your government. Full of seals and stamps. We need that, and maybe we'll issue a visa."

"Sonny boy, I'm the sheriff, and I'm coming in, and I'm on a diplomatic mission."

Rusty laughed. Diplomat, that tickled him.

"Stay there. I will be right back," the cowboy yelled. The man hopped a nag, and a few minutes later he returned. "You got to leave your arms off, and I'll take you in."

I unbuckled my gun belt and laid it over the pommel, anchored by the saddle horn. Rusty wasn't wearing anything, but he just got off his buckskin nag and let the sheath hang.

"Leave your nags here and walk," the cowboy yelled.

Some fellers came out from the breastwork and collected the two horses, and me and Irons started up the gray road with two riders behind us. It was going to be a long walk on a hot summer afternoon, and I hoped there'd be some cider or something when we got up to the ranch house. I realized I didn't even have the arrest warrants; they were in my saddlebags. But I probably wouldn't need them.

Throckmorton's ranch wasn't imposing, except that he'd added a pillared portico on front, making it look like a southern plantation ranch. It reminded me of a false-front store, the high front concealing a humble one-story building snaking back from the street. But now some glistening white paint had cleaned the building up, and another Shorthorn Republic flag drooped from a pole.

In the shade of the lofty portico, some men lounged on wicker furnishings, enjoying the shade. And there was Throckmorton, awaiting us, and armed with shiny pearl-handled revolvers.

"Knew you'd be coming," he said. "Welcome to the White House."

"This is your government?"

"It is, and this is the future Throckmorton City. I am the father of my country, and it will be named for me."

Me and Rusty stepped into the cool shade and found the rest of the perpetrators there, enjoying mint juleps. There was young King Glad, lounging in a squeaking chair; mustachioed Andrew Cockleburr, sipping on a frosty glass. Rocco Benifice, wearing a flat-crowned black hat and a bandolier. Consuelo "Bully" Bowler, smooth, distinguished, a pencil mustache under flint-gray eyes, and Alvin Ream, ratlike and plainly least of these insurgents.

"Guess I've got to take you in, fellows," I said. "There's warrants in my saddlebag."

"Your writ doesn't run here," Bowler said.

"This is the Shorthorn Republic, and your law stops at our line," Cockleburr said.

"There, you see? You're out of luck," said Throckmorton. "But gents, do let us serve you a julep."

I suggested some cool water.

Rusty, however, had other dreams. "Suits me," he said.

Throckmorton acted crisply. "Two juleps and a glass of water, too," he said. "Now, you arrived just in time for the inauguration."

"The who?" I asked.

"Shortly, I will be installed as president of the new republic, and Mr. Bowler will be installed as vice president, by its executive council, who are sitting here. There's going to be some inaugural addresses and some fine music. Take any hundred cowboys, and you'll find plenty of musical talent. We have fiddlers, drummers, trumpet players, and more. We're just delighted you showed up. We were hoping someone would; we want the world to celebrate the new republic."

"Ah . . ." I said.

"Sure, what a hoot," Rusty said.

"More than a hoot, young fellow. The beginning of the first true tax-free American republic. There will be no taxes. The government will run on toll road revenues. There shall be liberty and fraternity and prosperity."

A gray woman emerged from the house bearing three frosty glasses, one with water and two with juleps. These were handed to me and Rusty, and we were invited to sit with the founders of the new republic, plainly a favored perch on that shaded porch.

Out on the verdant lawn a small platform rested with a lectern on it, and a few benches.

"We've appointed our friend Rocco, here, as chief justice, and he will administer the oath of office," Throckmorton said.

"Well, mostly I need to take you fellers into Doubtful and get you in front of the judge," I said.

"Oh, do relax, Pickens. You're such an old ninny. Have a chair. The show begins when you're about two sips into that julep."

"Maybe we ought to go, Cotton," Rusty said.

"No, you'll both stay and witness this great event," Bowler said.

"I think they outnumber us, Rusty," I said. The julep tasted real fine on a hot afternoon. And the water, too.

We settled into the wicker just as the band emerged from the bunkhouse, toting fiddles and drums and horns. They sure looked spiffed up. I had rarely seen a washed cowboy. They didn't come washed, except once in a while when they were courting. But there they were, hair fresh-dipped in the horse trough, pants scrubbed and dried, shirt pummeled with suds, and beards scraped a few layers closer to cheek. They sure were fancied up. Even their boots had some fresh axle grease shining them up.

They plunged right in, first with "Skip to My Lou," then "Across the Jordan River," and then "Pick Up the Pieces of My Heart." That was all fine with me; a mint julep and a live band and shade on a hot day were something to remember.

Next came Rocco, wearing a black robe that might have been borrowed from a minister, but would do for a Supreme Court justice, and a moment later, Throckmorton and Consuelo Bowler appeared, Throckmorton in a swallowtail, and Bully Bowler in a tuxedo, but at least they were all in black.

Rocco administered the oath, and both the president and vice president swore to faithfully administer the laws of the Shorthorn Republic, defend its borders, and see to the prosperity and peace of its citizens.

"Amen," said Throckmorton.

He approached the lectern as the band swung into "Dixie," and then "Carry Me Back to Old Virginny," and then he cleared his throat, settled his notes, which kept blowing away until someone handed him a rock, and plunged in:

"Gentlemen, ladies, and fellow citizens," he began. "This is a momentous occasion, a signal event, a turning point of history, and a revered moment in the evolution of mankind from apes into cattlemen. We have arrived at the sacred moment of the birth of a new republic. We have pledged our fortunes and honor to this creation, and if we lay down our lives for the new republic, let no one say it was in vain.

"For we stand firm and tall against tyranny, taxation, waste, regulation, fraud, dishonor, and oppression. In the creation of this new nation, we have thrown off the chains that oppress us all; we have torn ourselves free from the fiendish designs of those in Wyoming and Puma County who would oppress us with their shackles, their whips and scourges, their fees and imposts, their cruel and unusual punishments, and their contempt for our honor, our beliefs, our traditions, our rights!"

I sipped and dozed. I couldn't quite figure the meaning of half of it, and the other half got pretty boring. So I smiled and sipped, and confessed that whoever invented mint juleps had given the world a fine thing.

It sure was a stem-winder, that talk, and it took Throckmorton a long time to pry it out of his head and get it delivered, but eventually he got the whole thing said, and everyone began cheering.

Then Rocco Benefice offered a closing prayer that was quick and sweet, asking the good Lord to bless the new Shorthorn Republic and curse everything else. I sort of admired that prayer, which got right down to the bones of it, and in twenty seconds, too.

After that, there was a reception, and all those dignitaries and a mess of cowboys wandered around.

I was real curious about some things, so I corralled Throckmorton.

"What are you gonna do about brands?" I asked.

"About brands? What about them?"

"Your brands ain't any good in the county anymore. They got to be county brands. How are you gonna ship?"

"Ship?"

"Takes a brand inspector to load cattle onto the cars these days. If there's no recognized brand in the books, them cattle can't ship out. That's true in Montana, too," I said. "And it gets worse. If you got an outlaw brand, you get rustled. No way you can prove up the ownership of your herd, because the brand isn't a Wyoming brand, not even a Puma County brand. Makes you fair game for anyone, seems like. But mostly, you can't ship your beeves, so you ain't gonna ever get yourself paid."

"We'll force our way out."

"Railroads, they won't take just any old cow, Throckmorton. They want papers these days. Seems to me, you want to get your cattle to market, you better get on down to Cheyenne and talk with all them fellows down there and do up a treaty."

"We've pledged our lives, our fortunes, and

our sacred honor," said Consuelo Bowler. "But there goes our fortunes."

"This sure is a tough turn of events," Cockleburr said.

"We'll fight our way out!" Ream declared. "We'll blow the railroads to smithereens."

"I think we better go into executive session," Throckmorton said. "You'll excuse us, Sheriff."

The bunch of them trooped off into the house, while the rest dug into the beans and beef. I liked the beans, even though I knew I'd stink up the boardinghouse for a week.

Andrew Cockleburr was the first out of the secret session. "You have to understand," he said, "it's the principle of the thing. We've pledged our lives and sacred honor, but those are disposable. There are larger principles. What's inviolate is our profit. What's inviolate is our wealth. No one touches our herds. No one must interfere with profit. No one must prevent us from selling and shipping every single animal we possess, including dogs and cats. Let one cow be rustled, let one steer be refused its sacred right to travel to the slaughterhouse, and we've been violated. That's the sacred principle. That's the granddaddy of all ethical and moral and social principles."

The rest emerged from the executive session looking solemn. There was big medicine going on in that house. Rocco Benifice had tears in his eyes. King Glad stared into the clay and wouldn't meet anyone's gaze.

Throckmorton corralled me and Rusty. "You mind taking me to the Puma County supervisors under safe conduct and diplomatic immunity? We've got some neighborly treating to do."

"Of course I mind. I've got arrest warrants for the mess of you."

"You think we can get our brands back and ship cattle?"

"I'm the sheriff, not the governor."

"All right. We're riding into Doubtful, but not with you and Rusty."

"Nope, you're coming with us, and under arrest."

"All right, dammit, Pickens. We'll ride with you," the president of the republic said.

"You got us, Pickens. We're ready to pledge our lives and sacred honor, but not our fortunes," Vice President Bowler said. "Hang us if you must, but don't touch our herds."

CHAPTER FORTY

And that is how it came to pass that Sheriff Cotton Pickens and Deputy Rusty Irons rode into Doubtful along with the perpetrators of the revolution. The county seat was only then recovering from the shock of the previous week's uproars, now being told on every street corner and at the Elks Club and the Moose bar. Tearful county officials, their lives spared at the last moment by the sheriff and his saber, were still recounting the awful events of that night to electrified audiences, and the town itself was brimming with alarm.

Count Cernix had swiftly formed a militia, and businessmen with shotguns patrolled the streets, prepared to stamp out any further insurrections. Lawyer Stokes had addressed a crowd in Courthouse Square, eloquently describing the night of horror and what steps would be taken to hang, draw, and quarter the instigators of this offense against humanity and the commonwealth.

The repaired telegraph hummed and the governor offered to send the militia, but the count replied that everything was now under control and legitimate government had been restored in much of the county and soon would be restored in the rest. Cernix wasn't quite sure how, but he didn't doubt that bravery, courage, excellence in the field, a knowledge of tactics and strategy, and a determined militia would restore order.

The governor wired back that he would be available day and night and would send troops if needed.

All of which was happening while me and Rusty rode out with arrest warrants in hand to bring the criminals into Doubtful and lock them up for life. Some favored the firing squad. This was an insurrection, after all, and the firing squad seemed the proper remedy. Citizens vied with one another to be elected to shoot the culprits, and Cernix eventually decided that the honor should be awarded by random cutting of a deck of cards, left over from the days when Doubtful was a gambling mecca.

It was decided that aces would be low, not high, and by the time me and Rusty and our prisoners rode into Doubtful, Mayor George Waller, One-Eyed Harry First, and Hubert Sanders had won the honor and were polishing their rifles.

Then Rusty and me and the prisoners started up Wyoming Street, while the whole town gawked. What's more, I was not wearing my gun belt, and the deputy's shotgun was in its saddle sheath. But there we were, along with the worst criminals in Wyoming's history, quietly clopping toward Courthouse Square, the criminals looking solemn and resigned.

No one was speaking. Men on the sidewalks bristled with arms, ready to assist if anything should be amiss. But in fact, apart from some nervous glances, the president, vice president, and executive council of the Shorthorn Republic seemed peaceable enough, and we were allowed to pass through and then to dismount and enter the jailhouse. A few moments later, after I locked the bunch up, I emerged and addressed the crowd.

"We've got them fellers and don't you interfere. They'll likely plead guilty, and this is only gonna take half an hour. So you go along home and eat your mashed potatoes."

But the crowd didn't budge. This was the most exciting thing ever to happen in Doubtful, and no one wanted to miss a trick.

Lawyer Stokes showed up, strutting around like a rooster and making cock-a-doodle-do noises. "We've conquered the scum. We shall prevail!" he said.

Judge Axel Nippers was persuaded to abandon

his evening double or triple libation at the new Elks Club, and Jerry Dolce Vita, the clerk and recorder, was gotten out of the bosom of his family, where he was playing checkers with his sons, and court abruptly opened at the awkward hour of six p.m. The courtroom probably held more spectators than was safe, but no one seemed to mind.

At six ten, that fierce August day, I escorted the insurrectionists into the chamber, where they lined up before Nippers.

"Identify yourselves before this court," he said.

The executives of the Shorthorn Republic confessed their names.

"I have it, Mr. Throckmorton, that you are the president, and you, Mr. Bowler, are the vice president of the Shorthorn Republic."

The arch criminals acknowledged this.

"You are all charged with ten counts of attempted murder, ten counts of kidnapping, plus insurrection and disturbing the peace. How do you plead?"

"Guilty, Your Honor," they all said, one by one, and the pleas were duly noted by the recorder.

"Since I was the only county official not dragged to the hanging tree, it behooves me to be fair and impartial beyond question. Do you understand? For the leniency you showed me, I must be especially severe with you, so it all balances out."

"Yes, Your Honor," Throckmorton replied. "I speak for us all."

"Throw the book at them," said Lawyer Stokes.

"Shut your trap, Stokes. We will proceed in a just and equitable manner."

"String them up," someone yelled.

Nippers banged his gavel and glared.

"I will proceed with the sentencing. Since you are all equally guilty, this applies to all of you. First, I will fine you two cattle each for attempted murder; if you bring in culls, make it three. Second, I fine you one additional steer each for insurrection and kidnapping, and I will dismiss disturbing the peace if you pay promptly, say within forty-eight hours. The sheriff shall pen these cattle and conduct an auction, the proceeds going to Puma County."

Throckmorton looked dazed. "That's worse than a property tax, sir. That's an invasion of our herds. That violates every guarantee in the United States and Wyoming constitutions. This is not a fair trial, sir."

"Oh, be still, Mr. President. You have led a conspiracy that committed heinous crimes against the body politic, and against innocent persons, and you shall suffer for it. Not only must you supply the cattle at once, but you must pay your property taxes at the same time. Every day you delay, you will owe the county one more steer, which the sheriff will auction off. Do I make myself clear?"

"Yes, sir," whispered Bowler. "But surely this violates the cruel and unusual punishment clause."

"I am a hard man, Mr. Vice President. Now then, I wish to return to my evening libations. Sheriff, hold these prisoners. No bail. Release them when their minions show up with the cattle and cash."

It was a tad unusual, I thought, but old Nippers wasn't going to put up with any more nonsense.

I escorted the forlorn and depressed ranchers back to their iron-barred temporary homes, let them instruct their employees about bringing in the cattle, and offered them meals from Barney's Beanery.

"I'm too ill to eat," moaned Throckmorton.

"Just leave the pisspot. That's all we need," said Bowler.

The iron doors clanged shut, and the county's leading ranchers settled into their iron bunks and waited for the time when they might win release.

"Be glad you're in here," I said. "There are some in town who'd just as soon haul you out to the hanging tree. Deputy Irons and I will be on guard. Not that I don't sympathize with the mobs. I think you'd do very well, decorating the hanging tree. I'm returning the compliment. You thought me and Rusty, we'd look just fine swinging in the wind."

"Don't let them use our rope. We paid good money for that rope," Cockleburr said. "If we have to die, don't do it on our dime."

"That's one of our principles," said Throckmorton. "A man has to live by principles. A man without principles isn't worth crap."

The crowd slowly dispersed, and Rusty and me settled down on bedrolls for a long night. But it was oddly peaceful. The town had already resolved the entire case and had gone to bed content.

Next day, drovers showed up with the cattle, so me and Rusty penned the bunch over at Turk's and wrote out receipts, one copy for the court, and then unlocked the ranchers.

"You fellers can go now. The county has the cattle."

"We gonna be able to ship cattle out of Puma County now?" Bowler asked. "Our brands are good now?"

"That depends on whether you quit trying to make a foreign country in the middle of my county," I said. "You fold up your Shorthorn Republic, and I'll call your brands good."

"Guess we better have an executive meeting," Throckmorton said to his fellow ranchers. "All in favor of quitting the republic, say so."

They were all in favor, and in that moment the Shorthorn nation got voted out of existence. I said I'd tell the judge, and let the governor know, too.

"The governor, he was fixing to send Gatling guns and some howitzers up here, but I told him me and Rusty could handle it."

"Gatling guns?"

"Yeah, the state keeps a couple down there, ready to knock back trouble. I sure would have enjoyed seeing them knock a few holes in your parade."

"Gatling guns. I never thought of Gatling guns. We should have got some ourselves, half a dozen maybe, even before we voted ourselves the Shorthorn Republic. Damn! Why didn't we think of that? If we'd had some Gatlings out there, Sheriff, you would've wet your britches even coming within half a mile of my place."

"Well, if you're gonna make a new nation, you'd better have an army," I said. "Bunch of cowboys with six-guns, that don't persuade anyone of anything."

"Right as usual, Sheriff. Well, this is a sad day for us. Here we are, twenty-four good beeves shorter than what we possessed a few hours ago. Twenty-four beeves. We could have paid the county taxes with about one quarter of one beef. So we've learned a lesson: if you're going to start a revolution, you'd better have the arsenal."

"Makes sense to me," I said.

I watched those ranchers and their drovers ride off into the August heat.

I went over to the weekly and put an advertisement in, saying there'd be a sheriff's sale of twenty four cattle in good flesh, proceeds to the county, cash only.

That went fine. A few days later the whole lot was bought by a Laramie packing plant man, and the cattle were on their way south. I gave the county treasurer a voucher for enough to keep Puma County afloat for a while. And the ranchers would soon pay up their property taxes, too.

At last, Doubtful slipped into peace and prosperity. Those cowboys who still wanted a nip could and did join the Elks or the Moose, and belly up to the bar as they did before, and sometimes they played penny-ante poker there. The drovers were full of pranks, some of them pretty mean, but they didn't wear sidearms into town. And now and then they could be seen bidding on some gal's box lunch at church socials, which made me mad because I was too cheap to bid on the best box lunches, being a penny-pincher from the get-go. I knew what gals had made the box lunch, but I was afraid I'd get a lousy sandwich for my dollar, or a decaying apple, so I always quit bidding so I wouldn't be rooked. So my old rivals out on the ranches were sparking all the girls. But at least I wasn't prowling town with two six-guns hanging from my hips, and mostly I did my rounds with nothing more than a billy club. I was very good with a billy club and could make a bratty boy quit pestering stray dogs just by waving that club.

The count and countess turned out to be fine supervisors, and there was money enough so that Puma County could fix the potholes in the roads and build some shipping pens outside of town where the brand inspectors could look over the brands and okay the herds for travel.

All this happiness in Doubtful did not go unnoticed in the great State of Wyoming, and one day Governor William Hale showed up for a little ceremony in the courthouse. I knew nothing of it until I was suddenly roped in. There, on a fine October day, a whole gaggle of officials had collected. I saw the supervisors and Judge Nippers, and a fellow I recognized as the governor. And then for some reason they invited me to step forward, and I couldn't figure out what all those people with their beaming faces were doing, but I was put there next to the governor, and the man began talking away. I didn't quite get it all, but it was all about acting beyond the call of duty, or rescuing a county from a foreign invasion, of preserving the peace, of courage and honor and integrity.

"And therefore, Cotton Pickens, I am making you a lieutenant colonel in the Wyoming militia," said Governor Hale. "Congratulations, boy."

I sure shook a lot of hands that day.

But it wasn't over. There was a box lunch social on the courthouse lawn that eve, and sure enough, every stray drover in the county was on hand ready to bid on those lunches. A fiddler played, and then the count announced that the bidding would begin. For some mysterious reason, the countess Sally had insisted that I bid on a box with a green ribbon on it, and to keep on bidding for whatever reason, to bid even if I spent my last dime on it. There sure were a lot of people in town, and the bidding went high, but I for once cut loose and laid out one bid after another on the box with the green ribbon, even when the price went to seven dollars and twelve cents. "Seven and a quarter," I bid, and that settled it.

"Now go collect that box," Sally said. "That lady over there made the lunch."

I went over to get the box from the stranger, who looked sort of familiar, but somehow different, all fancy in a pleated white skirt and white blouse and shining hair all done up fine. And then I stopped, poleaxed, and my knees gave way. It was Pepper Baker, the gal I'd loved once, who got sent away to finishing school by her pa. And there she was, smiling at me, her eyes big.

"I'm glad you bid, Cotton," she said.

"So am I, Pepper. My ma, she always said to take a chance if you want anything good to happen."